FOR

PRO.

FORWARD

This is a story about Cold War soldiers/warriors using intellect rather than arms to confront the enemy. The enemy being the Soviet Union and their Eastern European subordinates who intended to occupy and rule all of Europe.

These are the recollections and memories of one of those Cold War *warriors*. He reminisces, as he awaits aboard a troop ship docked in New York harbor to muster out of the United States Army. He is returning from Germany where he served as a signals intelligence analyst assigned to an intelligence gathering and processing unit.

It encompasses the time from the latter part of World War II through the height of the Cold War in the early 1960s.

Soviet Premier Khrushchev is alleged to have once said something along the lines of, "Berlin is the testicles of the West, every time I want to make the West scream, I squeeze Berlin." A great deal of this story relates to the Soviets' genital compressions of Berlin—the airlift, erecting the wall, Checkpoint Charlie, and the Cuban missile crisis. The latter occurred halfway around the world from Berlin, but it inarguably involved Berlin. The airlift was the result of the firm testicular clinch by Khrushchev's predecessor, Joseph Stalin.

If Berlin were to fall to the Soviets, it would only be a matter of time before West Germany and almost certainly all Western Europe would follow suit. And if the Soviets attempted to take Berlin, there were no alternatives—Fight a conventional war the Western Allies were sure to lose because of the Soviets' overwhelming military advantage, or resort to nuclear Armageddon! Maintaining the status quo in Berlin became paramount.

This tale has a background and a foreground.

The background consists of two parts. The first relates to the German people's experiences at the end of the war and the years following that resulted in their subsequent attitudes and actions, at the time of this narrative, toward the occupying Allied troops. The counterpoint, then, is the GIs' attitudes and reactions toward the Germans.

The foreground is about the antics and accomplishments of a unique group of intelligence soldiers and is written in a manner as to counterbalance the serious historical events whose narration is rarely entertaining or amusing, but nevertheless an essential part of the story. Throughout the book, these episodes are scattered about to demonstrate the GI vocabulary, sarcasm, cleverness, and humor.

All of these accounts were based on actual individuals or incidents and conversations experienced by the author. Names have been changed to shield the innocent and protect the guilty. Yes, there were some fictional liberties taken, but, for the most part, this a factual accounting of what occurred at the time.

It was written to be both historically informative, as well as, an enjoyable narrative.

PROLOGUE

Aboard the *USS Gordon* in New York Harbor

26 September 1963

After ten days at sea crossing the Atlantic from Bremerhaven, Germany, to New York City, Army Specialist 5 (Spec/5) Leland Wolfe along with 4,000-plus other GIs had been rousted out of their bunks at four-thirty in the morning. The early awakening wasn't just another of the army's traditional hurry-up-and-wait drills. It was to be the last one these troops would have to endure. Few complained because this was the wake-up call all had marked on their calendars for months.

The GIs were alphabetically grouped throughout the ship in preparation for disembarkation and mustering out of the active army into active or inactive reserve duty. The hurry-up went quickly—but for Leland, or Lee as he preferred to be called, and the other W-surnamed troops—the wait was going to be lengthy indeed. Not only must the other soldiers disembark, but they also had to out-process from the active army into reserve units, which at best was a time-consuming bureaucratic drill.

The Ws were on the deck near the fantail, with those whose surnames began with X, Y, and Z even further back. Being nearly the last off was the bad news. The good news was that being on deck was much better than waiting in the bowels of the ship.

By mid-morning, the fog had burned off. Lady Liberty in all her elegance gazed down. Lee lowered to the deck and made himself comfortable using his duffel bag. With the Lady standing watch, he reflected on the last three years of his life.

His first thoughts turned to his arrival in Germany and his experiences in the days and months that followed.

ARRIVING IN GERMANY

Gutleut Kaserne, Frankfurt am Main, Germany

8 August 1961 – Six days before the Berlin Wall went up.

Lee had always envisioned that when he reported for military duty, it would be something like an old Western movie. He would enter the commanding officer's presence, come to attention, and offer a sharp salute, saying, "Private Wolfe reporting for duty, Sir!" with the officer responding, "Welcome aboard. Great to have you with us!"

It had been an arduous and sleepless journey to report for duty. It started at Fort Devens in Massachusetts, and now he could hear the squeal of tires on the runway as his plane touched down at the Frankfurt am Main airport in central Germany. After deplaning he and the other arriving soldiers boarded the equivalent of the army's shuttle-bus service.

Lee was dropped off at Gutleut Kaserne.

Instead of his visualized company commander's greeting, Lee was met by an overweight, unshaven staff sergeant whose uniform was wrinkled and grungy. And, who badly needed a haircut, not to mention a shampooing of the oily tangle of bristle atop his head.

The sergeant, with Lee in tow, labored up the steps, opened a door, and pointed inside, saying, "Find an empty bunk and stow your stuff.

The uniform of the day is full combat gear. Then go down to the armory and check out your weapon and get a pot."

"Pot?" Lee asked, thinking perhaps the army now issued individual port-a-potties.

"A helmet, you dumb shit. I'll be waiting for you outside on the bus to take you up to the Farben Building."

Lee did as was told.

Finding an empty bunk—although he had to settle for a top bunk from the double-tier bed offerings—and an empty locker was easy. Getting into all the parts and pieces of the full combat uniform of the day was a challenge.

As he entered the armory, he encountered another staff sergeant; this one was as professional as the first one was unprofessional. He was physically fit, his uniform was immaculate despite always being in contact with oily weapons, and his haircut was regulation. He took an M-2 carbine off the rack, checked the serial number, and had Lee sign for it. Reaching behind him, he grabbed a handful of ammunition clips and plunked them down on the counter.

This is not good. I have a weapon I've only fired once, and the army doesn't issue rounds unless they expect them to be shot.

The sergeant found a helmet and handed it to Lee who said as he tried it on, "Sarge, this doesn't even begin to fit."

"None will. Here's a tip. Find a piece of an old towel. Stuff it in there until it feels comfortable with the chin strap tight. That does two things. It keeps it on your head, and it absorbs sweat ... which is a given when you wear that thing."

"Thanks. I'll bet you served in Korea."

"Afraid so."

I like this gun guy.

Lee had been told the uniform of the day was full combat gear, though not why. So, he asked, "Hey Sarge, what the hell is going on? Full combat gear and all this ammo. What's happening?"

"The Soviets have gone on alert, ergo, you get to cart all this extra crap around. Standard operating procedure. The Soviets go on alert, and you weigh fifty pounds more when you step on a scale."

Lee gathered up all his gear and went outside, where surprisingly, a shuttle bus was waiting. He clambered aboard, awakening the dozing staff sergeant. Lee held forth his helmet, saying, "Look, Sarge. Now I know what a *pot* is. Thanks!"

He was soon to learn that the enlisted administrative cadre of the ASA 251st Processing Company—platoon sergeants and their ilk who did not hold an intelligence Military Occupation Specialty (MOS)—were mostly clones of his current escort. The first sergeant and the armorer were the exceptions. All the rest were substantially overweight, fell somewhere between one to three standard deviations on the low side of the intelligence bell curve, and only did the minimum necessary to get by. Their lack of professionalism matched their slovenliness. 'Indolent and congenitally incompetent' would have been a fitting descriptive term—the ASA GIs had nicknamed them the Fat, Dumb, and Lazies (FDLs).

Lee encountered his first German, the bus driver, a scrawny little guy in civilian clothes was wearing an Afrika-Korps-style forage cap. The FDL barked, "*I G* Hochhaus" (I G High-rise) at the driver before nodding back off.

They exited the Kaserne onto the cobblestone streets of Frankfurt.

As the shuttle-bus bounced over the cobblestones, narrowly missing an oncoming, clanging, shrieking steel-on-steel *Strassenbahn* (streetcar), Lee gazed out the window and mused to himself.

Well, it seems like I got here just in time to get shot at.

Lee dug an ammo clip from his gear and inserted it into the carbine to ensure he remembered the process. Satisfied, he ejected the clip. He then pulled back the bolt and checked to make sure he hadn't chambered a round.

The bus passed untold numbers of the same, drab, ashen hued two and three-story buildings as Lee stared out the window.

This scene doesn't appear at all like what I thought a German city would be. Every street looks just like the next. The only paint they must have had during reconstruction was gray and painted everything that wasn't already that color in myriad shades thereof. And, how does anyone find their way around? There are no landmarks to reference. At least there's the sun, so I'll know north, south, east, and west.

Little did Lee know that soon his only reference point would be hidden behind a gray moisture-laden sky for much of the next two years. In fact, he would learn that Germany, for the most part, would be a cold place to live, with short days and long nights accompanied by mist, drizzle, and rain. Days with the sun shining would be rare. Even when it did shine, he would be working in windowless environs. Given the short days and long nights, combined with long hours on the job, one may well go months without seeing the sun. As a young man, Lee had spent much of his time atop a horse herding cattle on the high plains of New Mexico. The sunny Southwest—Germany was not. This was going to be a much different environment and undertaking.

Lee continued staring out the window as he began to nod off.

A tidy bunch, these Germans. The sidewalks and streets are immaculate. And the signboards are a jumble of every letter in the alphabet where they concatenate a whole sentence into one word. Ausfahrt must be a major suburb of Frankfurt because all those little black and white signs with two arrows seem to point there.

Lee's chin dropped to his chest, and suddenly he jerked awake.

I'm exhausted. Can't remember the last time I slept.

Lee had every reason to feel as he did. It seemed like it had been days ago when, in the early morning, he and eight other soldiers were loaded into a van at Ft. Devens, Massachusetts. It was at Ft. Devens where he completed his advanced training and was granted a Top Secret (TS), Sensitive Compartmented Information (SCI), security clearance. He also now held one of the rare—and at that time, classified—98 series MOS. Specifically, that of a radio traffic analyst.

Their final journey's end was Germany. They left for the long trip southward to McGuire Air Force Base in New Jersey. As soon as they arrived, were ushered onto a cargo plane, a C-some-unknown number. Seated in tightly spaced canvas bucket seats along the bulkhead, meaning they would be up close and personal, flying backward for heaven knows how long. There were two small portholes, one on each side of the plane, for their viewing pleasure. Immediately in front of them was a huge cargo net whose purpose, it would seem, was to separate man from the material.

Even if this sucker doesn't crash, just a hard landing and it will take them a week to dig us out from underneath all that shit towering above us.

The airplane took off immediately, bound for Newfoundland, where they stretched their legs and used the facilities while the aircraft refueled. Next stop was Prestwick, Scotland. It soon became evident that food and beverage service was not an amenity on this flight. The food wasn't a big deal, but those little bottles of booze found on other airlines would have been much appreciated as they flew through the turbulent air over the Atlantic. Relief on the passenger's faces was palpable when the coast of Scotland came into view. At Prestwick, the plane again refueled. The GIs were allowed off to pee and poop. During the brief stop, the GIs became enamored with the beautiful lasses and their wondrous Scottish accents. After twenty-one hours in the air, they finally arrived at Frankfurt am Main. They hadn't crashed, nor had there been any hard landings. Lee now realized he was, at long last, in Germany—fatigued, yet still alive.

THE WORKPLACE FOR THE NEXT TWO YEARS

As they came close to the Farben Building, Lee noticed some of the façades around one window were missing. It was evident they had been taken out by gunfire. Fifteen years had elapsed since the end of the war. The army likely had the funds to repair damage to a major army headquarters building.

I'll bet our guys left it that way just to remind the Germans who won the war.

The shuttle bus parked at the west end of the imposing building. Passengers exited the bus and entered the building, where Lee encountered an elevator contraption the likes of which he had never seen before. It was called a *paternoster*. With some reluctance, Lee followed the FDL on board. Very slowly, but surely, up they went.

Chief Warrant Officer 2 (CW2) McDuff took possession of Lee from the FDL as they stepped off the paternoster at the sixth-floor landing. He escorted him up the narrow steps to the Secure Compartmented Information Facility (SCIF) on the seventh floor and indicated a chair for Lee to sit in. A SCIF is nothing more than a room where top secret materials can be processed, discussed, and stored. The warrant officer was short and rotund and claimed to be Irish. It soon became apparent he had a Napoleon complex with an ego to match his girth but lacked anything close to the usual Irish sense of humor. Polite small talk with which to begin a conversation was one of the classes the warrant officer had missed while attending Civility 101. The only introduction of himself was that he was the facility security manager. Without inquiring Lee's name, he began the top secret security in-briefing, referring to Lee only as Private.

"Private," Chief McDuff said in a tone of voice commonly reserved for judges castigating retarded juvenile delinquents, "You will be exposed to some highly-classified data. Should you reveal this to anyone not authorized, you will spend ten years in prison at Fort Leavenworth and pay a ten-thousand-dollar fine. Your MOS and your SCI Crypto clearance are classified, so make damn sure you don't reveal them to anyone outside this facility."

About this time, a GI with a camera showed up and took a picture of Lee.

I suppose that's for the Most Wanted poster they expect to hang in every post office in America.

The warrant officer then went into his ego mode. "Private, besides being the security chief, I also maintain the classified document library," sweeping his arm at the bank of file cabinets. "And I handle the destruction of classified documents and equipment, if necessary."

The GI who had taken the picture arrived with a laminated picture-badge for Lee. The badge was on a chain and was color-coded. The warrant officer handed it to Lee saying, "Private, you will wear this exposed at all times when in this facility. And you will not discuss what you do with anyone who does not wear a similar badge. When you leave here, you will without fail, not show it to anyone. Otherwise, you will be subject to spending ten years in prison at Fort Leavenworth and a ten-thousand-dollar fine."

Enough already with Fort Leavenworth and a ten-thousand-dollar fine.

"Private, stack your weapon. Wait here. Perhaps if you are lucky, your boss, His Lordship Mr. O'Donnell, will get around to seeing you," said the warrant officer as he waddled away, resembling an arthritic penguin. He sat down next to one of the file cabinets with a clipboard in hand.

Oh, boy! As if I don't already have enough to worry about, now I've got to deal with what appears to be an in-house pissing contest.

Lee sat down looking out over an open bay where GIs were thumbing through little yellow sheets of paper. It seemed as if someone had come in and dumped a trash can full of those yellow pages onto each desk. The GI would pick one up, scan it briefly, then almost always drop it into a classified burn bag at his feet. A few of the yellow sheets were set aside.

THE NICKEL TOUR

After about a half an hour, a civilian approached. He had only one arm, his left; the sleeve of the missing limb was pinned up at the shoulder. He was a big man—tall, broad-shouldered, large-chested—with an unlit half-smoked cigar clamped in his mouth. His necktie was loose at the neck, and his shirttail was nowhere close to being tucked in. As Lee would soon find out, he was gruff of voice and had a propensity for profanity.

Unkempt and intimidating would be the best adjectives to describe this guy. Give him some slack, he only has one arm. His missing arm along with his size and demeanor would likely scare the bejesus out of most folks.

The civilian sat down next to Lee saying, "Sorry to keep you waiting, but it's a little hectic right now. I'm Mackenzie O'Donnell. We will be working together."

Lee noted he didn't say, "I'll be your boss" or "You'll be working for me."

"What's your name?"

"Leland Wolfe, Sir."

"What do you like to be called?"

"Lee, Mr. O'Donnell."

"I have this rather simpleminded management philosophy that people who work together should be on a first-name basis. I prefer to be called Mac. So, dispense with the Sirs and Misters unless somebody outside our working group is present. Got that?"

Yes, Si ... Mac."

"Well, somewhat better. You'll get the hang of it."

This is the guy Chief McDuff called His Lordship? It beats the shit out of me as to why.

Without preamble, Mac began. "Our primary mission here is to keep an eye on the Group of Soviet Forces Germany ... the GSFG ... and their East German counterparts. Those are the bad guys on the other side of the border. Let me clarify just who the bad guys are. Most of the world incorrectly refers to them as Russians. Those steel-toothed bastards come from all over the Soviet Union ... thus, we refer to them as Soviets. Case in point, their main man, Khrushchev, is Ukrainian.

"We are looking for their threats of Imminence of Hostilities ... IOH. That's bureaucratic speak for an invasion into Berlin or Western Europe. Our powers that be have deemed Khrushchev and his East German stooge Ulbricht to be unpredictable. As such, right now their pucker-factor is tight. Such threats would include GSFG going on high alert, a significant increase in comm traffic volume, especially encrypted traffic, movement or the preparation for movement of troops. All the above is now happening, and our military muckety-mucks don't know whether to shit or go blind."

Lee was paying attention despite his fatigue.

"After World War II ... per the Potsdam Conference agreement ... Germany was divided into three portions of land, or zones, to be administered by the conquering Allies. The Russians, the British, and the Americans each acquired a chunk. Along came the sniveling French claiming they deserved a share, so the Brits and the Americans each ceded a portion of their allotment to the Frogs. The Russian zone became known as the German Democratic Republic ... the GDR. The GDR is what the rest of the world knows as East Germany. The Commies themselves call it the *Deutsche Demokratische Republik* ... the DDR. The British, American, and French zones became the Federal Republic of Germany (FRG) ... West Germany. Most folks know this, but what they don't know is that we have intercept stations strung out along the East-West German border, plus one up above Kassel. Also, to the south of us is Herzogenaurach, aka Herzo Base ... for apparent pronunciation reasons. And one in Berlin, some hundred-plus miles inside the GDR. It's called Teufelsberg or Devil's Mountain. It is an absolute intel gold mine. It's on top of an immense pile of rubble left over from World War II, and right where the action is. Those stations provide us with all these little yellow sheets of paper you see lying around. They are hard-copy of clear-text voice, and Morse code intercepts that have been recorded and then translated into English. Most are Russian, and occasionally some German. We have a good handle on the frequencies at which the different Soviet units transmit. Thus, all this stuff is sorted accordingly before it gets brought here for the analysts to look at, then it's either kept or discarded. The encrypted traffic gets sent off to the National Security Agency ... the NSA.

"What we do is comparable to putting together a mosaic of all the little bits of information contained on those yellow sheets. Scratch that … that's not a good analogy." Mac thought for a moment, then continued, "It's as if you've been given a ten-thousand-piece jigsaw puzzle, where there's no picture on the box to know how it looks. A whole bunch of pieces are missing and replaced with pieces from other puzzles. Our job is to try to make some sense out of that kludge. And, while I'm at it, here's my cardinal rule. Gathering intelligence is not an end unto itself. If it is not disseminated and used without delay, it is worthless! You'd be amazed at how many in our business don't realize that. Gatherers, disseminators, and users alike."

Lee sat in awe.

"About ten years back, the Russians learned we were reading their mail and appreciably improved their comm security. They went to using landlines whenever possible and to using one-time pads for the high-grade stuff going through the air. Thus, we've ended up working with the low-grade stuff. However, we do manage to glean a substantial amount of intel, specifically when it comes to their Order of Battle … OB."

"I'm not sure I know what that is."

"Order of Battle is a misleading term. It's nothing more than an organization chart with location and time attached. It uses four of the five W words. Who and what, where, when. Remember that! Who, what, where and when are the four things our combat commanders most want to know. An example of what they want to hear is … the Eighth Guards Army, commanded by General Ivan Ivanovitch, consisting of one tank division and three motorized rifle divisions, is in garrison in and around Magdeburg, East Germany. What they definitely don't want to hear … because it means World War III is well underway … is that the Eighth Guards, with all its divisions, is now located in and around Frankfurt, West Germany. With that primary OB in place, we try to fill in the blanks with the unit names and numbers, commanders, and locations of subordinate units. The why … we leave that to historians."

Lee was overwhelmed with this information dump.

Mac was just starting. "Let me give you the nickel tour, and let's begin with the big picture," he said, as he walked over to a map hanging on the wall. "This is what we face. The Soviets have five so-called armies in East Germany." Placing his one hand at the top of the map, he continued, "Up here we have the Second Guards Tank Army. It has one tank division, the 9th; and three motorized rifle divisions, the 21st, the 94th, and the 207th."

Whoa! Too much information. No way in hell am I going to remember whether they are a tank or motorized rifle division, much less their unit ID. I'm just going to count divisions. Nevertheless, he certainly knows his shit.

"Motorized rifle troops are nothing more than infantry grunts who ride into battle in trucks and get hauled out in ambulances. The Soviets have a bad habit of leaving their dead behind for someone else to bury.

"Here, between Berlin and us, is the Third Shock Army, with three tank divisions and one motorized rifle division." The tank and motorized rifle divisions along with their ID numbers rolled off Mac's tongue but went ignored by Lee, who, despite his weariness, was paying attention and counting the number of divisions.

"Around Berlin, we have the Twentieth Guards Army, which includes three tank divisions and one motorized rifle division. The Soviets don't keep any troops or tanks in Berlin itself. What I speculate is … if the Soviets decide to invade Western Europe, the Twentieth Guards will join up with the Third Shock before they take Berlin and head west."

Lee was somewhat surprised by the number of Soviet units. Nonetheless, he kept on counting.

"Down here we have the Eighth Guards Army, which is right across from the Fulda Gap. We pay special attention to it. The reason being, almost everyone, myself included, believes the Fulda Gap is where the Soviets will start their invasion of West Germany. For starters, it's their shortest route into central Germany. It's an ancient trade route connecting Frankfurt with points east, and Napoleon used it when he visited in the late seventeen-hundreds … your history lesson for the day. As you can see, it's where East Germany bulges out into West Germany. And, if they can control the Rhine Valley and the bridges across the Rhine, for all intents and purposes, it cuts the Allied armies in half. Those are the Brits, the Germans, and other NATO units to the north of the Rhine and ourselves and the French to the south."

Mac continued, "The Eighth Guards consists of one tank division and three motorized rifle divisions. Behind them is the First Guards Tank Army, made up of two tank divisions and one motorized rifle division. As above, before the balloon goes up, I believe the First will join up with the Eighth.

"Probably, there is at least a division of artillery deployed with the other units in East Germany. The Soviet battle plan is quite elementary. Artillery, followed by tanks, then infantry—allowing these units to leapfrog each other. They brought it to an art form as they came from Stalingrad to Berlin. If that's not enough, there's two East German tank divisions and four motorized rifle divisions scattered around the GDR. And, if that's still not enough, there's six Soviet tank divisions and five motorized rifle divisions in Poland, Hungary, and Czechoslovakia."

"If I counted correctly there are twenty Soviet divisions here in East Germany alone. How many troops do the Soviets have in those twenty divisions?" Lee inquired.

"I'm impressed! Here's a GI, who can count higher than ten without unzipping his fly or taking off his shoes … you'll go far in today's army. No, seriously, that's an excellent question. In fact, it's the sixty-four-dollar question. Nobody knows. I doubt even those steel-toothed bastards themselves know how many troops they have. I've seen estimates, more akin to wild-ass speculations, from three hundred fifty to eight hundred thousand. In my opinion, it's somewhere around five hundred thousand. Anyone whose IQ is at least as high as their body temperature has concluded that we are woefully outnumbered, out-armored, and outgunned. I've seen estimates anywhere between five to one, all the way to ten to one. By we, I mean ourselves, the Brits, the Germans, and a few NATO troops. I don't include the spineless Frogs. The French will run up the white flag as soon as they hear the first round go off. And regrettably, in the mindset of most of the military and civilian population here in Western Europe, it isn't a matter of *if*, it's only *when!* Our job is to help keep that from happening."

Lee, a somewhat skilled gambler, understood odds spreads.

Five or ten to one! I'll never smile again.

"And all of this is happening at the wrong time of the year. We see small unit training going on in the spring after the Soviet troops rotate in and out because of their conscription cycle. Then, we don't see large-scale exercises at the army and GSFG level until late fall. So here we are smack-dab in the middle of summer ... but, they're acting as if it's November ... with every unit in East Germany looking like it's getting ready to leave garrison. Damned if I know, and, here's the kicker in all this ... what the Soviets are capable of does not necessarily indicate what they are planning to do. On the other hand, it may. Or, are they just jerking our chain, wanting us to believe they will try to take Western Europe, thus pinning down our troops in Europe while they are planning something somewhere else in the rest of the world? The bottom line is that we don't know diddly-squat. And uncertainty leads to a bunch of anxiety and sleepless nights."

Mac then went into a synopsis of the Soviet military personnel. The officers and NCOs were almost all from Slavic-speaking countries. The ordinary soldiers were, for the most part, of Asiatic heritage, and then Mac added, "They are considered more expendable than bullets." He continued, noting the Soviets did not have a strong NCO corps as the Americans and Brits did, concluding, "Their junior officers do most of the functions our NCOs perform. They have a two-year conscription. As with all soldiers, it takes them time to get up to speed. Then, like soldiers everywhere, develop a short-timer's attitude. That means they only get about one good year of soldiering from their troops. Factor that into the equation, along with however many troops are on the ground, to get some idea of their real strength."

Lee just continued to listen.

"Be apprised we get outstanding intel from the American and British Liaison Missions out of Potsdam. The US, the Brits, and French all entered separate agreements with the Soviets to allow the so-called liaisons to travel within their zones. These liaisons are nothing but authorized spies. Our arrangement provides for fourteen Soviet military personnel at a time to wander about in the American zone, and we get to have fourteen of our troops in East Germany. The Brit's agreement is, I think, for thirty-one on each side. It doesn't matter how many the Frogs have since they never turn up anything of value. We go out in two-man teams, an officer and an enlisted man, who is the driver. The Brits go out in three-man teams. With their cameras and recorders, they come back with great stuff. Our missions have recently turned to scavenging in Soviet trash dumps. As it turns out, the Soviets are sloppy about what gets tossed into the garbage. So, if anything comes across your desk from the BRIXMIS or the USMLM, treat it as if it were gospel. Somewhat along the same lines is the West German intelligence service, the BMD. A lot of the old Afrika Korps soldiers were Prussians. After the war those troops who survived returned to their homes in East Germany. The BMD has recruited these old Afrika Korps guys as informants against the East Germans and Soviets. So occasionally we get some good intel from the BMD. On the other hand, we're cautious as to what we provide them. They've been thoroughly infiltrated by Soviet agents."

Lee, feeling as if some response was necessary, said, "I get it."

"Now as to what's happening here today. Frankly, we don't have the vaguest clue or inkling, other than something big is coming down. What we do know is that the Soviets are on heightened alert, and several units appeared to be prepped for movement. Throughout East Germany, the liaisons at Potsdam are telling us that rail cars used to transport tanks are being moved to railheads, which is their fastest way to move armor to Berlin or to the border. This looks a whole lot like what happened five years ago when the Soviets invaded Hungary. The good news ... if there is any ... is there doesn't appear to be any movement of troops from the other Soviet bloc countries toward East Germany, just the preparation for movement of those GSFG units already here. The other thing that scares the shit out of me is the fact they have extended fuel pipelines for their tanks to near Magdeburg and almost all the way to the border across from the Fulda Gap. As a rule, when they deploy on exercises, they try to camouflage those pipelines. This time, they didn't. Perhaps it's nothing more than a bluff … but if it's not … we had better batten down the hatches."

Not news Lee wanted to hear.

"There's not a hell of a lot you can do here today, so catch the shuttle bus back to the Kaserne and get some rest. I have a feeling we're all going to need it before the next few days are done. I'll see you back here in the morning. Oh, by the way, welcome aboard!"

Mac left.

Nickel tour my ass. I've been on the job for two hours and have already been exposed to more top secret information than most people will ever receive in a lifetime.

Lee gathered up his weapon and gear and went looking for the shuttle bus back to the Kaserne. Once there, he found his bunk. His last bed had been at Fort Devens all those many hours—or was it days—since. Having only fitfully dozed on the flight over the Atlantic, he slept as soundly as a log.

THOU SHALT NOT SPEAK WITHOUT PROFANITY

A few years later, the above phrase was codified as the Ninth Commandment of the satirical *Army Ten Commandments*. This edict had been in effect for as long as there had been an army and was certainly prevalent at the time of this story.

The GIs found themselves in an all-male environment without the constraints imposed elsewhere in polite society. Profanity was not only allowed but expected.

There were all those wonderful, pithy, vulgar, ribald, obscene, scatological, and profane monosyllabic Old English and Anglo-Saxon words that might be mixed and matched, whether with themselves or with other words. This gave the GI a very extensive, albeit not rich, vocabulary.

The f-word was predominant, as a verb and all its variants. And, as an adjective it was inexhaustible. It would find itself embedded in multiple syllable words and phrases, both English and German—the possibilities were endless. Also, the f-word adjective intermixed with proper Christian nouns brought blasphemy to a new high or low, depending upon one's commitment to the biblical Third Commandment. F-word usage was so common that it was often considered to be colloquial and conversational rather than profane; and, it could be used as a noun base. Quite often, the GIs' use of the word *mother* turned out to be only the first half of the utterance.

When the GIs varied from f-word usage, they tended to take a scatological track, bilingually at times. They routinely uttered, "*Verdammte Scheisse!*" (Damned Shit!), after being in the country for a while.

There must be at least twenty euphemisms for someone who is inebriated, yet most GIs utilized only two. Whenever a compatriot was a falling-down, drooling, and slurring drunk, his companions deemed him to be shit-faced. Or, they regarded him as totally-pissed. Not angry, just intoxicated.

At the time, the army in all its misguided wisdom had a recruitment poster, somewhat on the order of 'Join the army for Fun, Travel, and Adventure,' with FTA displayed in huge letters. This almost instantly became an unfortunate choice of an acronym. It took on two meanings. The polite one standing for the intended fun, travel, and adventure. For the not-so-polite one—Fuck The Army!

To their credit, the GIs of that era made a significant contribution to profanity. They outed the f-word in FUBAR and SNAFU from their World War II acronym closets and in their place created a new word encompassing all f-word situations: Clusterfuck. For generations to come, this word would remain in the GI vocabulary.

Aside from the profanity, other words and phrases were routinely used by the GIs.

A *keeper* was used to identify a young single woman with whom they would consider entering a long-term relationship, whether because of physical appearance, personality, and perhaps even intellect. Brainpower alone, however, was almost never a qualifying criterion. For those of the chauvinistic ilk, they didn't care if she was dumb as a rock, provided she was attractive and fun to be around.

The GI rated everything on a scale of one to some characteristic or definition. For example, "On a scale of one to Coyote Ugly, how would you rate the flat-chested broad sitting over there?" The responses were then numerical—one being the absolute minimum, and ten, the maximum. "Oh, she's somewhere between unattractive and hideous. I'd give her at least a seven, maybe an eight." This scale was used to rate things both good and bad.

Schatzi is the German word for girlfriend or sweetheart. The GIs realized that it rhymed with Nazi. Thus, the term *Nazi Schatzi* was often used by the GI, not in a particularly pejorative sense, but only to indicate the girlfriend was of German descent. However, if a GI wanted to positively piss off some frau or fräulein he had just encountered, all he had to do was to refer her as schatzi. Hell, hath no fury like a German woman being called *sweetie* by the hated *Ami*, which was the Germans' standard and often derogatory reference to American soldiers. Almost always, the Germans added a Teutonic invective or two along with Ami for good measure.

Career soldiers were referred to as 'lifers,' 'retreads,' or simply 'treads,' and those with several in-service stripes were known as 'zebras'—always uttered as uncomplimentary.

Straße or *Strasse* translates to 'the street.' The GIs would figuratively say, 'Going out on the Strasse' or 'Hitting the Strasse,' as nothing more than getting out of the barracks and involved in whatever was going on.

The GI phonetically adopted the German *macht nichts*, roughly meaning 'it doesn't matter.' It was, as a rule, used by the Germans as a reply to an apology. The GI corrupted it to "mox nix," or "mox no nix" and used it frequently.

The GIs in the intelligence business also picked up on the Russian pejorative term for Germans—*Dubs*. Phonetically, doobs. Semantically, it meant someone who was oak-headed.

A RUDE AWAKENING

Lee was startled awake the first morning hearing a booming, "*Guten Morgen. Y*ou fucking Krauts!" Standing in his skivvies at an open window was a barrel-chested, three-stripe buck sergeant Lee had seen on the floor of the SCIF the previous day. Not satisfied with the echo coming back from the adjacent apartment buildings, he again bid his beloved Germans another, even louder, good morning.

Well, no need to worry about having an alarm clock with that guy sleeping in here.

Finished with this portion of his rat-killing (all those things one feels obligated to deal with as life and shit happen) the sergeant headed down the hall to continue his morning routine, the three Ss. Or, as a Hispanic from a barrio somewhere in the Southwest had so articulately put it during basic training, "*Cheet, chower, y chave.*"

THE FIRST DAY

After being awakened by the buck sergeant bidding the Germans a good morning, Lee climbed out of his top bunk among his roommates preparing for the day. He had no clue as to the location of any facilities. His lower bunkmate introduced himself as Tim and, seeing the confused look on Lee's face, said, "I'll bet our FDL so-called platoon sergeant just dumped you here and didn't explain shit."

"You got it."

"Well, at least that worthless tread is consistent. The showers are down the hall on the left. Shaving is a problem. If you use a blade, you have to do it by feel since there aren't any usable mirrors."

"I have an electric."

"Good. Don't plug it into an outlet unless you have a transformer. Otherwise, it will go up in a cloud of black smoke."

"I don't have a transformer."

"Here, you can use mine until you get one. After you get cleaned up, I'll take you down to the company clerk, get you a mess hall pass, and introduce you to our wonderful dining facility."

On their way to the mess hall, his bunkmate showed Lee where to catch the shuttle bus to the Farben Building.

"Hey, thanks. I might never have done it without you."

"Don't worry. Your turn will come. I guess you know you arrived on-station at just the wrong time. Now is about the only time of the year we get any sunshine. The Russians have made a point of mucking things up, so we can't enjoy it."

"Yeah. I kinda got that idea at the in-briefing yesterday."

After consuming what the army called breakfast, Lee boarded the shuttle bus and rode to the Farben Building, then braved the paternoster to the sixth-floor landing while pulling out his security badge. He made his way to the seventh-floor SCIF, where Mac was waiting for him.

"Did you get squared away down at the Kaserne?" asked Mac.

"After a fashion. They don't seem to be the most organized bunch, but a guy I saw here on the floor yesterday pointed me in the right direction."

Mac led Lee to a desk piled high with yellow intercept sheets. "This is now your domain. Our daily take from two divisions of the Eighth Guards, the 79th and the 27th. On-the-job training, and like nothing you encountered at Devens. Your job is to make your way through this pile and pick out the good stuff."

"And exactly what is *The Good Stuff?*"

Mac chuckled, "It will become intuitive. Set aside anything that appears to be a fact. Unit IDs, commander's names, physical locations both by name or by grid coordinates, whatever is definitive.

"Okay," replied a somewhat skeptical Lee. "I'll give it my best shot."

"Pay attention to operator chatter. You'd be surprised what you can learn from their attitudes. If they're bitching about chickenshit officers, they're likely to be in garrison. If their gripe is about living conditions and food, they're probably on exercise. If they're concerned about what is happening, they may well be in a deployment mode. Don't dally too long over each intercept. Otherwise, you'll never get finished. Set aside anything you think might be of interest. At the end of the day, I'll go through your take. Any questions?"

"What's the rules for breaks and lunch?"

"No rules on breaks, and whenever it starts to all run together, get up and get away from it for a while. If you're a smoker, it's best to go outside. Absolutely no smoking here in the SCIF. There's a German shop as you get off the paternoster on the first floor that has good pastries. We take a long lunch break since you guys must be shuttled back and forth to the Kaserne. There is a cafeteria midway down the building, albeit pay-as-you-go." What Mac didn't tell Lee was that he took lunch at what was indeed the most opulent officers club in the entire army. Also known as the Casino, it was located directly behind the Farben Building.

Mac concluded saying, "Starting today, at the end of the day, I'm going to gather everyone here in the SCIF for an exchange of any information gleaned in the last twenty-four hours, plus a briefing as to what I have learned from outside sources. Last, but not least, I prepare a report on the status of the GSFG, which gets sent off to the powers that be. It goes without saying, the next few days are gonna be doozies."

With that, Mac left, and Lee attacked the pile of little yellow sheets with a classified burn bag at his side. It soon became evident that the Morse code and linguistic intercept operators at the outstations copied everything going through the ether, regardless of how trivial or incomplete it may have been. Lee set an occasional sheet aside, though the bulk went into the burn bag. He did encounter one that got his attention. It was operator chatter. A couple of Soviet troops were speculating about why they had been issued ominously more live ammunition than was usually the case when they went on exercise maneuvers. Lee drew a big question mark on it and placed it at the top of his save pile.

Later in the afternoon, Mac stopped at Lee's desk, "How goes it?"

"Not much here, I'm afraid," he said as he handed Mac his little stack of saved intercepts.

Mac briefly scanned through the sheets saying, "You're getting the hang of it. This one about 'Why the additional ammunition?' is precisely the kind of thing we are looking for." With that, he dropped all the saved intercepts into the burn bag except for the one about excess ammo. He patted Lee on the shoulder saying, "Good job," as he walked away.

So, this is what I'll be doing. Spending a whole day sifting through thousands of pieces of paper, only to find one of interest.

THE END-OF-DAY BRIEFING

At the end of the day shift, Mac went to the center of the SCIF and boomed out, "Everyone, gather round, and listen up!" Those nearby remained at their desks. Others meandered closer. Mac continued, "Here's the situation, as best I can tell. Throughout East Germany, the GSFG is on heightened alert, although not as high as we saw back in fifty-three when they put down the revolt in East Germany or in fifty-six with the Hungarian revolution. The Potsdam liaisons report that units around Berlin appear to be getting ready to move out of their garrisons. They also note that most of their forces between Berlin and the border are doing the same. Okay, what do you guys have to add?"

One of the analysts offered, "Traffic volume for the units around Berlin is sky high, and I get a sense of urgency, which makes sense with what Potsdam is saying."

Then, other analysts responsible for the rest of East Germany indicated this was the case throughout the GDR.

Mac again, "And, oh, by the by, we have a newbie with us today. Lee, stand up so everyone can get a look at your scrawny ass."

Lee complied saying, "Thanks. I appreciate such a laudatory introduction."

Mac chuckled, "You're welcome. I could've told them you came up with the best intel of the day, to wit, that units are being issued more ammo than they usually leave garrison with. But, that would have gotten you off on the wrong foot with this bunch of egotists."

Mac concluded, "I want all of you when off duty to not wander too far, or for too long, away from the barracks. Remember the midnight to six a.m. curfew that was imposed last week. Try to stay reasonably sober in case this situation turns to total shit. Keep up the good work!"

These end-of-the-day briefings would continue for some time as the imminence of hostilities indicators increased with the preparation for movement, then the movement itself, of large numbers of Soviet and East German troops.

THE FIRST NIGHT ON THE TOWN

The second night after Lee had reported for duty at the 251st, he and three other newly arrived slick-sleeved privates were gathered up by a PFC who had some time on the ground saying, "Newbies, you wanna go see what Germany is really like?"

Of course, they did.

Then Lee remembered Mac's earlier admonition about not straying too far from the Kaserne saying, "You're sure this is okay?"

"Yeah, *no problemo,* where we're going ain't all that far. We'll be back by midnight." He then led them down Gutleutstrasse to the Hauptbahnhof and then onto the adjacent Kaiser Strasse, which was Frankfurt's red-light district. Lee had experienced the Juarez equivalent while in college. It was Yogi Berra's "It's like *déjà-vu,* all over again," with some cultural and linguistic differences. Sleazy bars with shills out on the sidewalk, speaking German-accented English rather than Spanglish while urging the foot traffic to come inside. The same for pimps soliciting their trade. Hard liquor was s*chnaps* instead of *tequila, bier* rather than *cerveza.* The music was oompah-pah replacing mariachi. When they came alongside one establishment, their guide warned, "Don't ever go in there, that's a blacks-only bar."

The newbies raised their eyebrows, then one asked, "Does that mean there are whites-only bars?

"You got it."

"How about bars for both blacks and whites?"

"Are you kidding me? They don't exist. And everybody prefers it that way ... the Krauts, the army, and most of all the police. It keeps bloodshed to a minimum. The US Army may be integrated, but welcome to Germany, where it's not."

After about a block, Lee had enough. "Thanks for the tour. I'm going to head back to the Kaserne and get some shut-eye." The other three newbies followed Lee.

Undaunted by the newbies' lack of interest the PFC continued his night on the town—different strokes for different folks.

As the foursome headed back to the barracks, one commented, "Surely this isn't what Frankfurt and Germany are really like." Except for the self-segregated boozing establishments, Lee soon learned that what they had just experienced was not at all representative of Frankfurt and Germany. However, what would come as a surprise, as he later discovered, was that some remnants of the German mindset of the '30s and '40s lingered.

A few days later Lee came across an intercept that got his attention. He passed it on to Mac. It was sent by a Russian Major at the Soviet Babelsberg autobahn checkpoint to his headquarters in Berlin—He was very pissed off about being pissed on!

A convoy containing a company of American troops on their way to training in West Germany, while traveling on the East German autobahn, had encountered one of the typical chickenshit Soviet inspectors. The inspector insisted all be lined up shoulder to shoulder, so he would be able to look at faces and haircuts as he counted. Perhaps he hoped to spot someone who wasn't a GI being smuggled out of Berlin. There were 110 of them, according to their paperwork. On the Russian Major's first count, he had come up with 112. The second time through the tally, the number was 111. By now the GIs had been standing for an extended period and were getting fidgety. The first sergeant suggested to the company commander that the troops needed a pee break. The CO agreed.

As the inspector began his third count, the first sergeant issued a loud set of unusual commands that went something on the order of this: "Unbutton trousers! Hang it out! Relieve yourselves!"

The next morning, Mac, chuckling to himself, came in amongst the analysts saying, "All listen up. Lee, you remember that intercept from the Soviet autobahn checkpoint leaving Berlin? It turns out the Russians issued a complaint and the army investigated. Now the story is all over the net." Mac told the episode, ending with, "Can you imagine a hundred or so guys all lined up, with dicks in hand, pissing on command?"

One GI piped up, "That is a funny story. I can see why it *leaked* out."

A second GI added, "Marching units should incorporate it into their *short-arms* drill."

A third completed the thought, "Yeah, and the final command should be, *Preeezent arms!*"

After a good laugh, the GIs went back to scanning intercepts. It seemed they spent a little more time before dropping the yellow sheets into burn bags. Perhaps looking for a small gem as good as the one the newbie Lee had found.

After this incident and until the wall came down, Soviet inspectors never again insisted that American troops be lined up to be counted.

BACK ABOARD THE USS GORDON IN NEW YORK HARBOR

As they waited to disembark under the vigilant eye of Lady Liberty, Lee struck up a conversation with the guy behind him in line, a Spec/4 wearing the USAREUR flaming sword patch that Lee had worn before the ASA had been reorganized. "Where were you stationed?" asked Lee.

"Heidelberg. I was a clerk-typist. Not much glory and grade in that MOS."

"I suppose not, but you were at the prime duty station in all of Europe. I was a signal intelligence analyst and spent most of my time in Frankfurt. Rank came quickly, and there was a little bit of glory ... none of which was ever recorded because of the classification. My name's Lee, by the way."

"Mine's Isaac. I had a safe ... although crappy ... job. Get up, go to the same office, sit at the same desk, type out the same forms on the same typewriter, day, after day. But I did learn a lot about office politics working at a headquarters. That was kinda enlightening. Officers were covering their asses while at the same time trying to sabotage someone else. We lowly enlisted even had office pools as to who would succeed and who wouldn't. For us lowly grunts, temporary duty ... TDY ... wasn't an option, so the only parts of Germany I saw was on my own. I'll bet your being in the intelligence business was kind of interesting, huh?"

"If by interesting you mean being scared shitless at times, then yes. However, I did get to see a lot of Germany on Uncle Sam's dime." On the scary side of things, Lee went into some depth, being careful not to reveal any classified information. He continued, explaining how he came to realize how overwhelmed the Western-allied troops would be if the Soviets decided to travel westward. Then confided to Isaac his nagging concern or fear throughout his tour about the Soviet menace. He even mentioned his plans to get out of Germany if the balloon went up. Lee then recounted the Checkpoint Charlie incident where Soviet and American armor and troops with weapons locked and loaded, had faced off at point-blank range in Berlin and—how, in his opinion—the world came nearer to going up in a radioactive cloud than it did in the Cuban crisis.

"I had no idea. And I suspect many like myself didn't realize how serious Checkpoint Charlie was. After hearing all that I'm glad to be on this side of the Atlantic and about to get out of the active army."

With that, Lee dropped beside his duffel bag and reflected on some of the dicier times.

WHY THE BERLIN WALL WENT UP

Berlin was divided up, again per the Potsdam conference dictate, as was the rest of Germany. Those portions of the city were referred to as sectors. The Russian sector, known as East Berlin, was controlled by the Soviets while West Berlin was administered by the other Allies, each with their separate sector.

Late in the war, General Eisenhower informed the Russians that the Western Allies planned to stop their advance at the Elbe River—as per the Yalta Conference accord—and the Russians were free to take Berlin. Which they did, at a horrific cost—some 300,00 casualties. The Soviets believed, having paid such a price for the taking of Berlin, that it was now exclusively theirs to control. This division of Germany in general—and Berlin in particular—became a major bone of contention in the international arena in the years to come.

The FRG residents enjoyed a prosperous capitalist economy and newfound freedoms of a democratic parliamentary government. In the GDR, the inhabitants under the Stalinist Walter Ulbricht endured a stagnant socialistic economy; and, those hapless folks had merely exchanged one brutal, stifling dictatorship for another with a different ideology.

There was a vivid and unmistakable contrast between East and West Berlin. East Berliners saw the difference every time they were permitted to travel between the zones, and some fifty thousand East Berliners had worked in the western sectors before the wall went up. Visitors from elsewhere in the Eastern Bloc were also exposed to the polar-opposite ideologies. It was not a positive image to present to visiting comrades. Hence, Berlin became the focal point of the Cold War, in Berlin and around the world.

Stalin, and later also Khrushchev, wanted East Berlin and East Germany to be the models of Sovietization to which other Eastern Bloc countries should aspire. The Marxist bosses knew Allied control of West Berlin, some 110 miles inside East Germany was a severe threat to their plan.

The Marshall Plan was implemented, which Stalin unsuccessfully did his best to prevent. Once the plan was instituted, he stopped the Eastern Bloc nations from joining. Czechoslovakia and Poland had very much wanted to join

As an outcome of the Marshall Plan, the FRG entered what the Germans called *Ein Wirtschaftswunder* (an economic miracle). And, the people detained in the East German *Workers Paradise* wanted to be part of that action.

In the early 1950s, East Germans began defecting to West Germany in droves. In 1955, the Soviets closed the inner German border and erected a barbed-wire fence along its length. The barbed wire fence was a minor impediment. However, the punishment for those caught attempting to cross the border was severe, long jail terms—assuming one wasn't shot in the process. In 1957, East Germany instituted a passport law severely restricting the number of citizens leaving the GDR.

In Berlin, however, travel between East and West Berlin was thus far relatively unhindered. Consequently, Berlin became the funnel for this enormous flow of humanity making its way out of the GDR to points west.

By August 1961, some 3,500,000, or 20 percent of the GDR's population, had fled. The number of defectors was of grave concern, but the demographics of those fleeing was devastating to the East German government. They were the young, professional, technical, and well-trained individuals from the core of that society. At that time, it was estimated that scarcely half of the remaining GDR population was of working age, and its economy on the verge of collapse. Khrushchev feared that if East Germany went down the tubes, there would be a domino effect, starting with Poland and taking down the rest of his Eastern Bloc satellites.

For years, Ulbricht had urged Khrushchev to stop what historians called the hemorrhaging of the lifeblood of the GDR. In public statements in late July 1961, both President Kennedy and Senator Fulbright told the East Germans and Soviets they could do whatever they damn well pleased in East Berlin and East Germany, to the consternation of the other Western Allies. Kennedy's only concern seemed to be the Allied access rights to and within Berlin. Khrushchev ultimately agreed with Ulbricht.

THE END-OF-DAY BRIEFINGS AS THE WALL WENT UP

At the close of each day shift, Mac would gather the soldiers in the SCIF around him for a daily briefing as to what was happening in East Germany and specifically what was going on in Berlin. There was a free exchange of information, with most of the relevant material coming from Mac.

Thursday, 10 August

Mac opened, saying, "Well shit guys, I don't have much good news. GSFG is still on heightened alert. The Potsdam missions are reporting that GSFG units around Berlin appeared to be preparing to leave their garrisons, and flat cars for rail transport of tanks are being moved into position for loading. Yesterday, an interesting bit of information was in an intercept picked up at Teufelsberg in Berlin. It was a vague reference that the East Germans going to restrict foot traffic in and out of the Soviet sector. It didn't say where or when. It's been forwarded to NSA, and perhaps they have other intel that ties in with it.

Friday, 11 August

After getting everyone's attention, Mac stated, "Things are getting a little dicey. Potsdam reports all units around Berlin and between Berlin and the border seem to be getting ready to hit the road. It's too early in the year for large-scale maneuvers by those steel-toothed bastards. As a rule, we don't see this kind of activity until late fall, around the October–November time frame. Let's just hope this is nothing more than a GSFG-wide training exercise that is ahead of the normal schedule. Nothing new on the intercept at Teufelsberg about restricting foot traffic. However, the MPs roaming around the Soviet sector in Berlin have recently reported what appear to be stockpiles of sawhorses, barbed wire, and concrete posts. Perhaps they're going to do some fencing, but this doesn't seem to be of concern to our so-called decision-makers."

Saturday, 12 August

Mac started by saying, "Pretty much the same on the Eastern front today. Heightened alert and lots of activity within the garrisons themselves. That's relatively good news. The bad news is … All Soviet troops have been ordered off leave and are to remain in caserne!

"The even possibly worse news is … I'm worried about what our President may, or may not do if this turns to shit. After his experience with Khrushchev at the Vienna Summit, the last thing Kennedy probably wants is another confrontation with the Soviet boss. Especially since it's only been a few days ago that he implied in a public speech that they could do whatever they wanted in regards Berlin.

"The really bad news for you guys is … I'm restricting you to stay within the Kaserne until we have a better idea as to what in the hell is happening."

A murmur of discontent arose from the troops. One GI was heard to mutter to himself, "Really bad news, my ass. The proper adjective would be either shitty or crappy."

Mac continued, "I know, I know. You and your Nazi Schatzies are not going to be happy campers, but that's the way it's going to be.

Console yourselves with the fact you have an EM club, and … please … limit your consumption of booze in case this thing goes completely tits-up."

Sunday, 13 August

Mac was somber, not his usual easy-going demeanor when he called the troops together. "What we have in Berlin and throughout East Germany appears to be a massive clusterfuck. I'm not sure what's happening, but here's what I do know. Early this morning the East Germans turned off all the streetlights and shut down all public transportation in the Soviet sector. Then they brought in an inordinate number of the armed police and militia forces to close off the border between the East and West sectors and around the perimeter of West Berlin. According to reports, in some places, standing almost shoulder to shoulder. The MPs in Berlin estimate there are at least twenty thousand police and militia scattered about. Then they began laying rolled barbed wire on sawhorses and setting prefab concrete posts to hang the wire on. In the process, they closed off all except thirteen of the crossing points between the sectors."

A GI asked, "How might they have possibly gotten an estimate so quickly? And that's a hell of a lot of barbed wire. Where did it come from?"

Mac continued, "For the estimate … maybe they counted the number of troops within a given distance, at a few places around the city … getting an average of troops-to-distance. The distance around the Allied sector is a known, then it's just a matter of arithmetic. The barbed wire is a good question. To the best of my knowledge, none is produced in the GDR. So, they apparently went into Western Europe to buy it. If somebody shows up with marks, francs, or pounds, whoever is selling doesn't give a shit who is buying or what it is to be used for. While all this was going on, the East Germans moved troops toward East Berlin from their Eighth Motorized Artillery Division and the First Motorized Division garrisons, along with a couple of hundred tanks. There are now an estimated ten thousand East German soldiers in East Berlin, which is ten thousand more than allowed by the Potsdam Agreement. That's the situation in Berlin as best I know it."

By now, the troops in the SCIF joined Mac in his demeanor. During his narrative, frequent expletives could be heard muttered within the group.

Mac continued, "The Potsdam missions have been active and report three nearby Soviet divisions, along with two East German divisions, are moving towards Berlin. The four Soviet divisions between Berlin and the border are also positioning behind the East German divisions right at the border. It appears as if they plan to let the East Germans be the cannon fodder should there be an attack from the west. Either that or they don't expect the East Germans to hold the line. The effectiveness of the Potsdam missions is going to be zilch since the Soviets have declared the areas surrounding Berlin, and between Berlin and the border, as 'Temporary Restricted Areas.' The missions aren't permitted to travel in these areas, so we must rely on our radio direction-finding folks, the duffers, for the location of all these units being repositioned. I must give those steel-tooth bastards credit, they didn't declare the restricted areas until already on the move, as to not give a tip-off about what was coming down. Bottom line … My guess is, Berlin is now entirely surrounded!"

During this portion of the narrative, the expletives heard were no longer muttered, they were loud.

Mac then announced that to provide twenty-four-hour coverage, shifts would be extended from eight hours to twelve hours in length and would be divided into two groups. One group would be on duty from four in the morning until four in the afternoon and the other from four in the early evening until four in the morning. This way, all would be able to attend the daily briefings. Surprisingly, there were no complaints.

Thus, on this date, a wall began to be built—not just within Berlin itself, but the entire length of the border between East and West Germany. Ultimately, it would become a barricade complete with watchtowers, searchlights, sirens, and tank traps; and, a no-man's land of minefields and cleared areas to provide a field of fire to shoot anyone attempting to escape.

They did, however, establish crossing points in the wall for vehicular travel like the one at Friedrichstrasse, aka Checkpoint Charlie, and not try to restrict Western sector vehicles from entering and exiting East Berlin. That would happen a couple of months later.

A line was drawn in the sand of international confrontations.

Monday, 14 August

Mac started, "Needless to say, the people of Berlin are big-time pissed off, on both sides of the border. The East Berliners because they are trapped in the so-called *Worker's Paradise*. Specifically, those fifty thousand border-crossers who live in East Berlin and until yesterday worked in West Berlin. The West Berliners as well, because, the Allies ... namely the Americans ... haven't responded. There have been a bunch of demonstrations on both sides of the border, but none seem to have gotten out of hand. The duffers in West Germany have been hard at it. Regrettably, their triangulation is iffy, and it's difficult to determine which units are located on the east versus the west side of Berlin. Nevertheless, they have identified and located two units ... the Sixth and the Nineteenth Motorized Rifle Divisions. And, here's the kicker ... Soviet missile forces have been placed on full alert throughout Eastern Europe!"

The usual chorus of expletives arose from the group.

Tuesday, 15 August

Mac began by saying, "The state-of-affairs in East Berlin has calmed down, and it appears the deployed troops are in defensive rather than offensive modes."

One GI immediately popped up saying, "I thought you told us that the Potsdam missions couldn't travel in the so-called restricted areas around Berlin. So how do you know whether it's offensive or defensive?"

For the first time in days, Mac smiled. "Our Potsdam guys are known for not playing by the rules, but you don't need to repeat that. The duffers have now also identified the Tenth Guards Tank Division all snuggled up next to Berlin."

An obviously frustrated senior GI uttered, "Why the hell are we letting this happen? Give every trooper in Berlin a pair of wire cutters and let them go to work. This is all Ulbricht's idea, and if we show just a modicum of balls, the Soviets will back down. I'm almost ashamed to say I'm an American."

"My sentiments exactly," declared Mac. "However, someone way above our grade is making that decision. We just need to concentrate on doing our job and see where it goes."

Wednesday, 16 August

"Well, it's happening," said Mac. "The East Germans are sealing off East Berlin. They are moving in prefab concrete slabs and setting them in place to form a wall and bricking up doors and windows that open out into the Allied sectors. A few people are still getting through the wire, and they have begun to shoot at those attempting to escape. However, the autobahn to West Germany remains open, as do the air corridors. Disappointingly, no hint of any action or force by our powers that be. The Potsdam missions report that throughout the GDR, units are moving to fill the gaps left open by the divisions now around Berlin and those between Berlin and the border. It also appears that GSFG units are positioning behind East German border units throughout the country. I think it tells a great deal about how the Russians feel about the reliability of the East Germans should the balloon go up."

Thursday, 17 August

"Pretty much the same as yesterday," said Mac, after getting everyone's attention. "A wall is going up all around Berlin, and our guys are just standing around with their thumbs up their asses watching them. Still a little movement of units throughout East Germany. And, they are still at the same alert level. By the way, I do appreciate all of you *hombres* putting in the extra time and effort and not bitching about it."

Friday, 18 August

"Potsdam reports that most of the GSFG seem to have settled in place," was Mac's leadoff. "Yet they continue to be on heightened alert. That's the trivial stuff. This is important ... yesterday, the president announced that Vice President Johnson and General Lucius Clay will be coming to Berlin tomorrow. Johnson is only coming for a visit, but Clay is going to be the president's man in Berlin. The word is, Johnson isn't at all thrilled about coming. Perhaps it has something to do with a bunch of armed guys standing around with their fingers on the triggers. The good news, no, it's great news … General Clay is coming to stay, and he has *cojones* the size of basketballs!

"Also, the president is, at long last, starting to develop some spine … I suppose to show a token of resolve to the international community … and has ordered the 1st Battle Group, 18th Infantry to enter West Berlin through East Germany via the autobahn, starting near Helmstadt.

It'll be a perfect setup for the bad guys if they decide to start shooting, our guys lined up like ducks in a shooting gallery … I sure as hell wouldn't want to be in that convoy! If the shit is going to hit the fan, it's going to happen tomorrow. So, get some rest and stay off the booze."

Saturday, 19 August

"The Battle Group from our Eighth Division is now strung-out along the autobahn from Helmstadt to Berlin," Mac opened. "The Soviets and East Germans are just sitting there, watching them go by. Who would've guessed? Between Johnson and Clay showing up and the Battle Group starting to arrive in Berlin, the Krauts in West Berlin are going ape-shit."

Indeed, the West Berliners did give the soldiers and dignitaries a massive, rousing, and enthusiastic welcome. The convoy consisted of some fifteen hundred men in full combat gear in tanks, armored personnel carriers, howitzers, and support vehicles and were inundated with flowers—and likely with some *bier und wein*—showered upon them by the welcoming Berliners. It took most of the next day to tidy up their vehicles.

Sunday, 20 August

Mac's mood bordered on jovial when he started, "Well, the battle group made it into Berlin unscathed. We now have about twelve thousand Allied troops in Berlin, about three brigades. Realistically, only two brigades, once you factor in the Frogs' history of fighting wars. They are now surrounded by *only* four or more Soviet and East German divisions. I'm reminded of what Marine Corps General Chesty Puller stated under similar circumstances during the Korean War. Something along the lines of, 'The enemy is to the right, to the left, in front, and behind. They can't get away this time.' The same condition here. Now, Berlin is better defended, and we have those steel-toothed bastards right where we want them. The battle group brought with them a battery of one-o-five howitzers. Those buggers are anything but defensive weapons. Go figure. The guys at Potsdam report that throughout East Germany, both the GSFG and the East Germans are returning to garrison.

"The president along with his advisers ... contrary to reason and understanding ... appear relieved that a wall is going up. I guess, in their opinion, Berlin will no longer be a flashpoint in world political relations, but it's certainly not my take on it. Well, at least the Soviets didn't attempt to block access to West Berlin from West Germany."

As the group broke up, one trooper inquired, "Why does Mac always refer to the Russians as *those steel-toothed bastards?*" Lee flippantly responded, "Otherwise, he would often be saying, *those motherfucking, cunt licking, sonofabitches!* This way he gets to clean up his language a tad while still demeaning their dental work."

Monday, 21 August

Mac was brief, beginning with, "The Soviets are headed back to garrison and have gone off their alert. So, have we. Back to regular eight-hour days and no more end-of-day briefings. It's been a pleasure working with you guys through all of this. Get back and make up time with your schatzies, and perhaps suck down some beer in celebration. You certainly deserve it!"

THE BEER BARGE

The GIs took Mac's suggestion about guzzling some celebratory beer as if it were a direct order from the army's Chief of Staff.

Thus far, all Lee had seen of Frankfurt, except for Kaiser Strasse on his first night on the town, was the route to and from the Kaserne and the Farben Building.

After returning from duty that afternoon, Tim offered, "Lee, some of us are headed over to Herr Burke's beer barge. Wanna come?"

"Is the Pope Catholic?"

Five of them piled into Tim's car and crossed to the south side of the Main River, heading eastward. By now, Lee had learned that Main was pronounced as Mine and rhymed with Rhine. Speaking German was going to be a challenge. They passed through suburbs—all painted depressing shades of gray, like the rest of Frankfurt—and parked near the river. Nearby, what had once been a small river barge was now a floating outdoor *Bierstube* (beer pub).

To the south could be seen the imposing structure housing the Binding Beer brewery, whose advertisement 'Du und Mir und Binding Bier' (You and me and Binding Beer) seemed to appear on every billboard.

As they came down the gangplank, a short-of-stature fellow greeted each by name. When it came Lee's turn, Tim said, "Herr Burke, this is Lee. Lee, Herr Burke." Herr Burke gave a firm American-style handshake saying, "Lee, welcome aboard my humble enterprise and my even more humble abode."

You must be kidding me. This German has a better command of the English language than most of my recent so-called professors.

They were soon seated with a bottle of beer in hand—Binding Beer was, of course, the only option.

Must be like trying to buy something other than Coors in Golden, Colorado, which would border on sacrilege for the local folks.

Lee looked about. Spanning the river was a green-painted pedestrian bridge connecting the Altstadt with the suburb of Sachsenhausen. The pedestrians were scurrying along, headed for home after a day's work, or more likely, for a stop at one of the *Apfelwein Stubes* (hard cider pubs) for which Sachsenhausen was famous. Across the river were medieval church spires poking up toward the heavens.

Now, this is more like how I expected Germany to be.

A small group of fräuleins came aboard for a beer. To Lee, they didn't seem to be there to meet GIs, only to flaunt their ample wares. For the horny young men—who hadn't any exposure to the opposite sex for several days—this display resulted in a significant shift of blood flowing from one brain to the other. One of the observers muttered, "Those broads are nothing but a bunch of prick teases." Another GI alliterated, "Yeah, right. Just twits with tits and twats."

On board was a dispensing device that, if one inserted a five-pfennig coin, out dropped a handful of salted peanuts, which the beer drinkers consumed with gusto. The GIs tossed them into their mouths, looking as if pounding their faces with closed fists. The fräuleins seemed to think this was hilarious. This induced the GIs to eat more peanuts and thus drink more beer. No one would ever say Herr Burke didn't know how to sell beer to American troops.

Much later in the evening, as dusk approached, and the barge's clientele thinned out, Herr Burke joined them at their table. He was unsparingly reducing his beer inventory as he reminisced about his time in America. Burke had been a conscripted *Kriegsmarine* (wartime sailor) on a U-boat during the war and had been captured. After spending some time in a prisoner of war camp in Florida, he, along with almost two thousand other submariners, were transferred to the Papago POW facility near Phoenix. Like oil and water, their captors thought. The desert was a perfect place to send enemy sailors, and the two would never mix. *Au contraire!* The enlisted were permitted to volunteer for work on local cotton and citrus farms, earning eighty cents a day, payable in a script which was spendable at the prison commissary. This pittance kept them in cigarettes and toiletries. Because of his treatment by the farmer's family for which he worked, Burke came to respect the Americans. When it came time for the noon meal, the farmer and his family sat down with the POWs and shared the same food. Occasionally, on Sundays and almost always on religious holidays, the POWs were invited to the farmer's home to spend the day and share a meal. At the end of the war, Burke wanted to remain in Phoenix and work for the farmer, and the farmer desired that as well. They tried, but the military bureaucracy insisted all POWs return to Germany.

The GIs respectfully, albeit somewhat indifferently, listened as Burke continued.

Security at Papago was slack at best. The POWs dug a tunnel about two hundred yards underneath the prison fence, exiting into the bank of a nearby irrigation canal. On Christmas Eve, Burke and twenty-four other prisoners—about an even number of enlisted men and officers—supplied with phony documents, civilian clothing, water, and provisions made their escape. They had planned well for their existence on the run, although they had overlooked the Phoenix weather: they expected it to be hot and dry, but instead, because of a rare winter storm, it was cold and wet.

Burke now had the GIs' complete attention. Here before them was an actual, honest-to-God, real-life POW escapee—Stalag 17 in reverse!

Burke continued.

The officers intended to head to Mexico via the Gila and the Colorado Rivers. The enlisted, realizing the war was lost and nearing its end, planned to hide in the nearby mountains and wait out the war. Two of the officers made it to the Gila River, only to find a half-mile-wide dry arroyo. For the officers and the enlisted alike, their escape was short-lived. One of the escapees was a conscripted non-German who, without delay, went to the local authorities and informed them of the breakout while seeking asylum. Thus, it was the local authorities who told the Papago command there had been a large-scale escape, even before the prison officials knew it. Within two weeks, all the absconders were back behind the wire, dining only on bread and water for their derring-do.

Herr Burke was now selling beer to and sharing war stories with, those who a mere fifteen years previous had been considered the enemy.

This is, without a doubt, going to be a regular stop in my travels around Frankfurt.

Involve a bunch of folks who, for the most part, appear to be masochists that believe in applying the Golden Rule, and —

Who perceive a single leader's ideology is the only pathway to a nation's preeminent status in the world.

Who take solace in their self-inflicted pain and suffering.

Who have had ingrained in them for centuries that there are only two classes of people: those who give orders and those who follow orders.

Who, throughout time, had Aryan precepts embedded in their DNA.

Whose belief is not to reason why, but to do or die.

Who are fervent nationalists and believe the good of the state triumphs over the well-being of the individual.

Who foster an ethnic hatred of the French and Russian people going back a millennium.

Whose psyche possesses a victim mentality.

Who experience pleasure in the misery of others—so thoroughly is this ingrained into their culture, they have a single word for this phenomenon: *Schadenfreude*.

Who enthusiastically engaged in a little experiment in eugenics. It didn't turn out all that well, not to mention engendering some appalling bad publicity. Genocide tends to have that effect.

And who are thorough to a fault.

Take all these ingredients, add a dash of paganism and a pinch of the occult, and as a final component, a generous ration of anti-Semitism. Blend them together for twelve years and what do you get? Millions upon millions of dead, untold suffering, and an entire continent in ruins!

The German people were that bunch of folks. The end result of their generation's Nazi-indoctrinated ideology was World War II and its aftermath in Europe.

ATTITUDES AT THE TIME

Not unlike almost all young GIs who—in the 1960s—ended up in the army stationed in Germany, Lee was almost entirely and blissfully ignorant of World War II history. Most were too young to remember much about the war when it occurred. Some vaguely recalled movie newsreels of Holocaust horrors and multitudes of Germans with their *Heil Hitler* arms upheld during Nazi rallies. But in their minds, that was long past. They also were unaware of the German people's suffering in the latter years of the war and the period immediately following. Before deploying these young soldiers to Germany, the army did not attempt to instruct them about the European campaign and its negative impact on the lives of the German people or about the horrendous environment and experiences of the survivors afterward. The GIs had no concept what the German people had suffered. They naively arrived in Germany with an open and ambivalent attitude toward the Germans.

In their minds, they pictured a welcoming German people living in quaint, picturesque, medieval villages. In their libido, they imagined fräuleins hopping in bed for a Hershey bar or a pack of Lucky Strikes. None of their imaginings were realistic. The German populace was at best barely tolerant and at times downright hostile to the occupation troops. The GIs did not know that virtually every village and city with a medieval heritage had been bombed into piles of rubble. Few of the almost two hundred towns and cities with medieval cultures and architecture escaped the British and American bombs. And it was true that German women had been sexually vulnerable as they struggled to survive the war's aftermath, but this was no longer the case.

After World War II, Germany was in chaos, a word often used when one has no other vocabulary to describe appalling situations and circumstances.

All major cities and the communities surrounding industrial and military compounds had been reduced to giant piles of rubble. What remained was building materials, ashes, destroyed personal property, and an untold number of decomposing human bodies.

At the end of the war and the years immediately following it, the German people lived in a state of anarchy, combined with a dearth of infrastructure: no water, sewage, transportation, or communications services. The two winters following the war were brutally cold. Life consisted of only trying to survive the lack of food and fuel.

The Germans had plundered, pillaged, and raped as they went eastward in Operation Barbarossa—the planned conquest of Russia. Some twenty million Russian citizens perished in the process. For the Soviets moving westward following their victory at Kursk, it was now payback time. An estimated two million German women were viciously and serially raped as the Soviets advanced across eastern Germany. The French soldiers on the Western front weren't much better. Both continued their sexual exploitation throughout the early occupation of Germany. In the two years following the war, there were an estimated two million annual abortions by German women. Add to that 150,000 to 200,000 *Russkie babies* born to German women each year. For many such pregnant women, suicide became the only option.

The Americans and the Brits—to their credit—kept it in their pants unless it was consensual.

Throughout Germany, the situation was further compounded by the fact that some seven million slave laborers the Nazis brought into Germany were now free and on a spree of rape, pillage, and murder. There were also about twenty million ethnic Germans who had been run out of Eastern Europe, now roaming about without food or shelter. All of them were called *displaced persons*—as if the native Germans themselves were not. These displaced persons lived like rats in the rubble in cellars and basements while scavenging for food and fuel. Germans looted each other. Prostitution was rampant.

And, as a closing warning, the Allied victors had to deal with all those damned Nazis. Those who had been genuinely evil needed to be tried and punished. Those not quite so bad were denied all except manual labor positions. The top German engineers and scientists, many of whom were Nazis, were snatched up and hustled off to America before the Soviets could grab them. General Reinhard Gehlen's organization, replete with Nazis—which had spied on the Russians during the war—became the fledgling West German intelligence establishment, currently spying on the Soviets.

Now another problem arose: Who was going to maintain and operate institutional and governmental functions? It was soon learned that about the only folks available with those talents were ex-Nazis. Thus, a blind eye was often turned as they began to infiltrate back into those governing posts. Denazification was slowly but surely being pushed to the back burner.

The enormity of the German's plight was mind-boggling. Their society had reached a moral, functional, and economic nadir— Germany was undoubtedly in chaos.

Even after some fifteen-plus years, most of the German people remained somewhat hostile or at best uncertain in their attitudes towards the GIs. Some Germans would never admit they lost the war. For them, it was still going ongoing and continued to fight on in their pathetic little ways. None would openly admit to having been Nazis or having fought on the Western front against Allied forces.

The German people, young and old, either by coercion or acquiescence, had Nazi ideology branded into their brains since at least 1933. The anti-Semitic and *Deutschland über Alles* brain-numbing propaganda continued with a vengeance until the war ended in 1945. No one over ten years of age was exempt. The math was easy. If a German was ten years old in 1945 and it is now 1961, that German is now twenty-six. Thus, anyone over that age was suspected of having *Der Fuhrer's* mindset.

A nationwide poll was taken following the war with a statistically significant number responding to ensure accuracy. Even after calculating the carnage, more than half of the Germans surveyed thought Nazism had been the path to follow and had unfortunately just made a couple of wrong turns along the way. And, for many

Germans, it wasn't so much the Nazis had taken them into war but that those Fascist despots had the timidity to lose it.

The good news for the GIs was that most of the nubile fräuleins were under twenty-seven years of age. Focusing on this demographic, GIs discovered three strata of young unmarried women within German society.

At the societal top were the *nice* German girls who, by their own choice or parental and peer pressure, did not date American soldiers. Razor-phobic, these young women were easy to identify by their unshaven legs or underarms.

The next level down were young women who dated GIs with some Nordic resemblance. Most of those *not so nice* fräuleins were unopposed to body hair removal. However, there were occasional trimming holdouts in this group and whose GI boyfriends were often made fun of by their peers.

At the bottom were those females who, in the indoctrinated German's minds, dated African-American soldiers. Or, as these soldiers were deemed by the ex-master-race faithful, *Untermenschen* (subhumans). Rooted deep within the Aryan mindset of most Germans at the time was, *Rassenmischung ist absolut verboten*! (Racial mixing is absolutely forbidden!)

To further aggravate the racial situation was that *Neger* was the German word for Negro, which was emphatically, and at times violently, not well-received by African-American GIs. As such, the Krauts quickly learned to instead use *Schwarzer* (a black man).

As with soldiers everywhere, the American GIs were in the community, but never of the community. They adapted. Even though a long way from home, the weather dreadful, and the Krauts—except for the fräuleins—for the most part, passively ill-disposed toward them, they hung tight and endured.

Mac and Lee were taking a break after Lee had gone down to the first-floor German-run snack bar and bought two cups of coffee and two apfelstrudel. He made his way back to the SCIF, being careful not to spill the coffee when stepping on and off the paternoster.

"Since I don't have a clue, how did the ASA come into existence?"

"We have a long history. It all started back in World War I with a little cryptanalysis going on. Then in the 1920s, there was the so-called Black Chamber, where the Western Union allowed sneak peeks into international communications. Secretary of State Simpson shut it down, claiming that gentlemen do not read each other's mail. When things in World War II turned to shit, he changed his mind. During the war, the Signal Security Agency was created. After the war, it became the Army Security Agency."

As Mac licked the remnants of the strudel off his fingers, he continued. "Harry Truman was an ole country boy of whom Roosevelt didn't think favorably. He was given Roosevelt's mushroom treatment ... kept in the dark and fed manure. Can you imagine Roosevelt not telling his second-in-command about the Manhattan Project and the atomic bomb? Once he became president, Truman turned out to be an absolute genius when it came to organizing intelligence units. He took the old Army Security Agency, the air force equivalent, and the Naval Security Group and combined them under one controlling organization, the National Security Agency."

Mac paused for a moment, and Lee interjected, "These strudels are great, but this so-called coffee sucks."

"Did you know that *muckefuck* is one of the German words for ersatz coffee? Appropriate don't you think?"

Lee considered the dregs in his coffee cup. "You know what? I believe we've just been muckefucked."

Mac chortled and then continued his story. "Truman then left the ASA and the others as intact units, but under the control of NSA. This way the DOD picked up the bulk of the manpower costs, leaving the NSA budget available for buying computers and intercept equipment. There were three pluses to this arrangement. First, the military branches could share intelligence. Second, it exponentially expanded our signal intelligence ... SIGINT, capabilities. Third, it kept those assets out of the clutches of the FBI. Can you imagine the clusterfuck, given the particularly dicey situation in Berlin, and Germany in general, that we would be in today if J. Edgar Faggot were our boss?"

Lee laughed as he took the last swig of what Germans called coffee.

"Truman also took the World War II Office of Strategic Services, OSS, whose assets the military and the FBI were trying to gobble up after the war and made it a separate foreign intelligence agency. You know it as the Central Intelligence Agency ... the CIA. It's pretty much of a clone of the Brits MI6, but hopefully without the evident and apparent buggers and their Soviet ideologies and sympathies we saw with the Brits earlier."

Lee nodded, now somewhat in admiration of Truman, a man who in the past he had merely regarded as a piano-playing country bumpkin.

Mac concluded, "Who knows where Truman's intellect came from? Perchance it was the shot of whiskey with which he started each day."

OH, BY THE WAY

Before the establishment of the Military Intelligence Corps in 1962, for a GI to end up in the ASA, he had to be recruited into the ASA based on the Armed Forces Qualification Test (AFQT), an intelligence quotient (IQ) and aptitude testing at the time of induction.

The army did some things well enough and others not so competently. The aptitude and IQ testing were one of the former. The army took the top qualifiers of these tests and developed rosters of potential applicants for such things as special forces, officer candidate schools, helicopter pilots, and intelligence technicians.

A little-known, and unadvertised fact—for obvious reasons—is that to be recruited into the ASA, a GI was required to have a substantially higher army entrance exam score than was the prerequisite for officer candidates. The average joe need not apply.

Was it prudent to have quick-witted subordinates with more intelligence, aptitude, and ability than their superiors? Perhaps, that is why the Cold War was won the hard way.

CHECKPOINT CHARLIE

Checkpoint Charlie would go down as a minor footnote in the Cold War history books. However, those who had been there or observed from the sidelines knew the Friedrichstrasse standoff was closer to Armageddon than most would ever realize. If a single round, accidental or intentional, had been fired at Friedrichstrasse, that projectile would have brought return fire, then the conflict would spread into all West Berlin, then into West Germany. The Allies would not have been able to contain the overwhelming Warsaw Pact forces, and would likely have resorted to using nukes. American schoolchildren would have climbed under desks as sirens went off, except this time, it would not be a drill.

For those who experienced both, the Checkpoint Charlie incident appeared much more volatile than the Cuban Missile Crisis. In the missile crisis, there had been a physical distance between the opponents and a time lag between significant events. Also, by the time of the Cuban fiasco, leaders on both sides knew catastrophic destruction would result if they made a wrong decision.

Such was not the case at Checkpoint Charlie. American troops faced off with their Soviet and East German counterparts. They were eyeball-to-eyeball with their tank guns and weapons locked and loaded, fingers on the triggers. The Soviet nuclear forces had been put on the highest-level alert, which was the first ever witnessed by American intelligence. Charlie had everyone's undivided attention.

After the wall had gone up, Checkpoint Charlie was the only entry and exit into and from East Berlin for Allied forces, diplomats, and other non-Germans.

The checkpoint itself wasn't all that impressive. On the American side, it resembled a small white tool shed with windows. On the Soviet side, there were zig-zag concrete barriers with raisable barricades above.

Checkpoint Charlie was a relatively short but exceptionally stressful time in the lives of the 251st troops. Because of the nearly real-time flow of information—although happening more than one hundred miles inside East Germany—they sensed what was going on as if it was occurring just beyond the windowless SCIF.

After the debacle of the wall going up under their noses a couple of months earlier, without Mac's asking, all the 251st troops volunteered for extended duty hours. A few, including Lee, volunteered to be on the job twenty-four hours a day when events became threatening in Berlin. They grabbed an occasional bite at the German pastry shop or the Farben cafeteria, paying out of their pockets rather than make the long trip across Frankfurt to the mess hall. And when fatigue overcame them, they found out-of-the-way corners to catch cat naps. They learned a classified burn bag full of discarded intercept sheets made a passable although somewhat noisy pillow when they napped. One of the often-overlooked self-disciplines the army taught GIs—was the ability to sleep anywhere.

The analysts and linguists knew a great deal about what was going on because of the intercepts. To those, Mac added comments obtained from his reliable but unidentified sources about the previous day's events in Berlin.

It all began Monday evening, 22 October 1961, when Allan Lightner—the senior American diplomat in Berlin—and his wife planned to attend a Czechoslovakian theatre group's performance in East Berlin.

On 23 October, Mac got everyone's attention in the SCIF saying, "Well, the East Germans are at it again. Last night our top American diplomat and his wife decided to attend an opera in the Soviet Sector. When they attempted to cross the border, were stopped by an East German border guard who insisted on seeing their passports. The agreement with the Russians is that any vehicle bearing a US

Forces license plate is to be allowed to pass in and out of East Berlin, regardless whether the occupants are in civilian or military attire. Also in the agreement is that only Russian officers are permitted to verify Allied travelers' documentation because East Berlin is under Soviet jurisdiction. Lightner refused to show their documents to the East German and insisted on speaking to a Russian officer. The guard refused to call a Russian officer and continued to detain the them. An armed squad of MPs with bayonets unsheathed was sent, and they returned the Lightners to the American sector. You'd think that bozo had better things to do than mingle with a gaggle of Marx-spouting card-carrying Krauts, so he can hear a fat lady sing. I expect more of the same since that buffoon Ulbricht thinks he's the tail that wags the Soviet dog."

On 24 October Mac began, "Thank Heaven General Clay is now in charge in Berlin. The East Germans are doing the same shit they did with the diplomat the night before. Vehicles with US Forces plates driven by anyone in civilian attire are stopped and not allowed to enter the Soviet sector unless they show their IDs to the East German guards. Our guys refused and asked to see a Russian officer as per protocol. The East Germans wouldn't let them through the checkpoint. So, Clay ordered in escorts … convoys of jeeps, one jeep in front of the escorted vehicle and two behind … with bayonet wielding troops aboard, to ensure they could go into and around the Soviet sector as they damn well pleased. No problem with the escorted vehicles or military vehicles or civilian vehicles with drivers in uniform. However, private vehicles with US Forces plates and their drivers in civvies, are not being allowed through. And, are being told by the East Germans guards that they were now in total control of the border crossing; and, anyone in civilian garb passing through must first provide them with identification. Knowing General Clay's reputation, things are about to change."

"Am I a prophet or what?" bragged Mac on 25 October. "As a test, General Clay sent two officers in civvies driving a private vehicle with US Forces plates to Checkpoint Charlie. Sure enough, the East Germans wouldn't let them through until the jeep convoy showed up as an escort. Clay made his intentions clear. He rolled ten M-48 tanks to within seventy-five yards of the border, with their muzzles pointing into the Soviet sector at Charlie. We'll see what those steel-toothed bastards and East Germans do now. So, pay damned close attention to those little yellow sheets. I appreciate the extra time you're spending here, especially those of you working around the clock."

On 26 October, Mac began the daily briefing saying, "Last night, the Soviets or the East Germans moved thirty-three tanks into Berlin and parked them near Brandenburg Gate. T-54s I think. That's more damned armor than our three brigades combined have in Berlin. Then this morning, they moved ten of them just across Friedrichstrasse from our tanks, back seventy-five yards on their side of the crossing. Just so you know … in tank-speak, one-hundred-fifty yards is point blank range. We don't know whether those ten tanks are East German or Russian since all markings have been painted over, to obscure who they belong to. If they happen to be Russian, General Clay may not act. On the other hand, if they are East German, he will not be a happy camper. As per the Potsdam Agreement, there are to be no East German army troops in Berlin. When the wall went up, some ten thousand moved into Berlin. Clay let that slide, but he has made it abundantly clear he will not tolerate East German armor in Berlin. Period."

On 27 October Mac got everyone's attention, saying, "This will make your day. Soviet missile forces throughout the Warsaw Pact have been placed on the highest alert we've ever seen. As you can tell from the enormous number of intercepts we're picking up, the situation in Berlin appears to have Moscow's complete attention. Most likely, the same is happening in Washington. We now know who the tanks belong to. Some GI took a stroll among them, found one that appeared unoccupied, climbed in, found and swiped a newspaper in Cyrillic. Ergo, Russian tanks. That GI is either a bona-fucking-fide hero or a total idiot. No, I'll take that back … He's almost certainly both! Those in Berlin seem just to be sitting there looking at each other, hoping and praying someone on either side doesn't decide to pull off a round. If that happens, the shit will hit the fan. First, Berlin, then West Germany, then Europe, then the whole world will go up in smoke."

On the 28th, after some very tense time, the end of the crisis came none too soon with Mac's announcement late that day, "Well, at long last, it looks like common sense prevailed in Moscow and Washington. Earlier today, a Russian tank withdrew from the border, then an American tank withdrew until all were gone. All that remains at Checkpoint Charlie is the little white shed and the barricades on the other side. Vehicles with US Forces plates, driven by someone, not in uniform, are no longer being stopped by the East Germans. General Clay made his point, but it sure as shit got downright dicey while he was doing it."

He concluded, "I'm proud of you guys. Now get your asses outta here, get cleaned up, and get some rest. I don't want to see you until Monday. Oh, did I ever mention the Germans brew decent beers? Now might be a good time to try one of each brand or a bunch of the same label. That's my plan."

End to end, it had been one hell of a week on Friedrichstrasse.

SECURITY CLEARANCES

Per United States law, there are only three levels of security classification: Confidential, Secret, and Top Secret. Some people claim to hold or have held a clearance above top secret. What they had, was, in fact, a top secret clearance with access to sensitive compartmented information on a need-to-know basis.

Confidential is seldom used and requires minimal clearance.

Secret clearance requires not much more than a database check. That includes such things as outstanding warrants for arrest or when your name appears on the membership list of an organization known to have the intent of overthrowing the government.

Top secret clearances and SCI eligibility—almost always granted together—are a much different story. For those within the intelligence community, the SCI clearance was known as a *crypto* clearance based upon the so-called cryptographic duties. However, few within ASA were actual cryptographers or cryptanalysts, who were identified outside the intelligence arena as *code breakers*. Both the TS and SCI clearances require a Single Scope Background Investigation (SSBI). It is a rigorous and thorough check for the last ten years—or to the age of 18 for younger applicants—into every nook, cranny, and closet of the applicant's life, including financial and credit history, affiliations, citizenship, employment, education, personal associations, and possible criminal activity. It also includes interviews with people the applicant had given as references, as well as spouses, family members and other individuals who surface during the investigation. The investigators homed in on ex-spouses. If there were any of the applicant's dirty linen lying about, he or she would know where it was stashed away.

The investigating agents have a specific interest in closets. If the applicant supplied information not positive to himself, the investigator's attitude was something along the lines of, "This guy admitted he screwed up and was upfront about it. We like that. It shows character." On the other hand, if the applicant had not disclosed his stashed pile of bones and the agent found them, his chances of getting a clearance were none and never. Not only were these good investigators, but they also kept records that seemingly had no expiration dates.

After the defection to the Soviet Union of some of the Oxford Five (aka Cambridge Five) turncoats who held high-level positions within British intelligence; and, subsequently, the American traitors Martin and Mitchell—most of whom had a homosexual or sexual deviation bent—the intelligence community became paranoid about homosexuals and sexual deviants in their midst. This was long before the army's Don't-Ask-Don't-Tell era and those who were *a little dainty when dancing* sure as hell didn't tell, but those with a run-of-the-mill dosage of testosterone in their system were, at times, vociferous in their biases and opinions. This paranoia continued for decades. The homophobic mentality began following the Oxford Five debacle. At President Eisenhower's direction, FBI's J. Edgar Hoover hypocritically developed an enormous volume of files of those within government—and conspicuously those within the intelligence community—suspected of not being exclusively heterosexual. Even those with just a hint of a limp wrist received particular attention. Following the Martin and Mitchell fiasco, the

NSA jettisoned more than two dozen whose proclivities were suspect. Within ASA, linguists were often singled out for additional scrutiny.

Sexual preference wasn't on the SSBI investigator's official list of traits to investigate. However, it seemed to be the first thing that caught the agent's attention. If an applicant was a skirt-chaser, a womanizer, or even a philanderer, he likely received positive points in the investigation.

When the investigators showed up in small towns and communities with their suits, ties and wingtip footwear to investigate the ASA recruits, it set in motion the local rumormongers. "What has Johnny boy down the street gone and done this time? I always knew he was up to no good," were the words expected to spew forth from the local gossip queens, much to the distress of the soldier's family.

For ASA recruits, obtaining the SCI clearance was somewhat of a roll of the dice. Before the advent of the voluntary army, the army had no obligation to give a GI a specific duty assignment. These troops signed on for an additional year of duty, and if they didn't meet the SCI requirements, spent that extra time as an infantry grunt. The same was true if they failed their advanced training courses.

THE ASA MILITARY OCCUPATION SPECIALTIES

These inimitable ASA troops with their unique set of abilities, talents, and idiosyncrasies had been assigned a Military Occupation Specialty based on testing.

Those outside the intelligence community commonly identified all those on the inside as *spooks*. However, the ASA personnel did not regard themselves as such and only referred to covert personnel by that term.

The Morse code interceptor operators, nicknamed *ditty-boppers* or *mill-monkeys*, were a breed apart and unpredictable in their behavior, both on and off the job. During advanced training, they had the highest wash-out rate of any of the ASA GIs. They were known to throw their mill—a typewriter-like device—out of windows or against a wall. Who could blame them after they listened to nothing but dits and dahs for hours on end while looking at a blank wall? They had to be pure masochists to succeed at this endeavor. The ASA had psychiatrists on call for these guys as well as for the drunks coming out of Shemya and Sinop. Booze and babes were about the only off-duty soldiers' alternatives, and at these stations in Alaska and Turkey babes weren't available, either because of the remoteness or cultural taboos or both, and alcohol abuse was common.

The radio direction finding technicians, also known as *RDFers* or *duffers* were a resilient and adaptive lot because they were always on the move. They tended to misbehave when duty wasn't calling.

The voice intercept operators, linguists, were an interesting study. Most received their training at the Defense Language Institute in Monterey, California. A few others were native speakers because of their ethnic heritage. Within the ASA European Theater, they spoke and translated Russian, German, and a smattering of Eastern European languages. As a rule, were more intelligent and better educated than the other ASA troops. Many seemed effeminate and received additional attention due to the intelligence community's paranoia about sexual deviation. One linguist, after being hassled by army counterintelligence (CI) agents, was overheard to say, "Those frigging CI assholes bring a new meaning to chickenshit." They preferred brandy and ballet to other GIs' favoring beer and babes. They were given the nickname *Monterey Marys*.

The communications security specialists didn't monitor Soviet traffic. Instead, they watched transmissions within ASA itself, while looking for internal communication breaches. These fellows were collectively referred to as *buddy fuckers* and were, with few exceptions, disliked and ostracized by other ASAers.

Then there were the computer system operators. The term *computer geek* had yet to come into the modern lexicon, even so, these dudes were the vanguards bearing the geek banner. Their barracks area was always obscenely clean and well organized as if ready for an immediate IG inspection. Neat freaks, each and every one. And they never got into trouble.

Lastly, there were the communications traffic analysts who were the antitheses of the geeks and always in trouble when off the job. They had no nickname, but without a doubt, conjured up every profane and invective word available in their regular army superior's vocabulary.

One senior official was overheard commenting about the collective ASAers, "As soldiers, they are one sorry, pain-in-the-ass bunch of misfits and mavericks, but we couldn't survive without them."

The RDFers roamed about Germany. The ditty-boppers and most of the linguists manned the intercept stations. The geeks, some linguists, and almost all the analysts composed the Frankfurt contingent. Heaven knows where the buddy-fuckers hid out.

LIFE AS AN ASAer IN THE 251st

Being in the military was a matter of establishing priorities. The officers had two priorities. One was determining whose ass to kick. Second, for the sycophantic ilk, was deciding whose ass to kiss. The enlisted, however, had three priorities. Booze and babes were their first two priorities, not necessarily in that order and preferably occurring in tandem. Their most important priority was to ensure that the army negligibly interfered with their pursuit of the first two. The GIs of the 251st Processing Company took these priorities as covenants.

The troops in the 251st were an eclectic mix: rural and urban, affluent to bordering the indigent, Christians, Jews and most had some college experience. There was a high percentage of Jews in the mix who were well-schooled in their faith. They would engage in arguments, sometimes bordering on fisticuffs, as to some article of faith. As best as Lee could tell, those confrontations often seemed to do with whichever tribe the offended had descended. On the other hand, most Christians didn't know if they were on earth because of the planning of an omnipotent God or were the fortuitous outcome of a serendipitous mix of primordial mud, billions of years past.

The GIs didn't earn much money, but if they were careful, a dollar went a long way. For starters, they were guaranteed room and board, though certainly not at the Ritz. And you didn't have to worry about medical expenses if you didn't mind the hurry-up-and-wait routine while in agony or thinking you were breathing your last. Theirs was a tolerable existence.

The dollar was strong against the Deutsche Mark. The exchange rate was roughly four marks to one dollar. Out on the German economy, a mug or bottle of beer was, as a rule, *Fünfzig Pfennig* (half of a mark). Put it this way: a GI could really tie one on with eight mugs or bottles of high alcohol content beer for a dollar. Good white German wines, even *Sekt* (the German equivalent of champagne) was moderately inexpensive. Except for *Schnaps*, hard booze was expensive out in the community. However, at the enlisted clubs, you were served your martini—stirred, not shaken—for a dime. Meals, even at upscale restaurants, were reasonable. Cigarettes were available for $1.14 a carton. Gasoline, if you were lucky to own a vehicle, could be purchased at a Post Exchange (PX) station for a small fraction of what Europeans paid. Then there was the PX. Among other things, one could buy a tailored English wool suit or a Harris Tweed jacket, complete with leather elbow patches, for a pittance.

The specialist pay grades were established when the army, at long last, realized it required soldiers with more skill than just pounding a tent peg and should be paid accordingly. The specialist grades began at Spec/4—the pay grade equivalent of a corporal—and continued up. Although the specialist rank extended on paper up to Spec/9, they realistically topped out at Spec/7, and very few achieved that pay-grade. However, the Spec/4 thru 6 grades were a bonanza for those with applicable Military Occupation Specialties.

For army soldiers with a *crypto* security clearance—the situation for almost all in the 251st Processing Company—they had to utterly screw-up not to get their promotion with a minimum time in grade. These were real-life issues their bosses had to deal with regarding supply and demand. There was a finite number of soldiers available with these particular abilities, and at times, that part of the world seemed to be on the verge of nuclear Armageddon. Where might the bosses draw the line when it came to be determining if an offense was severe enough to take the offender offline, or just to let it slide?

As such, close disciplinary/punishment calls, by and large, went in favor of the ASA GI, much to the chagrin of the hardcore regular army dudes. Also, most of the 251st soldiers received a supplement pay based on their MOS.

For some of the army incoming, it had been either enlist or go to jail, and none of this group ever reenlisted. Among the draftees, damn few reenlisted after their first tour of duty. Unlike the army, the air force was replete with volunteers who reenlisted. However, the army did have some perks. Case in point: Spec/5 intelligence specialists, with scarcely more than two years in service time, worked alongside their air force grade equivalents who had put in six or seven years of rank-and-file duty. So much for the benefits of being part of the Wild Blue Yonder.

There was a phenomenon about ASA troops. Off the job, they could be and often were irresponsible jerk-offs. When at work, however, dedicated entirely to their jobs and doing them correctly. This on-and-off-the-job disparity in the troops' regard of responsibility caused their superiors untold grief. They desperately needed this limited number of specially trained soldiers on the job because their expertise was unavailable from any other source. However, they realized the need for proper discipline when the GIs went astray. There was also the issue of morale. The 251st had an excellent esprit de corps, and the last thing their bosses wanted was to mess with that. It was a delicate balance between looking the other way or taking punitive action that would remove the errant soldier from the workplace. The bosses only hoped their underlings didn't get caught in whatever they were doing when not on duty— No news was good news!

The ASAers were a discriminating bunch when it came to what they took into their bodies. Almost all were nonsmokers, and most didn't partake of the hard liquor available at the EM club or the army's Class VI stores. The only thing they bought at the Class VI store were cartons of cigarettes to be used as trade goods. A remnant of the black market even now flourished in parts of Europe in the early 1960s. Marijuana was readily available in Amsterdam, but ASAers avoided it here like the plague, unlike the indulgences of their Vietnam era compatriots. Aside from their security clearance interests, they didn't want to be mellowed out and hungry. Instead, they wanted to get into the action and be ready to jump into the bed of an accommodating female if given the opportunity. They were content to drink inexpensive beer, whose only drawback was creating a frequent need to urinate. When *Fasching* (pre-Lent celebrations) or a wine fest occurred, were more than willing to drink the excellent German wines.

To whom the ASAers reported, was a mystery to most, and a definite bone of contention for many. What particularly rankled the non-ASA military superiors was the fact that the ASA soldiers allegedly under their command were controlled by the NSA and not them.

A persistent story circulated from time to time. A major general had gotten himself into an embarrassing and career-ending public pissing contest with the NSA as to what the ASA troops should be doing. Per the story, the two-star, in an issue of an above-the-fold front-page article of one of the army newspapers, asserted the ASAers were his troops. If he wanted them painting rocks or picking up cigarette butts, that was his prerogative. The NSA had a different opinion. The story continued. Shortly after that, the two-star retired rather than report to Eritrea as the protocol officer, a billet usually held by a major, not a major general. Whether or not the story was true, the non-ASA officers and NCOs treated it as if it were gospel and handled the ASA troops with kid gloves so as to not find themselves taking the many immunization shots required for deployment to an eastern African station. Was the eight-hundred-pound NSA gorilla real or imagined? For the ASA troops, it didn't matter. They were the beneficiaries either way. Although the ASA's 251st Processing Company soldiers were regular army, the 251st—to be candid—was anything but a *regular* army unit. There was no physical training. Their kitchen police tasks were performed by German contractors. There were no police or guard details, no barracks inspections other than the annual inspector general scrutiny. They rarely stood formation, and marching wasn't in the 251st's province.

Spec/5s served on a rotating basis as after-duty hours Charge of Quarters (CQ) for the 251st Company. CQ was considered a pain-in-the-ass assignment. Stay awake all night answering a phone that almost never rang and occasionally awakening senior NCOs too lazy or self-important to set an alarm clock. The only duty of significance was monitoring the sign-out and sign-in log of GIs heading to and from the Kaserne for the evening.

The dress code while on duty was the Class B khaki uniform or fatigues, the latter almost always the chosen option. Off-duty, outside the Kaserne, civilian attire was mandatory. The GIs' work environment varied little from that of a civilian desk jockey. The only differences were they had to wear a uniform to work, and the unmarried troops had to eat and sleep at the Kaserne.

For the most part, they worked the day shift Monday through Friday, unlike their counterparts at the outstations who had three shift rotations every day of the week while a fourth shift got time off. On occasion, some of the 251st troops, Lee included, worked the swing and mid-shifts when things got dicey with the Soviets and East Germans. When things took a serious turn, all were expected to be at work twenty-four hours a day—sometimes for days on end.

Everyone in the intelligence business eventually came to realize that access to secrets wasn't all the fun they imagined it to be before entering the service. Disquieting, on occasion. Boring, most of the time. Entertaining, almost never.

The only real aggravation—once or twice a month—an early morning bed check was held by the Company's FDLs in an attempt to curtail the number of soldiers suspected of violating curfew regulations. The Spec/5 CQs promptly learned how to mitigate this situation. The army had a curfew from midnight to six a.m., with an extra bonus hour thrown in on Saturday night. Anyone caught violating curfew—not possessing a valid leave or pass document—was subject to an Article 15 under the Universal Code of Military Justice (UCMJ). An Article 15, the equivalent of a civil misdemeanor, offered almost no due process for the accused. The commander, usually the company commanding officer, was judge, jury, and executioner. The only way a GI might obtain due process was to demand a high-risk court-martial.

The procedure at the 251st for anyone going out on the town during the evening was to go to the company clerk's office where the rotating Spec/5 CQ resided and sign his name and time of departure on the sign in/out log. When the GI returned, he entered the time of his arrival. The company's bachelor senior members—non-ASA NCOs—were billeted in private rooms in the barracks. When leaving for the day and too lazy or self-important to bother setting alarm clocks, they informed the CQ they were to be awakened at a specific time in the early hours, almost always between one and three in the morning—signaling a bed check was coming down that night. So, when GIs signed out for the evening, the CQ informed them, "There's going to be a bed check tonight. Have your asses back here by midnight." The 251st had a remarkable record of almost no one ever missing bed check.

The ASA took its concern about security to the absurd. It was a security breach if one of its soldiers revealed his name, MOS, unit, or commanding officer's name. Also, it was deemed that the ASA personnel should not wear name tags on their uniforms. The security folks' reasoning was this prevented potential foreign agents from knowing the soldier's name. The result was the opposite of that intended for security considerations. The lack of a name tag instead pinned a label on the GI, saying, "Look, here's a soldier with a top secret SCI clearance." It also made the ASA enlisted troops perfect targets for chickenshit junior officers from outside the unit. They dressed down the GIs for not having name tags on their uniforms. The encounter went something like this:

"Soldier," the officer inquired, "Why aren't you wearing a name tag as required by army regulations?"

"I'm not allowed to, Sir."

"That's ridiculous! What's your name, soldier?"

"I'm not allowed to say, Sir."

"Excuse me! What unit are you with?"

"I'm not allowed to say, Sir."

"Bullshit! Who is your commanding officer?" "I'm not allowed to say, Sir."

At about this point, things went downhill, the officer threatening an arrest by the MPs followed by a court-martial if the soldier continued not to respond. If the GI kept his cool, the officer, in due course, wore down. To save face on being outlasted by the GI and to have the last word, the officer departed with the threat, "I damn well better never again find you without your name tag," before striding off.

The GIs despised saluting vehicles, particularly those that did not contain high-ranking officers driven by chauffeurs too lazy to remove the rank flags on the front fenders. When GIs saluted, they extended only the middle finger as the arm came forward. The third finger salute was not strictly limited to vehicles.

KEEPING IN SHAPE

Because the 251st Company didn't have mandatory physical training, the onus was on the individual GI to keep himself in shape. Most considered lifting a hefty stein of beer to their lips was all that was necessary to keep them fit.

Within the Kaserne was a full-size gymnasium where guys like Lee's companions, Reese and Gus, engaged in a pickup game of basketball. There was also a three-lane bowling alley that had few if any users.

Lee enjoyed running, even on those typical German days when it was dreary, damp, and cold. He obtained a workout suit, a couple pairs of thick socks and a low-grade pair of KED sneakers. He donned his exercise gear, placed his ID and a few marks into a pocket, exited the Kaserne, and turned south the short distance to the Main River promenade to begin his run.

The Germans liked to walk, but running wasn't their forte. As Lee ran along the river with his long stride, Germans stopped to watch.

I bet these Krauts haven't seen anyone running like this since they did it themselves when leaving Stalingrad or the Falaise Gap.

WHO IS KEEPING TRACK OF THE TROOPS?

When Lee came into the service, there was no Military Intelligence (MI) branch. It wasn't until midway through his tour of duty that the army MI branch was created. As such, the officers put in charge of intelligence organizations came from the combat arms branches or the signal corps. They often didn't understand what was going on in the unit, and many lacked the political skills required to survive in that unique environment. They had yet to learn the kiss-or-kick-ass rules of engagement within the intelligence community. If they tried to kick rather than kiss the NSA asses, they were in for a harsh dose of reality.

When Lee arrived in Frankfurt, a new unit was being put together with personnel from the European and Middle East theaters along with recent graduates coming from advanced analytical or linguistic training. The chain of command in the new unit, or in this case, the lack thereof, was mind-boggling.

The commanding officer at the workplace was a combat arms *bird* colonel who seemed to not have any subordinates. One would expect a colonel to have a lieutenant colonel and a couple of majors along with a gaggle of captains and lieutenants on his organization chart. If they existed, were never visible. The colonel had an office on the seventh floor SCIF. He would arrive, go directly there, and almost never came out into the work area of the SCIF. Perhaps he didn't want to embarrass himself, in that he as a combat arms officer had no clue what the troops under his command were supposed to be doing. The only person seen entering his office was the civilian O'Donnell. There were a captain, a staff sergeant, and a couple of buck sergeants on the floor of the SCIF who performed technical duties and appeared not to be part of any chain of command. The colonel signed an occasional commendation but seemed to have little else to do. Was his assignment, perhaps, an end-of-tour figurehead posting?

O'Donnell was somewhere in the chain of command but did not have an office. Mac preferred to work on the SCIF floor with three desks shaped in a U around him.

A few miles away, under a far distant mindset, was the Gutleut Kaserne. Here the 251st Processing Company GIs were under yet another commander, a captain, who didn't seem to report to or communicate with the workplace colonel. The GIs were barracked and fed at Gutleut Kaserne with this captain as their CO. The indolent FDLs along with a couple of squared away sergeants were his subordinates. He, however, was a rare combat arms officer who held a top secret SCI clearance. The captain signed the usual pass, leave, and promotion documents and had Article 15 jurisdiction. The company administrative personnel appeared to have no inkling which of their troops were on duty at the Farben Building at any given time. They seemed to come and go anytime, day or night. Because of this disconnect between the workplace and where they had their bed and meals, the GIs, when the occasion arose, took advantage of the situation. For traveling soldiers, the army issued passes or leave documents that were recognized throughout Europe as a visa for GIs crossing international borders. On occasion, some 251st troops, when the opportunity presented itself, forged their own passes or leaves. The GIs only did this when relieved from duty at work for an extended period but didn't want the militaristic and bureaucratic company personnel to know of their absence.

Keeping track of the 251st troops was akin to herding cats.

A SIGN OF THE TIMES

It was the early 1960s, and America was awash in unprecedented racial issues and conflicts.

The ASA appeared to be ethnically whitewashed. However, almost none of the ASAers were racially or religiously prejudiced. One exception and one of the few slugs in the unit was a kid nicknamed *Baby Huey* from Alabama. He was, perhaps, thus tagged for his racial views that were in lockstep with Huey Long, the former racist governor of Louisiana. When a group of GIs was discussing their plans after mustering out of the army, Baby Huey offered, "A'm goin back'ta Alabama, be a sheriff's deputy, an' shoot niggers."

"So, hotshot, how are you going to get to be a deputy sheriff?" someone inquired.

"Piece a cake," responded Baby Huey. "Ma Uncle Elmer is the county sheriff."

Ah, shit! The county sheriff is unique in America. It's something to do with our English heritage. He doesn't answer to the governor, the state police, or anyone except his constituents. Huey is a shoe-in to get his dream job.

"Oh, jest so y'all know, ah really like being in the ASA with'n all y'all. None of youse, even if'n y'all be Yankees, ain't no jigaboos, spicks, or gooks mungst you."

Hearing that, the group immediately broke up. As Reese and Lee walked away, Reese opined, "I hate to admit it, but that fat, sorry, piece-of-crap barracks-rat is right. You don't see any blacks, Hispanics, or Asians."

"Right on, perhaps ASA being its usual compartmented self, has them working somewhere we don't know about," suggested Lee. "Aside from that, think about this ... Take Baby Huey, put him in a police uniform, a badge on his chest, a visor hat on his head, and add a pair of mirrored aviator sunglasses, and he would be the stereotypical southern cop."

"I don't even want to think about the possibility," Reese uttered with a grimace. "Let's get ready for a night on the Strasse and put that thought behind us."

A day or so later, Lee, Reese, Levi, and Eli were sitting at the front of the shuttle bus to take them back to the Kaserne for the noonday meal. They had learned that boarding first on the bus meant being first off, resulting in first in line at the mess hall. Not that the mystery-meat-*du-jour* offerings were all that good, but those at the end of the line received barely edible gruel.

Baby Huey's comments about what he wanted to do after the army lingered in the minds of those who had heard him. He came on board and took a seat at the back of the bus. After Huey had gone by, Levi said, "Someone ought to send a picture of Baby Huey to Trojan, you know, the condom guys. They could use it in an ad saying, *this is what could happen if you don't use our product.* Sales would skyrocket."

"How did that douchebag ever get into the ASA?" Eli asked. "He never leaves the compound. Only occasionally goes to the EM club. Spends most of his time lying on his bunk. I suppose that's where he fantasizes about shooting niggers back in Ala-fucking-bama."

"Well," Reese jested, "you know in the enlightened and sophisticated State of Alabama where they have turds like Huey who refuse to flush, they grade IQ scores on a curve. Fortuitously for him, although not for the army, he floated up."

"That may be true," Lee said while attempting unsuccessfully to cross his long legs in the narrow space between the bus seats. "But, seriously, army recruiters have a number to meet. I suppose they occasionally must scrape the bottom of the barrel to meet their quota. Huey was the slimy piece of whatever the recruiter scooped out."

"I think Reese's argument of grading IQ scores on the curve is the right one," opined Eli as the shuttle fired up and left the Farben parking lot.

THE OLD NAZI BAR

Jimmy Joe and Lee had been roommates when they first arrived at the Kaserne. Jimmy Joe was a descendant of a Revolutionary War general, albeit on the British side. He was big, strong, and had the bothersome habit of engaging in fisticuffs with the Germans. One evening Jimmy Joe left in light-colored garments. When he returned, in the dim natural light of the barracks room, he appeared to be wearing camouflage. Lee flipped on the lights. Jimmy Joe was splotched and splattered with blood. As it turned out, none of it was his. Jimmy Joe's only apparent damage was his bruised and scraped knuckles. After that, when they went out on the Strasse, Lee's admonition was, "Remember, we are here to bed fräuleins, not to pound their brothers about the head and shoulders." Jimmy Joe usually complied.

On a side street, the second block down Gutleutstrasse going towards the Hauptbahnhof, was a unique bierstube. Lee and Jimmy Joe had found it by accident on one of their early trips out of the Kaserne.

They first discovered the proprietor brewed a beer that was superior to any they were to experience in Germany. It was full-bodied and aromatic, and it had a full and lasting head. As such, this establishment became the first stop for them when they hit the Strasse.

What the establishment offered in excellent libation it lacked equally in ambiance. Dingy would be the best adjective to describe it.

It was dimly lit, which may have been intentional considering the accouterments. There was a rough-hewn bar in front with a beer tap on one side and a half dozen bar stools on the other. A few bottles of schnaps on the shelf behind completed the motif. The large windows in front had been coated over with white paint, so the only image of one coming into the establishment was a silhouette.

They next discovered that it was a hangout for old Nazis. In the back were tables where the former Third Reich faithful played cards or dominoes or whatever geriatric Nazis did in their leisure time.

Jimmy Joe brought a new component to their entrance into the bierstube saying, "Those old farts back there can't see diddly when someone comes in. Just for shits and grins, why don't we give a Nazi salute every time we enter?" And so, it went, a stiff-armed mock salute delivered at an upward forty-five degrees every time they arrived.

Everyone was content. The old Nazis were confused but perceived these Ami GIs were showing them respect. Lee and Jimmy Joe were drinking world-class beer at low cost. And the owner was making a few pfennigs.

On one occasion as they departed, Jimmy Joe said, "Part of our mission here is to establish a rapport with the German people. I think we're doing a hell of a good job with those old Nazi bastards."

THE BOMBING OF GERMANY

Alfred, aka *Bomber,* Harris was one-of-a-kind. Unquestionably, he alone contributed more to the German peoples' misery during the latter part of the war and afterward than did Generals Patton, Montgomery, and Bradley combined. He unrelenting held a single-minded conviction: you could force your enemy into submission and surrender through *area bombing* without setting a pair of boots on the ground.

The innocuous-sounding term—area bombing—implied bombing of military and industrial facilities as well as civilian populations. Quite often, it turned out to be the bombing of the civilian population only.

Harris was considered rude and abrasive and often bordered on insubordination that made him few friends with the powers that be. His payback would occur after the war. He had come up through the ranks of the British Royal Air Force (RAF) in bomber units and would become the Commander-in-Chief of the RAF Bomber Command in February 1942.

Harris viewed himself as a strategic thinker. He didn't want to get caught up in what he considered trivial actions when conducting a war. Those little specific things that other civilian and military commanders desperately needed at the time, such as supporting the Allied invasion of Normandy or bombing oil processing facilities, transportation routes, ball bearing producing plants, or aircraft manufacturing facilities. "I will pick my own targets, thank you. Your interest is noted. Now, bugger off!"

Early in the war, the RAF bombers had a miserable performance record when bombing the continent. They first tried daylight bombing in the Ruhr and Rhine valleys and lost aircraft and crews at an unsustainable rate. Thus, they gave up attacking during daylight hours and attempted nighttime attacks. It was considered acceptable targeting if their bombs fell within three to five miles of the target. The number of bombs that fell on a target was in the single-digit percentile. Harris, nevertheless, seemed content to just drop bombs somewhere over Germany. A brutal statistic revealed their lack of success—Early in the war more RAF crewmen perished in the air over Germany than Germans died on the ground!

To negate the risk of anti-aircraft fire and fighter aircraft when flying over land, the RAF made what they considered low-risk bombing raids on the lightly defended Baltic coast, coming in from over the ocean to bomb Lübeck, Rostock, and Hamburg. When bombing Hamburg, they unexpectedly created a firestorm, killing some twenty thousand Germans, almost all civilians.

A firestorm is a meteorological phenomenon. A large area burning at a high temperature creates a chimney effect. This updraft causes a vacuum that sucks fire-laden debris along the ground with torrential force winds toward the updrafts, thus igniting other fires, consuming all oxygen, and leaving behind poisonous carbon monoxide gas.

Enter Bomber Harris as the commander of RAF bomber forces. The Hamburg raid became his model of what he wanted to occur throughout Germany for the rest of the war. To create a firestorm, it first requires the right combination of explosive and incendiary bombs dropped into a congested area of structures. The Brits usually dropped six tons of incendiaries for each four tons of explosives. The Americans—who attacked during the day—and were considerably more precise than the nighttime bombing Brits, used roughly the opposite tonnage mix. When the Americans bombarded under clear skies, by and large, they were reasonably accurate. When having to use radar because of cloud cover, they weren't much more precise than the RAF.

To create the firestorm, the area had to be prepped by first dropping explosive bombs. The intent was to blow out walls, take off roofs and blast open doors and windows to allow updrafts in the buildings. The explosive bombs were, for the most part, five-hundred and thousand pounders, with a few air weapons called mines weighing two and four tons thrown in for good measure. The mines exploded above rooftops, taking off protective roofing that would have negated the incendiaries that followed. Four-pound incendiaries then saturated the area. These were nasty little dudes. They contained a thermite igniter made of powdered iron oxide and aluminum (which generates its own oxygen) to start its magnesium content burning, which in turn ignited nearby flammables. Thus, if the exploding bomb didn't kill you, the falling rubble from roofs and walls might, if not the following fierce hot wind. If those didn't do it, you would die from asphyxiation or carbon monoxide poisoning. The survival rate for those caught in a firestorm was near zero. German cities and noncombatant civilians paid a terrible price for the Allied bombing.

Early in the war, the Germans indiscriminately bombed English cities—London and Coventry in particular—resulting in enormous loss of life and limb. Late in the war, the V1 and V2 rocket bombs again fell randomly over England. Therefore, there was little moral outrage concerning Allied bombing of mainland Europe, and Germany, least of all.

The main cities in Germany were repeatedly bombarded with a vengeance, leaving behind piles of rubble and soot-blackened walls as far as the eye could see. Berlin was attacked 363 times from the air during the war. At times, more than a thousand Allied aircraft appeared over Berlin and the Ruhr industrial cities. Their destruction was enormous but paled in comparison to the damage inflicted upon Hamburg, Kassel, Leipzig, Darmstadt, Magdeburg, Würzburg, and Pforzheim, all of which were firebombed. Pforzheim was particularly hard hit and lost more than a fourth of its population in a single raid.

Then came Dresden. After numerous false alarms, the people of Dresden came to believe the city would not be bombed due to its cultural and architectural legacy, and it was obvious the war was soon coming to an end. The lack of bombing, combined with the belief held by Germans outside the city that Dresden was not contributing to the Reich's war industry, led to a false and tragic sense of security. In turn, this resulted in woefully inadequate air raid shelters for protection against the ravages of a firestorm.

In fact, Dresden was replete with small, high-tech precision war industries and had become a critical rail junction for German troops going to and from the front as the Soviets approached Saxony. Those elements alone would have justified its wartime destruction. Also factored into the equation was that the people of Dresden were ardent Nazi supporters. An analysis of pre-raid aerial photographs revealed the city would likely burn well. It did.

There was no moral outrage regarding firebombing until the attack on Dresden, often referred to as *the Florence on the Elbe*. Well known for its history, culture, and architecture, it was firebombed less than three months before the end of the war. Twenty-five to forty thousand people in Dresden, predominantly civilians, were believed to have perished in the two-day raid. This number was greatly exaggerated, first by Nazi propagandists and later by the Soviets and East German GDR regime during the Cold War.

Harris himself was no more culpable than other Allied leaders in the decision to bomb Dresden but, based on his previous track record, he got the credit for the carnage and the destruction of the city.

At the end of the war, Arthur Harris was knighted. However, he was the only high-ranking British Officer not made a Peer of the Realm (a member of the nobility entitled to sit in the House of Lords).

FRANKFURT AFTER THE WAR

Frankfurt was no different than any other major city or town in Germany that had experienced the Allied World War II bombing. The RAF had bombed Frankfurt fifty-four times by mid-1942. Their targets were war production facilities, bridges, and rail junctions. From a strategic military point of view, because of the Brits' imprecise targeting, their efforts did little damage other than force Frankfurters into bomb shelters and denying them a good night's sleep. When the Americans began with their B-17s in January 1943, the targeting was somewhat more accurate. The Americans sometimes joined the RAF to area bomb the city. There were major attacks in January, April, and October 1943, followed by similar attacks in January, February, and March 1944. By the time it ended, more than two-thirds of prewar structures were destroyed. All that remained of Frankfurt as far as the eye could see were soot-blackened walls rising as sails on a sea of medieval rubble.

The *Altstadt* (old city, aka *Römer*) area of Frankfurt was repeatedly bombed—at least six times. Surprisingly, the so-called Kaiser *Dom* (cathedral) named in honor of St. Bartholomew, whose construction began circa 1200, and *Paulskirche* (St. Paul's church), circa 1800, survived. As did *Sankt Nikolaus Kirche* (St. Nicholas church), circa 1300, and the façade of the *Rathaus* (city hall) circa 1400–1700. Most were structurally intact but burned out. These still-standing structures were a testimony to the skill of stonemasons long past. The half-timbered structures and the *Seufzerbrücke* (the German version of the Bridge of Sighs) were rebuilt after the war. What did not survive, with a few exceptions, were all the bridges and most structures within greater Frankfurt. One notable loss was the *Alte Oper* (old opera house). It had been built at enormous cost by the citizens of Frankfurt in the late 1800s. It was world renowned and could seat more than two thousand. For decades, it was considered the finest in the world.

During World War II, the opera's basement had been used as a Wehrmacht communication center. As the Allies approached, the Germans booby-trapped the underground facility before abandoning what was left of the once magnificent structure.

In the reconstruction of the city, there had been two attempts, involving loss of life, to clear those booby-traps. There had even been discussions about excavating underneath the entire area, then dropping it into a hole in the ground using explosives. Instead, the Germans gave up and built a fence around the perimeter with concertina wire on top. Here in the middle of Frankfurt was a remembrance of the war that refused to be hidden. All that remained of it was the frieze inscribed with *Dem Wahren, Schönen, Guten* (The true, the beauty, the good).

A mere fifteen years after the war, Frankfurt had arisen from the ashes like the Phoenix. In this case, it was literal rather than mythical. There was no evidence of the war bombings other than the booby-trapped opera house. All the rubble was removed or recycled. The historic structures, principally those within the *Römer* or *Altstadt*, were authentically restored or reconstructed. The bombed-out bridges over the Main River repaired. A bustling major airport was nearby. The streetcar system—complete with all its squealing, screeching, clanking, and klaxon horns—was restored all the way to the Taunus Mountains. The city was again an important railway hub. All the population appeared to have be housed, albeit in block-looking structures painted in dreary shades of gray. The business community was becoming the primary financial center in all of Europe. The streets were still paved with cobblestones, but all pothole bomb craters were filled in and again spotlessly clean. Restaurants and drinking establishments for all levels of the socioeconomic population were available.

A GREAT PLACE FOR A GI TO SPEND THE EVENING

One such *Gasthaus* (restaurant) was Dault Schneider's on Neue Strasse in Sachsenhausen, a suburb of Frankfurt south of the Main River. (This locale should not be confused with the infamous Nazi concentration camp of the same name.) It was a *gemütlich* (friendly, genial, pleasant) kind of place and was the favorite in all of Frankfurt for the troops of the 251st to spend an evening.

Sachsenhausen was a blue-collar neighborhood. Dault's had been owned and operated as a family enterprise for centuries catering to that clientele. They specialized in serving a hard apple cider and a limited meal menu. The cider tasted somewhat akin to sweet, diluted battery acid, leaving its drinkers with a god-awful hangover because of the unfermented sugars it contained.

Their offerings included:

Rippchen (smoked and brined pork spareribs)—a halfway decent meal.

Rindertartar (beef tartare) chopped raw meat and a raw egg with a dash of pepper on a slice of dark bread—salmonella and E. coli just waiting to happen—but it was tasty.

Gebeizt Schweine Knöchel (pickled pig knuckles)—frequently and ravenously eaten by the middle-aged German men. Was their appetite for pigs' feet conceivably a contributing factor in losing two World Wars in a row?

The restroom facilities were typical of most German establishments selling alcohol-based libations. The *Herren* (men) urinated on a tiled wall that drained into a trough on the floor and eventually found its way to the Main River. After a couple of visits, the GIs became accustomed to the female attendant responsible for keeping the place relatively sanitary and who sold condoms to supplement her income.

The patrons sat on hard wooden benches and linked arms with those next to them, facing others across the table sitting on equally uncomfortable seats. Dault's had a band during the evening hours to which the revelers swayed back and forth, singing to upbeat German music, most of which was of the oompah-pah variety with an occasional folk song. The Germans sang with gusto. Not knowing the lyrics, the GIs merely mouthed some words.

The band almost always ending the evening with a variety of what seemed to be reruns of martial tunes from World War II. Occasionally a bit of *Horst Wessel* (the Nazi party anthem) made its way into the night's singing repertoire. A residue of Nazism remained.

Dault's had its enticements for the GIs. First, the apfelwein was damn near free—something to do with local liquor laws. Second and more importantly, it was a perfect place to meet German girls. The German girls would arrive with their effeminate German boyfriends, all of whom wore pointy-toed shoes—certainly not macho footwear. Many of the boyfriends had been raised by successive generations of women. Their fathers and grandfathers had gone off to war, and few returned. The German girls were looking for something other than a mama's boy. The GIs dripped testosterone, which seemed to be what the fräuleins sought. The GIs flirted with a nearby girl. If she responded, he made a head movement toward the restrooms. She nodded, excused herself, and started toward the *Damen* (women's) toilet. Knowing the fräulein was interested, he rose and make his way toward the Herren facility. Outside the peeing privies, they arranged a future date. The agreed-upon meeting place was often near the Eschenheimer *Turm* (Tower)—located near a major streetcar terminal—which allowed easy access for both to meet using the extensive rail system within Frankfurt. The adjacent area was also well populated with good restaurants and upscale nightlife possibilities.

The question was this: Would the fräulein show up for their date? There was a correlation between the fräulein's attractiveness and her likelihood to meet the GI. For the potential keepers, maybe three or four in ten showed up. For those not quite so *ziemlich und niedlich* (pretty and cute), the percentage was higher. Despite no-shows, GIs quickly learned the social life in Frankfurt was beyond their wildest expectations.

A GI could come into Dault's and scan for targets of opportunity, then worm his way into the crowded seats on the bench across from his selection. Flirt for a while, then, after meeting outside the pissers for a future get-together, he almost always encountered an authentic cultural and social experience. After a few dates, he might even find himself in bed with his chosen target. By late in the evening, the GIs had no idea how many Nazi rally songs they may have participated in, but they didn't care as long as their scheduled future dates showed up as planned. All in all, a GI couldn't find a more perfect place to spend an evening.

WHAT SURVIVED THE WAR

Among the few Frankfurt structures that survived the war were the Farben Building, Gutleut Kaserne, and a beautiful marble structure the army turned into a medical dispensary.

The rumor persisted that the Farben Building survived because General Eisenhower wanted it for his headquarters after the war. It did become Ike's command post, but most likely it survived because it was such a conspicuous reference point for Allied bombing runs during the war. It was almost eight hundred feet in length and seven stories high. The only visible war damages were a few bullet holes and chunks of missing façade around two windows.

The Gutleut Kaserne was adjacent to the rail yards that served the Frankfurt Hauptbahnhof, a major transportation center in Germany, which was subject to multiple bombings by the Allied air forces. The reason Gutleut survived was simple. The Nazis housed Allied airmen prisoners of war in the basement of the barracks nearest the rail yards and let that circumstance be known to Bomber Harris and his counterparts. This information didn't stop the Allied bombing of the railroad center, though being extra careful before announcing *bombs away*. As with the Farben Building, the only harm to the Kaserne was a few bullet holes and a missing brick or two around one window.

At the end of the war, Frankfurt was nearly destroyed and had no governing system or infrastructure. Without food, water, sewer, transportation, or communication systems, the remaining populace lived like rats in lice-infested cellars and basements where they scavenged for food and something to keep them from freezing. Most survived, but many did not.

Consequently, the older German population of Frankfurt weren't enamored with the occupying GIs when reflecting on the war and its aftermath.

THE FARBEN BUILDING

The IG Farben Building was built in the late 1920s as the headquarters for a vast chemical enterprise. It was the largest office building in Europe and continued to be so until much later. Despite its enormous size, the overall architecture design was aesthetically pleasing and surrounded by a large, well-manicured acreage. Once it became evident the Farben Building would not be bombed, some city residents during the World War II bombing went there for safety, rather than into underground bomb shelters. It had a stately set of stone steps leading up to a columned entrance. The only other entries or exits were two at the far ends of the building, which may possibly have been an evacuation nightmare. Most rooms and hallways had high ceilings, ideal for the Nazi flags and paraphernalia of an earlier era. There was substantial window exposure, except for the seventh floor. The Farben, which was built along a slight linear curvature, gave someone walking the length of the building the feeling they were walking through an endless tunnel. They were unable to see the end of the hallway until they neared the end. There was almost no vehicle parking—but back in the 1920s, who could have foreseen the glut of cars, trucks, and buses that would overtake the world? With limited parking spaces, anyone arriving and leaving had to be dropped off or picked up. However, there was a strassenbahn stop within easy walking distance. The IG Farben corporate executives didn't fare well at the Nuremberg trials because of their activities—including developing a chemical gas known as Zyklon B, which was used to execute concentration camp inmates by the millions. The locals, to avoid community embarrassment, began calling the building the IG Hochhaus. The GIs picked up that usage as well.

The ASA occupied some of the sixth and seventh floors at the west end. The only entrance and exit, to the ASA domain, was located behind an iron bar barricade, guarded by two armed soldiers. On the seventh floor was the SCIF. It was a large windowless open bay with desks scattered about and a couple of offices on the periphery. Along one wall was a bank of encrypted teletypes for communication with its outstations. The teletype encryption was so sensitive that it was maintained by an organization outside of the ASA and not even the ASA commander was allowed into the room where the encryption devices were located. Unless escorted, the only personnel allowed within a SCIF must hold a top secret SCI clearance and have a need to know. The area was frequently *swept* for electromagnetic and sound acquisition intrusions, aka bugs.

Over time, a lot of hype and a little bit of aura has been given to the Farben Building's paternosters. The Latin Lord's Prayer, beginning with Paternoster, with a capital P, may have had something to do with the naming of these devices. Perhaps one needed divine intervention when stepping aboard. The Farben Building's paternosters were nothing more than human dumbwaiters used to move bodies from one floor to another. They were small compartments with no interior lighting, designed to accommodate two people. Passengers required a certain amount of feet-to-eye dexterity to safely enter and exit the moving platforms in an open shaft environment. These were slow-moving devices, but when more than two riders came aboard and planned to exit the same floor, the passengers needed to be fleet-of-foot to avoid a very long and jarring step down.

For those who missed getting off on a lower floor or were out joyriding, as they reached the upper levels, the experience might be somewhat traumatic. The last exit going up was the ASA landing. There, behind iron bars stood two uniformed knuckle-dragging fellows with rifles slung over their shoulders. Thus intimidated, none of the egress-inattentive or joyriders stepped off on this floor. As they continued upward, there was no lighting. In the dark, passengers had the sensation, when reaching the top, they would be dumped over onto their heads as the compartment started its slow descent. Not to worry—the chamber was akin to a human birdcage, hung from the top, on a continuously rotating mechanism.

THE WANDERING GENERAL

A one-star general exited the paternoster and intimidated his way past the two security guards on the sixth floor. He climbed the steps to the SCIF on the seventh floor. As he entered the SCIF, he encountered the usually sequestered ASA colonel, demanding, "Why weren't these men called to attention when I came in?" The colonel replied that it was a working area where military courtesy was put aside.

"What kind of operation are you running here, anyway?" asked the miffed general. The colonel made no response.

The general walked into the work area and seeing the bank of teletypes said, "What is in that room behind them?" The colonel replied that it contained encryption devices.

"Well, I'd like to see them."

"Sorry Sir, I can't do that. I'm not even allowed in there," replied the colonel.

"What did you just say? That's beyond belief!"

Do all generals begin an utterance only with words starting with W?

Lee stood in his best attempt at attention as the general approached him, asking, "What do you do here, soldier?" Lee scanned for a security clearance badge around the general's neck and saw none.

"With all due respect, Sir, I'm not at liberty to discuss that with you."

"What do you think this is?" the general boomed as he pointed to his one star.

"Sir. It is an indication of your rank, not of your security clearance."

"Well, soldier, I'm giving you a direct order to tell me …"

At this point, Mac, who had been scurrying across the floor, took the general by the arm with his one hand and said, "This is a secure area. Allow me to escort you out."

The general jerked away, saying, "Who the hell do you think you are?"

Mac, in his most intimidating mode, stuck his cigar-embedded head into the general's face and stated, "Let me start again." Then, pausing between words, as if speaking to a child, articulated, "Either I accompany you out of this highly classified facility without a lot of trouble, *or* … I will have you taken into custody." He took his cigar out of his mouth and lowered his voice another octave, "Your choice."

The general paused for a moment while considering what might show up in his 201 Personnel File if he were taken into custody. He threw back his head in a pique and followed Mac out of the SCIF.

Mac and the general disappeared down the steps.

I'm in deep shit. Over my head in deep shit. I just told a general to fuck off. But it was kinda fun.

A few minutes later, Mac came back up and approached Lee.

"Mac, I'm sorry. I guess I screwed the pooch?"

"Quite the contrary. You did exactly what our so-called security chief and the colonel should have done before that asshole got to you." Mac patted Lee a couple of times on the shoulder saying, "Well done."

Lee's pent-up anxiety evaporated.

Mac continued, "First, I'm going to have a little discussion with Chief McDuff and the colonel, so this doesn't happen again. Then I'm going to find the building security manager and strongly advise him to give the general a block of instruction, enlightening the general as to where he is … and is not … allowed in this building. Then I'm going to insist, absolutely insist as per army regulation … I have no fucking idea which one it may be, although I'm sure there is one … that Chief McDuff debriefs the general up close and personal regarding his intrusion into this facility. That should make everyone's day, especially mine."

He pointed first to the warrant officer, then at the colonel, and then at the colonel's office. Once the colonel's office door closed behind the threesome, the only sound heard coming from within was a booming voice laced with profanity. It belonged to Mac.

That made my day as well. And now I know who runs this place.

THE GUTLEUT KASERNE

Gutleut Kaserne came into being as a cavalry post in the late 1800s and was constructed almost exclusively of stone, mortar, and brick. It was three stories high, four if one counted the basement, which was partially above ground. The front of the Kaserne faced Gutleutstrasse on the east, hence its name. The only exit from the facility was through a narrow stone arch onto the street. Two L-shaped barracks buildings laid topside end-to-end formed the west side of a quadrangle. It was a miserably cold place to reside, even in the summertime. One GI once asked, "Which is colder, a witch's tit, a well-diggers ass, or Gutleut Kaserne?" Another GI responded, "Well, I never had an intimate relationship with a witch … and for sure I never felt a well-diggers ass ... but I'd still bet my next paycheck that this pile of stone would win hands down."

The Kaserne was a bed-and-board facility for ASA and military police units. It contained some acceptable amenities. The consolidated mess hall was not one of them. As with mess halls everywhere, it reeked of grease and body odors. Big globs of bland, indistinguishable food were served, accompanied by a mystery meat with each meal. Dr. Seuss's green eggs and ham was the breakfast specialty. The ham was iffy, but the green eggs were authentic. Inmates of the adjacent Frankfurt Stockade also dined there.

The sanitation facilities within the barracks were somewhat of an enigma. There were ample communal shower facilities, but urinals were limited in number and not conveniently located throughout the compound. There was one commode each on the second and third stories shared by all the troops on that floor, resulting in there was almost always a waiting line. As one GI put it, "If you have a case of diarrhea, you are literally shit out of luck." The GIs drank copious amounts of fermented barley, apple, and grape beverages before hitting the sack. Once the urinary urge hit, the GI went to the nearest shower room, occupied or not, and peed down one of the drains not currently being used. On the positive side, ammonia in the urine kept incidences of athlete's foot to a minimum.

In addition to the boarding-house function, the Kaserne included an Enlisted Men Club, a small library, a full-size gymnasium, a tailor shop, and a barbershop staffed with German barbers.

The first trip to the barber for the macho GIs drove them up the wall. When entering, it was immediately apparent that all the barbers were homosexual, ranging from subtle to blatant. They liked to fondle the GIs' heads as they cut their hair, but it was the only choice the GIs had. The civilian German barber shops didn't have a clue how to give a military haircut, and the only other option was the barbershop at the PX across Frankfurt. It too was staffed with barbers of the same proclivities as those at Gutleut. One of the new arrivals, after his first haircut, was heard to say, "That's a fucking flock of flaming faggots in there."

His companion with more time on the ground said, "I bet you were an English major in college with minors in profanity and homophobia. You'll go far in this outfit. The next time you go in for a haircut, be sure to tell the barber that you have a date with your schatzi and want to look your best when you meet her. You'll get fewer head strokes. And never tip them the way you do a barber back home. Otherwise, your homo hairdresser will think you're signing on for blowing and buggering."

The Enlisted Men Club was in the northwest portion of the compound. It had a bar that sold beer for a nickel and mixed drinks for a dime, and it had a pizza oven that was popular with the GIs. The waitresses were a batch of local fräuleins. The club was run by ex-GIs who married into the local German community and appeared to be mafia types, and as such, brought in excellent entertainment for the GIs. The notable trappings were three slot machines and a well-stocked bar with a bunch of top-shelf booze. The most obvious accouterment was a glass dance floor on a hydraulic lift that could be raised a couple of feet and used as a stage when an entertainment group came to perform. To enter, a GI needed to present a minimal cost membership card. The club was situated so that if the 251st GIs didn't want to bother to go out on the Strasse to suck down beer but wanted a nightcap after a hard day of monitoring the Soviets, it was convenient and inexpensive.

Other than that, the club was little more than a retreat for the regular drunks, many of whom were FDL types from the 251st and *lifer/tread* equivalents from other units. It was also a refuge for those who never left the compound during off-duty hours. Those types were few and far between, and something was amiss with their psyches. They had a golden opportunity to go out, socialize, and soak up another culture, but they chose instead to stay with their introverted ilk.

Also within the compound were a small movie theater and a three-lane bowling alley that had few clients. The visitors those facilities did attract were the same types as with the EM Club nightly regulars, fellows who seemed reluctant to associate with the German people.

The parking lot behind the 251st barracks was a car salesman's dream. He would have a vehicle to fit anyone's budget. There was a bunch of clunkers, some that were not so bad, a few new VW, a half-dozen Porsche, and a couple of Alfa Romeo. This variety of vehicles revealed a great deal about the ASA—it recruited from all economic strata of society.

The recently constructed basketball gymnasium was open to anyone wanting to get involved in a pickup game. Basketball was popular and prevalent within the military units throughout Europe. ASA-Europe trained its team at Gutleut. A bunch of guys whose height was at least a head taller than those around them reported to the gymnasium as their duty station. These guys practicing basketball all day prompted a snide remark by a GI who wished he could play ball instead of working his current job, "I wonder what the MOS for a power forward is?"

Without a doubt, the most fascinating place in the entire Kaserne was the area where captured Allied airmen were held during the war by the Luftwaffe. These POWs were the reason Gutleut survived almost intact, despite multiple bombings nearby. Along the entire west basement wall, closest to the rail yards, was the POWs' domicile. These were not individual cells, but cavernous areas fronted with iron bars. There was no heat or running water. The only light that entered was through narrow iron-barred windows at the top of the walls.

What the Germans didn't realize was they had placed their prisoners in the safest place within the compound, below ground in a virtual bomb shelter. It would have taken a direct hit to get to those men. It was now used as a secure storage area.

THE CORNER LIBRARY

To orient himself to his new environment, Lee roamed the basement of the barracks of the Kaserne. In the far, deep corner between the armory and the World War II prison cells, was a library for the GIs. He entered and browsed the shelves to find that the books were old hand-me-downs and of no interest to him. The place was immaculate. The librarian was the typical stereotype: mild-mannered, middle-aged, her hair tied back in a bun. She was a German widow named Frau Müller who lost her husband in the war. She was outgoing and spoke English relatively well. Lee politely asked how to check out a book.

"I have, how do you say, *inventarisieren* in English?"

She must be kidding me. There must be at least nine syllables in that word.

Lee did pick up on the first three syllables and suggested, "Inventoried?"

"*Sehr gut ... Sehr gut!* (Very good ... Very good!) I inventoried all the books and put on a number, *und Ich habe ein Blatt* (and I have a sheet) for books that have been taken." She pointed to a check-out sheet. "You write your name and your *Einheit*, ah ... unit on the *Blatt* and I put the book number. Then the date for bringing back I put on a little card in the back."

Lee noted that it was at almost mid-month and the check-out sheet had no entries.

"You speak English very well."

"*Vielen Dank!*" (Thank you!)

"I've just arrived in Germany and would like to learn a little of the language. Perhaps, if it would not be too much trouble, you can help me?"

"*Wunderbar!* (Wonderful!) I will talk to you in English and you will a*uf Deutsch sprechen* (speak in German), and we will correct each other. That will help to pass the time."

And, so it went, for almost two years, with Lee learning to speak as much as was necessary *auf Deutsch,* to order food, drink, and occasionally get laid—thus satisfying the three quintessential needs of a young GI.

THE GUTLEUT WURST STAND

Throughout Frankfurt, as in all German cities, were *Würstelständen* (sausage stands), the German equivalent of America's fast food joints.

They were mobile and had some heating mechanisms to maintain the grills.

Their standard offerings were a few of the multitude of German wursts—the ever-popular *Bratwurst* and usually *Weisswurst, Bockwurst, Knackwurst,* and *Blutwurst.* They also provided a piece of dark bread and a glob of spicy mustard to go with the wursts. Some offered a helping of sauerkraut or potato salad on the side. Most of these stands also grilled *shashlik,* whose appearance on a spit resembled a miniature American kebab. Their ingredients were absolutely suspect. Perchance, roadkill *du jour*?

Lee considered one of the Germans' favorites, *Blutwurst*—whose only ingredients were pork rinds and pork blood—to be the worst of the wurst.

At the time, the East Germans had an organization known as the *Ministerium für Staatssicherheit* (Ministry for State-security) aka MfS, which was a clone of the Russian KGB and later known pejoratively as the *Stasi.* The MfS, with its *Teutonische Grundlichkeit* (Teutonic thoroughness), made the former Gestapo look like a bunch of rank amateurs. By the time they were done, it was an immense organization. It included a guard's regiment, a foreign intelligence branch, and, most amazingly, an agent or informer for every half dozen or so of the population of East Germany.

The MfS, along with its parent organization, the KGB, had been remarkably successful in placing agents at all levels within West Germany, notably within the West German intelligence agency, the BND. The infiltration had been accomplished by embedding agents among the displaced persons at the end of the war. Later they were effective in their penetration by being placed within the hordes of East Germans who voted with their feet by escaping Walter Ulbricht's version of Stalinism. American GIs involved in signal communications or signal intelligence were of particular interest to the MfS and the KGB. The GIs at Gutleut Kaserne received their share of attention.

In the late afternoon and around noon on weekends and holidays, a wurst stand would appear just outside the exit from Gutleut Kaserne. Its only customers were a half dozen or more middle-aged German men. The GIs gave it no business when they exited the Kaserne because they were focused on their destinations. When they arrived back, they just wanted to climb into a bunk and sleep off the effects of a night's imbibing. The stand appeared to receive few, if any, customers from walk-by German traffic. Perhaps those civilians knew more about its possible covert purpose than did the occupation counterintelligence people.

Early in his tour of duty, as Lee and a friend left the Kaserne, Lee stopped to retie his shoe. He glanced back and saw one of the customers who had been at the wurst stand was behind them. When they boarded the streetcar at the Hauptbahnhof, the same guy also boarded. At Dault's, the fellow sat down across the table from them and began buying their drinks while striking up a conversation. He asked their names and lauded the US military for all the good they were doing in Germany. Their trailer finally got around to asking what they did in the army. Herr Whoever subtly persisted on that matter while the security-conscious GIs remained noncommittal.

Then it happened again. This time, when about fifty yards down Gutleutstrasse, Lee intentionally tossed his keys on the cobblestones and took a quick look back as he picked them up. The rest of the evening was, as Yogi said, "*Déjà-vu,* all over again."

Lee was concerned. He went to the only security officer he knew, Chief McDuff.

He explained to the warrant officer what happened during the two previous evenings. He also mentioned that the Gutleut wurst stand appeared to have little if any, food-service financial support, suggesting it must be getting monies elsewhere. Lee concluded with, "Chief, I believe that set-up is a front to allow foreign agents to follow us when we go out on the town. And to try to get us to compromise ourselves, or at least identify us as targets for compromise."

"Private, who the hell, do you think you are, 007?" responded the warrant officer.

"No, but practically everyone who goes out through that gate has a top secret SCI clearance. I thought you as a security manager should be made aware of the situation."

"Private, well, now I'm aware of it. If you want to play James-fucking-Bond, then do it on your own time, because I've got more important things to do. You are dismissed!"

Yeah, your all-important library. I wouldn't want to take you away from sitting on your fat ass all day doing nothing except pulling folders out of a drawer and putting them back.

So, Lee did do it on his own time. First, he thought about what to say when asked what he did in the army and wrote it on a slip of paper. He took it to Frau Müller saying, "I want to be able to speak this in perfect German."

The librarian's eyes opened as wide as saucers when she read it. She reverted to her native German, *"Mein Gott, ist das wahr?"* (My God, is that true?)

"No," Lee lied. "It's not true … just a little joke I'm going to play on a friend."

The note read, "I am an espionage agent, looking for people like you. Thanks for the drinks and if you go now I will not bother to call the military police."

Frau Müller translated it onto paper in German, complete with the nasty little umlauts. It read: *Ich bin ein Spionage-agent, auf der Suche nach Menschen wie Sie. Vielen Dank für die Getränke, und wenn Sie gehen jetzt werde ich nicht die Mühe, die Militärpolizei zu rufen.*

It took Lee several iterations before Frau Müller was satisfied with his pronunciation.

The next day at work Lee explained the situation to a GI German linguist and then spoke the two sentences. The translator gave him a thumbs-up. That evening, Lee and three GIs left for a night on the Strasse. After some distance along the street, he threw down his keys and looked back. They didn't have a trailer.

Shit! I was all ready to show off. Now I'm just another lowly grunt like them.

The next evening was different. Lee, Eli, and Reese were at Dault's when their trailer sat down and began buying them drinks. The trailer got around to asking the ultimate question, "What do you do in the army?"

Lee performed his two-sentence spiel.

The trailer left. A puzzled Eli asked, "What did you say to him?"

"I told him to get his ass the hell and gone out of here," said Lee.

"I don't think so," Reese responded with his usual shit-eating grin. "I believe you told him to meet you out back and you'd give him a hand job."

"This is the thanks I get for keeping you out of Leavenworth?"

"Hey," declared Eli. "If any of us end up in Leavenworth, we sure won't just be giving hand jobs."

THE BURLAP BAG EXPERIMENT

Beginning with his first encounter of Chief McDuff, Lee suspected that the warrant officer wasn't the sharpest knife in the drawer.

His suspicion was further reinforced whenever he observed the warrant officer maintaining his so-called library of classified documents. The library consisted of numerous lockable file cabinets located in the SCIF. Apparently, the warrant officer was the only one with keys to unlock them and it appeared to Lee that no one ever checked anything out. Nevertheless, the warrant officer spent an inordinate amount of his time retrieving each file from every cabinet, checking it off a list, then replacing the file.

I ought to bring Frau Müller up here to give Chief McDuff a block of instruction on how to run a library. Inventory the damned things once, have a check-out sheet and be done with it. But then, the chief wouldn't have anything to do besides threatening everyone with ten years at Leavenworth and a ten-thousand-dollar fine.

The threat of being overrun by Soviet forces before classified documents and equipment could be destroyed was a real-life possibility. The SCIF on the seventh floor had no windows. The warrant officer correctly deduced there would not be enough oxygen to permit the burning of large volumes of paper. The nearest windows were on the sixth floor. The warrant officer, in his somewhat limited wisdom, decided the thing to do with the classified paper was to carry it down to the sixth floor, throw it out a window, then burn it on the Farben Building lawn where there was plenty of oxygen.

On the day of his experiment for the destruction of classified material, Chief McDuff showed up with a big stack of large burlap bags. He opened one of the cabinets and filled one bag with about two hundred pounds of classified documents. It took four GIs to manhandle it down the narrow steps from the SCIF to a window on the sixth floor.

On Lee's father's ranch during the winter, cattle were fed supplements of cottonseed pellets contained in burlap bags. If a sack filled with pellets fell off the tailgate of a truck, it would burst open.

That bag wouldn't hold together if dropped three feet. This idiot is going to throw it, filled with secret and top secret documents ... for a dry-run practice ... out a sixth-floor window? Un-fucking-believable!

"Chief, I don't think this is a good idea, I've had some experience with burlap bags. No way is it going to hold together."

"Specialist, if I want any advice from you, I'll ask for it," the warrant officer spat back.

Out the window went the bag.

One of the GIs who had tossed the bag peered out the window, saying sarcastically, "Congratulations, Chief! That's an impressive bunch of top secret paper you've got floating around in the breeze down there."

Fortuitously, Staff Sergeant Ramsey happened by and asked what was going on. He looked out the window, stepped back aghast, and commanded, "All of you, except the guards, get down there and try to control that situation! Use the stairs, the paternoster is too damn slow!" He raced up to the SCIF. A moment later, a flood of GIs spewed out, heading down.

The GIs picked up the classified paper and yanked it out of hands of passersby. An hour or so later, the cleanup was complete. One GI commented, "I hate police details, but this one was fun."

Another asked, "When the chief sticks his head up his ass, does he wonder why it's dark in there?"

On the paternoster, returning upstairs with his Jewish friend Eli, Lee asked, "On a scale of one to a total clusterfuck, how would you rate that little exercise?"

"An eight, maybe even a nine. For sure, Chief McDuff stepped on his dick big-time with that cockup."

"Yeah, it might have been worse. One of the guys who tossed out the bag may well have gone out the window with it."

"Methinks he had a *Brit Milah* ceremony. That, for you gentile heretics, is an abscission ritual. They just got the heads confused. Instead of the foreskin on the head of his dick, he was circumcised from the neck up."

Well, that would explain a lot. Lucky for Chief McDuff, the UCMJ precludes the army from court-martialing him for stupidity.

BACK ABOARD THE USS GORDON IN NEW YORK HARBOR

During one chat with Isaac, Lee said, "I knew an Isaac in basic training. He had a rough go of it."

"Didn't we all?"

Lee just nodded.

Considering your probable religion, my guess is you don't want to hear the story about that poor guy.

With that, Lee dropped back onto his duffel bag to reflect on Isaac, basic training, and the advanced training that followed.

THE SIBERIAN GULAG IN AMERICA

Few Americans realized there was a replica of a Russian Siberian gulag in the United States. Located in rural Missouri, it was called Fort Leonard Wood.

Lee arrived at Fort Lost-in-the-woods, as it was popularly known, on 2 January 1961 for basic training. Only two months prior, he had received the dreaded ORDER TO REPORT FOR INDUCTION notification, stating, 'Greetings. A local board of your friends and neighbors has selected you for training and service in the United States Army.'

It was snowing and bitterly cold. The new snow added to the accumulation that had slid from the rooftops, now at the barracks' window level.

Lee's basic training experience was the same as that commonly experienced by all GIs. Head shaved, belittled by the drill sergeant, innumerable push-ups, and repeating his army serial number until it was forever embedded in his brain. The drill sergeant gave him a nickname, the same one given to everyone in his platoon—Limp Dick. There were calisthenics, marching, rolling huge logs up a muddy hill, and kitchen police duty if you didn't pay attention to the drill sergeant. Add to this crawling through mud under barbed wire with machine-gun rounds going off above your head, a trip through the gas chamber, and firing the M1 Garand rifle at targets almost always obscured by snowfall. The most memorable of all was coming out of the bitter cold into an overheated tent to watch a color film of battle wounds while listening to fellow GIs vomit. Sucking chest wounds were the most effective to induce up-chucking.

A GI survived the ordeal if he kept his head down and his mouth shut. By the end of basic training, Lee was physically fit and came to understand he only had to deal with two classes of career soldiers—excellent leaders or total chickenshits. No one seemed to hold the middle ground.

The racial demographics of his training company's command structure was a white company commander, a black executive officer, a white first sergeant, one white and three black drill sergeants. A drill sergeant was often referred to as drill instructor or DI. Included in the mix was a black mess sergeant.

Lee was assigned to a platoon with a black drill sergeant. He had grown up in an entirely whitewashed environment. The only African-Americans Lee had encountered were a few on the sports teams while attending college. He understood few of the words his drill sergeant uttered, which was not good. Lee soon learned to just move with or mimic the other troops when the drill sergeant gave a command.

Soon after arriving and having their heads shaved, the Private E-nothings were issued uniforms and a pair of boots, then taken to the barracks and assigned a bunk. Shortly after that, the burly drill sergeant arrived with a box full of marking pens. He instructed them to print their name at the top of both boots saying, "Las na'm, comma, init'al of yo firs na'm. You limp dicks unnerstand? Fuckup, n you 'all be doin pushups in da mud fo th nex fo'ever."

Indeed, not all that articulate, but unquestionably intimidating.

Lee was a good printer and promptly finished his boots. He looked across the aisle to see an enormous young African-American, at least 250 pounds and 6'5" tall—a massive hunk of muscle.

Why isn't he wearing a Detroit Lions uniform rather than OD fatigues?

The black GI was sitting on the edge of his bunk, a boot in one hand, the marker in the other, and a look of despair on his face.

That poor guy is illiterate.

Lee picked up a boot, stepped across the aisle while showing his printing, saying, "Would you like me to do yours?"

Realizing he had just escaped a two-month purgatory of doing push-ups in the mud, the soldier nodded vigorously.

"What's your last name?"

"Qualls."

"Q-U-A-L-L-S?"

Again, a nod.

"And your first name?"

"Lester."

Shortly, Lester's boots were marked "QUALLS, L."

A few minutes later, the drill sergeant reentered, heading straight for Qualls. His apparent intent was to intimidate, berate, and belittle the biggest and strongest soldier in his platoon. He demanded, "Gimme yo boots, Limp Dick."

Qualls handed over the boots, saying, "Yes, Sergeant."

"What? I di'nt har yo!"

Qualls said a louder, "Yes, Sergeant!"

And, so it went until Qualls was screaming, "Yes, Sergeant!" at the top of his voice.

In due course, the sergeant got around to looking at the boots. He paused for a long moment before asking, "You do this'n yo'sef?"

Lee stood behind the sergeant, nodding his head up and down. Qualls bellowed out, "Yes, Sergeant!"

The skeptical sergeant asked, "Som'body hep you?'

Lee shook his head, and Qualls again at the top of his voice yelled, "No, Sergeant!"

"If'n you fuckin wif me an' I fine out … nigger, yo ass be grass 'n ah be de mower!"

Later when the drill sergeant was gone, Qualls came over, laid his arm—which felt more like a leg—on Lee's shoulder and said, "Yo ma man."

Thus, developed a mutual support system throughout their time in basic training. Lester the muscle and Lee, the so-called—albeit limited—brain power.

The E-nothings were the usual mix of urban, suburban, or rural environments. Black or white—a few well educated—but most were not. They were a mixture of religious faiths or lack thereof. Almost entirely missing were GIs of Hispanic or Asian ethnicity.

In Lee's platoon, all were in their late teens or early twenties, with one exception who appeared to be in his early thirties. This troop claimed to have reenlisted after being out of the army for a length of time, which required him to suffer through basic training again. Lee later found out there was an older reenlisted in each of the other two platoons overseen by the black drill sergeants.

Lee approached the thirty-year-old guy and asked, "What are you doing here? This is almost the last place on earth I'd rather be."

The older guy responded, "To tell the truth … when I got out of the army, I couldn't find a job. I have a wife and two kids to feed. I reenlisted."

"Gee whiz … I respect you for that."

Lee had a lower bunkmate by the name of Isaac, who was seldom there during the evening hours. Late one night, Isaac came in with his uniform greasy and muddy from being on KP and spending time in the mud doing push-ups. Isaac, collapsing in his bunk, asked, "When you came in, did you see a sign above the gate that said *Arbeit Macht Frei*?"

"What are you talking about?"

"They brought us here. Shaved our heads. Tattooed our brains rather than on our arms with a number. Put us in common dress.

They treated us as *Untermenschen*. I've been on KP duty almost every night since I came. I must have done a thousand push-ups in grease inside or in the mud outside. Do you remember pictures of concentration camps for the Jews, like Auschwitz? Doesn't this look and feel the same, as one of them?"

"Give me a break … at least we're not starving to death."

Lee glanced down, and before his words were out of his mouth, Isaac was fast asleep.

Lee had grown up with a rifle in his hands on his father's cattle ranch. It was just a .22 caliber, yet, over time, he became lethal with it. Lee had an intuitive feel as to the trajectory of an up or down shot, the impact of the wind on the projectile, and the effect of humidity when pulling off a round. He and his shooting buddies hunted jackrabbits. Becoming so accurate, they made the rule—you could only fire if the rabbit was running and you were shooting from the hip. As such, it was no surprise that Lee could occasionally shoot ducks out of the air with his small-bore rifle.

He considered the M1 Garand a dream come true. It was long barreled, hefty (nine pounds, plus), and difficult to tote around, but stable when pulling off a round. And it fired a cartridge with *oomph*.

Rifle qualification day was near the end of basic training. Pop-up targets on the shooting range were anywhere from fifty yards to what seemed like infinity. After Lee had knocked down the first few, the NCO behind him yelled, "Hey Bob, get over here!" When the range NCO arrived, he was told, "This kid can shoot the right eye out of a snake at a thousand yards." Lee finished knocking down the rest of the targets.

"Damn good shootin' there soldier, you just earned yourself the Expert Rifleman Badge," said the range NCO.

Lee's ego skyrocketed.

"I have somethin' you oughta consider. I have the authority to nominate candidates for advanced training at the army's sniper school. I would recommend you in a heartbeat. Whaddaya think?"

Lee put his ego on hold and reflected about what the recruiting sergeant in Albuquerque had passed along. "As a radio traffic analyst, you will have a cushy job and won't be anywhere close to the front line."

A sniper will be on the front line, and if you miss, the guy you shot at will likely shoot back.

"Sergeant, I really appreciate the offer, and as much as I like shooting, I'm going to stay with my current MOS."

The Expert Rifleman Badge was the only adornment or stripe on Lee's Class-A uniform, and he wore it proudly.

After the qualification shooting, an announcement came over the public announcement system: All Army Security Agency personnel were to report to Sergeant X, at location Y, for additional instruction Z.

A half-dozen ASA troops from various companies in the training command showed up at location Y where they found Sergeant X holding an M-2 Carbine. The M-2 was an upgrade of the M-1, which had a selector switch offering the option of semi-or-fully-automatic fire. "For you ASA guys, this will be your arms issue when you arrive at your duty station." He implied the weapon was accurate up to about as far one could to throw a rock and was designed for close combat, as in house-to-house urban warfare.

Whoa! This is certainly not what that asshole recruiter promised in Albuquerque. Maybe I should have taken the sniper school offer.

The sergeant provided the ASAers an opportunity to fire the weapon. Lee immediately volunteered and determined the as-far-as-you-could-throw-a-rock statement was correct. When set on full automatic, after three rounds, the three-pound short-barreled carbine was firing straight up.

Well, if I ever need shoot at something, I'll pick a point midway on the ground between me and the target. Pull the trigger and pray that it stitches him or it, as the barrel goes up.

At long last, graduation day arrived, and the troops were euphoric, except for another ASAer named Jesse from his platoon. Lee asked, "Why are you so down in the dumps? This is a great day! We are out of this shithole. Devens, here we come!"

Jesse hissed, "I've been fucked. Fucked with a fire hydrant. I'm on hold as a witness in the court-martial of the CO, the first-shirt, the three black drill sergeants, and the mess sergeant."

"You've got to be kidding. What are they charged with?"

"Anti-Semitism, conduct unbecoming, you name it. That older guy in our platoon who claimed to have reenlisted because he couldn't feed his family was a CID agent. There were two more, the likes of him, in the other two platoons with the black DIs."

Maybe Isaac was right. I'll take a gander on my way out to see if indeed there is an Arbeit Macht Frei sign hung over the gate.

ON TO FORT DEVENS

The day after graduation from basic training, Lee and others destined for advanced training at Fort Devens were loaded onto a bus and hauled to Lambert Field in St. Louis. There they boarded a commercial airliner headed for Boston.

The stewardesses fell somewhere between very attractive and downright gorgeous. (Remember, this was the early 1960s.) The comely flight attendants doted on the GIs and covertly slipped them those funny little bottles of airplane booze. This, Lee's first airline flight, would forever bias his perception of how the attendants should appear and function; and, over time he became disenchanted as the airlines' female personnel matured—as in aged, put on weight, and became surly.

After landing at Logan Airfield in Boston, they made their way to a train bound for Fort Devens. This was also Lee's first train ride, even though the Santa Fe railroad tracks ran through his father's ranch. Lee had an aversion to traveling by rail—and for a good reason. A couple of years earlier, he was one of the first to arrive on the scene where two passenger trains had collided head-on after a rail switch had been mistakenly thrown. Among the huge pile of steel and aluminum debris were bodies and body parts. Lee spotted an engineer who appeared to have nodded off while his engine sat on the tracks. When Lee crossed to the other side, he found the train engine and the engineer had been sliced in two and added to the pile of debris. With those memories, still somewhat fresh in mind, Lee was relieved when they arrived at Fort Devens without an accidentally thrown rail switch.

Lee's advanced training curriculum included network structures, memorizing one hundred words of Russian nouns, and a week of typing. As part of NSA, his schooling also included mandatory cryptanalysis instruction. Lee excelled in the latter and finished second in his class behind a guy named Eli, who would later become a close friend.

In Lee's class was a tall, rangy, competent, and confident Spec/4 by the name of James Thomas Davis. His classmates knew him as Tom. He, along with another RDFer who had completed advanced radio-direction-finding training, had been placed into the class to keep them from *casual duty* (i.e., KP) while awaiting orders to Southeast Asia. About midway through the course, they were sent on their way. Tom died in combat near Saigon in December 1961. President Johnson publicly misidentified him as the first American soldier to die in the Vietnam War. In fact, he was the sixteenth to die in that conflict. The news of his death had a profound impact on those who had known him. The ASA's Davis Station in Vietnam was named in his honor.

Also, one of Lee's classmates was a very atypical master sergeant. Master Sergeant Baker was always impeccably attired. He had re-upped for this class before his last tour of duty. Over time, Baker became akin to a compassionate uncle for his classmates. He admitted that the course subject matter was over his head and felt somewhat in awe of the young men around him. He gave them practical advice about how to get along and get ahead in the army. The GIs listened. After all, he was the only individual they had encountered with six stripes on his sleeve who talked to them rather than yelling. He was adamant about appearance, saying, "It doesn't matter whether you're out picking up cigarette butts or receiving the

Congressional Medal of Honor. Make sure you're appropriately dressed."

Not revealed to the students at the start of training was that their class position upon graduation would give them priority in choosing after-training assignments. Lee and Eli both picked Germany. Turkey was an option, but there, both booze and babes were off-limits. Eritrea (frequently misidentified as Ethiopia) in East Africa was not appealing. Heaven-forbid, Shemya, a little icebound rock at the end of the Aleutian chain, where many went through an alcohol rehab program before being reassigned elsewhere. Last on the list was Fort Huachuca, Arizona. Who in their right mind would choose to live anywhere near there?

Lee ran into Jesse, the fellow ASAer who had been held at Leonard Wood to testify in their basic training company's anti-Semitism court-martial.

With a hearty handshake, Lee greeted him saying, "I see you escaped from the armpit of America."

"Armpit of America doesn't begin to do it justice, Fort Lost-in-the-woods is the asshole of the universe."

"What was the court-martial all about? I didn't have the foggiest about what was going on because all I was trying to do was survive."

"As it turned out, there had been complaints from previous basic training cycles about the treatment of Jewish troops by the black DIs and mess sergeant in our company. Apparently, some senator or other heavyweight got in the loop, and an investigation followed. Hence, the alleged reenlisted guys desperately needing to feed their families ... who were CID agents ... got to enjoy redoing basic training along with the rest of us. It was ugly ... physical abuse, unwarranted punishment, ethnic demeaning, you name it. The company commander and the first sergeant, under duress, ended their military careers for allowing it to happen. The three black platoon sergeants and mess sergeant are currently residing in prison at Fort Leavenworth, and *Yid* and *Kike* are likely no longer in their vocabulary."

Isaac wherever you are, I hope you find some solace in this.

Due to the classified nature of the curriculum, there was no after-hours homework. Lee had hooked up with a retread Spec/4 who had used his reenlistment bonus to buy a new Buick, giving them wheels to travel. They first tried dance halls in the area that catered to big-band music. The New England dollies they encountered weren't all that appealing—prudish would be an appropriate adjective for them collectively. The two GIs liked to bet on races and spent a good deal of their off-duty time traveling to Boston, New Hampshire, and upstate New York to wager on the dog, sulky, and horse races. Considering the gas-guzzling Buick consumed most of their meager winnings, it was nevertheless fun.

There was also a lot of marching. Monday through Friday, the student marched almost two miles to and from the barracks to the fenced and arms-guarded red brick structure known as the Schoolhouse or the Bird Cage. If that wasn't enough, on Saturdays the powers that be regularly scheduled a Pass in Review for retiring personnel

On one occasion, there were two retirees—one was a two-star general, the other a two-stripe corporal. The general was no doubt delighted to share the spotlight with his illustrious counterpart.

During these ceremonies, the GIs were required to stand at attention or parade rest for extended periods of time. Some GIs invariably locked their knees and passed out due to an insufficient blood flow to the brain. Everything went downhill from there—literally. The soldiers almost always fell face down while still rigid at attention or parade rest. If the troops were in close formations when one soldier went down, he took out an entire column of soldiers. Medics and ambulances were present to deal with the collateral damage. For military ambiance, a band played something about caissons rolling along.

Well, that's history long past. I can't believe it was nearly three years ago. They say flies when you're having fun. Yeah right! Now, think about some things that were fun.

WHAT THE IDEAL WOMAN SHOULD LOOK LIKE

Lee and a bunch of his cohorts were drinking beer on Herr Burke's beer barge, soaking up some rare sunshine while solving the problems of the world. Then, an even more relevant subject came up: What should the ideal woman look like? They all agreed she should have a beautiful face. Anatomy was a different story. All except Lee were taken with women with ample bosoms. They opined, the bigger the boobs, the better; and reminisced about burying their faces in cleavage, which was almost certainly more wishful thinking rather than experience.

Lee was a leg man. In defense of his minority position he submitted, "They must be long-of-leg, trim-of-ankle, with just enough butt to top off firm, not flabby, thighs. And, with tits that stick out rather than hang down. As far as I'm concerned, their legs can come all the way up to their shoulders."

He continued, "What are now 38Ds will soon become 38XLs … extra longs. You know, Sir Isaac was right, gravity works. In about ten years, all of your big-busted women will be flopping those boobies up onto their shoulders to carry them around."

The problems of the world went unresolved that day, as did resolution regarding the anatomy of the ideal woman.

TO COPENHAGEN AND POINTS NORTH

It was the lull following the storm of the Berlin Wall going up, an unexpected quiet interlude since the Kennedy administration's response had, by and large, essentially been a nonresponse. The East Germans were resigning themselves to Stalinist encapsulation. The Soviets took their troops off alert and moved them back into garrison. And it was still August. Mac got his troops' attention within the SCIF and said, "Things have calmed down drastically. Now is a good time for some of you to take leave. Whatever you do, don't go to the shores of the Mediterranean. Throughout Europe, everyone takes August off and heads to the beaches."

Lee had accumulated some leave time and was recruited along with his friend Reese to take a tour of Scandinavia. Reese was a point guard on one of the major Pacific Northwest university's basketball teams before the army captured him. He was a large, muscular, athletic fellow who always had a big shit-eating grin plastered on his face. The trip recruiter, by the name of Gene, owned a late-model Ford station wagon. The Allies didn't have bases in Scandinavia where they could buy inexpensive gasoline, so they filled a half-dozen five-gallon jerry cans with petrol and lashed them to the rack on top of the station wagon before starting the journey—a mobile Molotov cocktail just waiting to happen. With their open-ended travel agenda, they took their sleeping bags with them, knowing late arrivals would sometimes preclude them from finding rooms for the night.

North, they went, through Germany into Denmark. A ferry ride and a short drive later were in Copenhagen.

Lee loved Copenhagen for many reasons. The Danes were outgoing and friendly, and most of them spoke passable English. The city itself was enchanting. Seafood, which Lee favored despite, or perhaps because of, having grown up on a cattle ranch, was the only thing on the menu. He went into an establishment offering at least fifteen different varieties of herring and pigged out. Above all, what Lee most liked were the Danish women. Anywhere and everywhere he surveyed, he saw a gorgeous creature—Lovely of face and trim of figure!

"I don't think I've seen even one overweight Dane. It must be all of those damned bicycles that keep them in shape," offered Reese.

"Suppose so. I want to come back to Copenhagen as a cobblestone when I'm reincarnated," said Lee.

"Huh?"

"That way I can spend eternity looking up at all those amazing female legs passing over."

"I knew you were a leg man, but how, as a cobblestone, are you going to get your hands on them?"

"Oh shit! Never thought about that. Better reconsider my reincarnation."

They did the usual tourist things—including visiting the Little Mermaid statue emplaced atop a boulder overlooking Copenhagen's harbor, and the massive nearby fountains that were much more impressive than the demure little sea creature. That evening they roamed through Tivoli Gardens with all its radiant aura, restaurants, and entertainment.

The next day they wandered around the city and, as evening approached, took the last tour of the day through the Tuborg beer brewery.

Their guide was a middle-aged man who instructed his followers: one first mixed malted barley, water, hops, and yeast together, then through a process of fermenting, carbon dioxide production, and some generated heat, you ended up a with a very drinkable albeit somewhat alcoholic thing called beer. Tuborg excelled in that endeavor.

Tuborg had a gymnasium-sized room where the tours ended with samples of different beers. There was no cleanup after each group was done. The next entourage used a different set of tables and left their debris behind, and so on throughout the day. The cleanup crew to remove the collective mess would show up at o-dark-thirty the next morning.

The guide took a liking to the GIs, and when the tour was over and the taste sampling complete, he offered them an extended stint of duty in the Tuborg brewery.

There appeared to be innumerable unopened bottles of beer. They gathered many of them to one table and began to consume. The beers were at room temperature, but the GIs didn't care. As Reese opined, "Beer is just like pussy. It comes at all different temperatures. Take and savor it at the temperature served."

Their escort had endured the Nazi occupation of Denmark. That night, he regaled his American drinking disciples of the many times he and his compatriots hid or protected their Jewish countrymen from the Nazis.

As it approached the ungodly hour of four in the morning, the guide stated, "Time to get out of here. The clean-up crew is due in soon."

The traveling threesome made their wobbly ways to the parking lot. As luck would have it for the totally-pissed beer imbibers, the station wagon was easy to locate because it was the only one left in the lot. After twelve straight hours of drinking beer, driving back to their hotel room wasn't an option. They unrolled their sleeping bags and slept off a humongous beer hangover.

Copenhagen had been a marvelous adventure.

Leaving Copenhagen, they crossed into Sweden and headed north along the Kattegat Sea, through Gothenburg, before entering Norway, and shortly thereafter, arriving in Oslo. Aside from driving on the wrong side of the road, this portion of Sweden was about as monotonous and boring as any spot on the globe. They arrived in Oslo to find a pleasant and somewhat picturesque community. After locating a room to spend the night, they went out for a meal at Gene's urging, as he had a fondness for dining. Lee spoke a little Spanish along with some German and his native English. The other two travelers, only the latter. They quickly learned that Norwegians were monolingual. Once seated, they were presented with a menu. It was undecipherable. They first tried to communicate in English. When that failed, they tried what little they knew of German. The waiter was almost immediately joined by an enormous fellow with what appeared to be an eighteen-inch-neck-size shirt. Unquestionably the bouncer. They didn't understand what was being uttered, but there was no doubt they weren't to let the door hit their asses on their way out.

"Madre de Dios!" exclaimed the cuisine-loving Gene. "We're going to fucking starve to death! We've just arrived in Norway and have to make our way all the way across and back again."

"These folks obviously have a serious hard-on about the Germans, and I suppose for a good reason. We'll just have to find a way to keep their nationalistic testosterone level in check. Speaking German is strictly verboten," said Lee.

"My guess is, that is exactly what that primate said in Norwegian when he so graciously asked us to leave," added Reese.

They made their way to another eatery. Again, the menu was in code. Lee asked the waiter if he spoke English. When the response was negative, Lee stood and led the fellow by the arm—wandering among the tables—until he spotted something that seemed appetizing. He pointed to the meal and then to himself. The waiter nodded. Two more iterations of the same drill for his fellow travelers, and were served an excellent fare. Primitive yet effective, and it didn't get them thrown out of the place. At mealtime, this became their modus operandi for the rest of the Norway tour.

The next morning, they headed west across Norway to the coastal town of Bergen. It was a two-lane macadam of gravel sprayed with oil. Their mobile Molotov cocktail was almost the only vehicle on the road, coming or going. Not only were there not any rest stops or gas stations, but there also were no signs of habitation.

"Damn, I'm glad we brought our own gas," said Gene. "Otherwise, we would be shit out of luck, along with the petrol."

"Yep," Reese agreed. "No different than the Viking days. They only travel by sea and just speak one language."

As they approached the fjord area on the western side of Norway, the vista became spectacular. Everywhere they looked were huge waterfalls cascading over cliffs from the melting winter snows. They pulled to the side of the road to stand by and take pictures of one of the torrents. Lee yelled at the top of his voice to be heard above the water's roar, "I don't know about you guys, but this made my trip!"

They made their way onto Bergen, disappointed to find a fishing and cargo port with a minimal amount of charm. The evening meal—again, just seafood choices—chosen by their pick-and-point routine was as impressive as the views coming into the city.

The next morning, back to Oslo for a ho-hum night, being careful not to utter a single German word. They then returned to Copenhagen for a night that was as entertaining as the previous one was boring.

The next night Lee climbed into his bunk back at Gutleut Kaserne with memories of time well spent.

Tomorrow it will be back to all those damned yellow sheets about what the Soviets are doing.

THE ALL-PURPOSE STATION WAGON

Shortly before Lee entered the service, he sold his vehicle and had a few bucks stashed away. After the trip to Scandinavia, he was convinced that a station wagon was the ideal vehicle for a GI wanting to travel around Europe. From Frankfurt, France, Luxembourg, Belgium, the Netherlands, and Switzerland were within a four-hour drive. Denmark, Spain, and Italy could be reached in a day. A station wagon wasn't a babe-magnet, but it was functional for the needs of the traveling GIs. They didn't have all that much money to spend on lodging, and their travel itineraries were at best unpredictable. Take along your army-issue sleeping bag. If you didn't have the necessary funds to book a room or you arrive somewhere too late at night to find a place to sleep the station wagon became your home away from home. One person could bed down on the front seat, another on the back seat, and the other one or two in the rear compartment of the vehicle. One in the rear was comfortable, although it was a tight fit with two occupants.

A GI who owned a 1958 Pontiac station wagon was returning to the States and asking eight hundred dollars. Lee bargained it down to six-fifty and became the proud owner of this big chunk of metal. He placed pads in the rear of the vehicle for the dubious sleeping comfort of any future occupants, obtained his international driver's license, and was ready to hit the road. When he did, the big V-8 engine kept pace with the fast autobahn traffic. Also, when it came to who had the right of way, the intimidating Pontiac almost always won

.

SMOKES

In the years immediately following World War II, cigarettes were the de facto currency throughout Europe. American cigarettes were considered the gold standard. Even fifteen years after the war, cigarettes were regarded a valuable commodity.

The Dutch unquestionably liked their smokes—in fact, the more carcinogenic, the better. Their coffin nails of preference were unfiltered Camels.

Now with an international driver's license, Lee decided to take his newly acquired chariot to Amsterdam on its inaugural crusade. In advance of the first trip, he sought out regular Amsterdam travelers, of whom there were many, asking their advice. Their counsel was, "You can never take too many cigarettes to A-dam." Over time and with experience, this became a routine for visiting the *Venice of the North*.

GIs could buy cartons of cigarettes at the Class VI store for a dollar and fourteen cents, with which they bartered for a night's bed and breakfast in Amsterdam. There was, however, the little matter of getting the cigarettes across the border into Holland. Those entering the Netherlands were allowed only a limited quantity for personal consumption. Lee and his traveling companions were nonsmokers. When they bought cigarettes to use for the B&B barter, they also purchased an extra carton or two to expedite their border crossing and for other bribing or gratuity purposes. It was surprising how fast they were seated in a crowded restaurant when the Dutch maître d' was offered a pack of those beloved Camels.

In preparation for crossing the border, Lee and whoever was riding shotgun would each open a pack and toss out a couple of cigarettes. When the border guard approached asking if they were carrying any liquor or cigarettes, Lee would respond, "No liquor, but we do have cigarettes," while popping one into his mouth as if to light up. He then offered one to the Dutch guard. After the guard took it, Lee would say, "Go ahead and keep the whole pack." He would turn to the front seat companion and ask, "Got any smokes?" Lee handed that pack to the guard saying, "For your friend over there." They were waved through the Dutch border faster than one could say the then-popular advertising phrase, 'Have a real cigarette, have a Camel.'

THE FIRST OF MANY VISITS TO AMSTERDAM

On their first trip to Amsterdam, after reaching the outskirts of the city, Lee and his compatriots were utterly lost. In front of them was a maze of canals and bridges, and they were engulfed in a sea of bicyclists seemingly going in all directions.

Lee pulled to the side of the road and took out a map. While studying the map, a car pulled up behind them. Out came a rotund middle-aged fellow, by all appearances a Dutchman. He approached and asked, "Can I be of help?"

"We are lost and need to get here," Lee said, pointing to the map.

"Just follow me," replied the Dutchman, after glancing at the map.

They followed their guide through a city apparently not intended for anything except pedestrians and bicycles until they arrived at their destination.

There, Lee got out of his car, took out some bills and asked, "What do I owe you for your help?"

"No, no, no, put your money away!" demanded the Dutchman. "The American airdrops of food after the war saved my family from starving to death. I will never be able to repay that debt."

Wow! How does anyone respond to that?

Lee reached into the car and grabbed a handful of cigarette packs and offered them, saying, "For your trouble."

The Dutchman had refused to take money but did not hesitate for an instant to accept the offered cigarettes. He extended his hand, giving a firm handshake. His grip was the kind Americans appreciated—not just one shake going up and one shake down, the dead-fish variety found elsewhere in Europe.

As did most GIs, Lee tolerated the French with their pompous arrogance and the Germans with their barely concealed animosity, but the thing that drove him up the wall was the wimpy European handshake. Lee avoided handshakes whenever possible, and when forced to proffer one, he ensured it was bone-crushing to the point the recipient's knees started to buckle. A career in the diplomatic corps was not in his future.

The Dutchman departed, saying, "Enjoy Amsterdam."

They did indeed take pleasure in Amsterdam and their many later returns. Thus, began Lee's sincere admiration of the Dutch at that time and their resistance against the Nazis during the war.

THE PROS AND CONS OF HUMINT VERSUS SIGINT

Shortly after the Berlin Wall went up, Mac disappeared for a couple of days, as he frequently did. When he came back, he called everyone together saying, "You all know the difference between Signal Intelligence ... SIGINT, which is what we do, and Human Intelligence ... HUMINT, which is what the CIA and a few others do."

One GI held up his hand saying, "No, I don't have the foggiest."

Mac went into a lengthy dissertation explaining the human intelligence side of things. It boiled down to this: the CIA sent agents behind enemy lines to gather classified information, which was a definite high-risk endeavor for said agents. Once they obtained something of interest, which was infrequent, they attempted to get that information back across the border by sending messages using invisible ink, encryption pads, or the actual documents themselves. The information was, as a rule, carried back across the line using couriers who were also at very high risk. It was a time-consuming process that resulted in most data being outdated by the time it got back. Some had radio transmission capability, but this was also high risk because the bad guys possessed the technology to determine from where the transmission was coming. Signal intelligence, on the other hand, was near real-time and it was voluminous.

"The construction of the wall will drastically alter the intelligence playing field. It not only will keep the East Germans in, but it will also keep potential agents out. Not to mention getting intel out. As such, SIGINT is now the primary if not the only source of intelligence as the HUMINT capabilities dry up. Bottom line guys … The ball is now in our court!"

The GI who didn't have the foggiest now said, "Okaaay, that was informative, although perhaps a bit more than I expected."

Mac was nowhere near finished. He went on at some length, concluding with, "SIGINT has its negatives. The biggest problem being its high-security classification to protect the source and method of collection. All you guys have top secret SCI clearances, but damned few of the people who should receive this information have that clearance. Then there's a problem with so much volume, which tends to overwhelm our analytical capability. Everyone is looking for a complete answer. We have a bunch of the pieces of the puzzle … but never all of it. Last, but not least, there are those egotistical assholes who do have the clearance. However, when the intel doesn't match what they expected it to be, they don't use it. Field Marshal Montgomery was a prime example. Or General MacArthur, who didn't believe intelligence findings to be credible. He wouldn't allow intelligence collection, specifically the wartime Office Strategic Services … the OSS, now the CIA … in his area of operation. They both believed in only using brute force to overwhelm the enemy. For them, intelligence was considered nothing but a bothersome annoyance. Any questions?"

No one dared to hold up a hand seeing as their derriere couldn't endure more minutes of Mac's expert, albeit lengthy, verbiage.

"Thank you for your attention. Now get your butts back to work."

On their way, back to their desks, Eli opined, "Mac is a bona fide genius. I just wish he wasn't so verbose when he gets started."

"I guess that's what happens when you know so much and want to pass it on to others," said Lee.

BACK ABOARD THE USS GORDON IN NEW YORK HARBOR

Lee and Isaac struck up a conversation about the antics, pranks, and misbehavior that had occurred within their units. After a few exchanges, they leaned back on their duffel bags to while away the time, privately reminiscing about other experiences not shared.

I don't know about Isaac, but I barely scratched the tip of the 251st iceberg. Unbelievable, the shit we got away with.

THE BONN FLAG

Shortly after Lee's arrival, a couple of 251st soldiers made their way to Bonn. There they imbibed of the local spirits and concluded that the flag atop the Swiss Embassy would make the perfect souvenir for one of them to take home. Somewhere late in the flag collection process, the Swiss guards took them into custody, turned them over to the German *Polizei* (police), who turned them over to the military police, who transported them back to Frankfurt and presented them to the 251st company commander. Throughout this custody exchange of the alleged flag thieves, no formal charges accompanied them back to Frankfurt.

The Status of Forces Agreement between the United States and the West German government mandated that German police could take a GI into custody but could only hold him until military police arrived because GIs were not subject to German courts of law. Turning a GI over to the Americans was a bureaucratic nightmare. First was the inconvenience of contacting the MPs and waiting for them to arrive. Then came a ton of paperwork, including writing up and translating the charges before transferring the miscreants into the custody of the MPs.

Clearly, some discipline was needed, but the company commander was in a quandary. He had no idea how troublesome the infraction was and hearing only the soldiers' accounts of what transpired, sat on it for a few days while waiting on the bureaucratic paper mill, before deciding on the punishment. After several days no complaint had arrived, so he opted to give each of the GIs an Article 15. He gnawed a chunk out of their asses—or, in army vernacular, gave them a verbal reprimand—as punishment and logged it in their 201 files. UCMJ precludes double jeopardy once the action taken is recorded in the 201. The company commander believed he was done with the matter. He could not have been more mistaken.

The Swiss filed their complaint with the State Department, which forwarded it to the Department of Defense, which sent it somewhere into the bowels of the army. By now, this well-aged bucket-of-shit was thoroughly putrefied and ready to be tossed into the fan. That was precisely what happened. When the Swiss government learned that the offending GIs were only given a scolding and could not be retried, they were anything but happy. Diplomatic traffic flourished. The State Department passed the Swiss complaints to the DoD, which passed them down through the army until they reached the ASA command in Europe.

Remember the adage, 'What goes up must come down.' That expression holds particularly true for feces under the pull of gravity—it journeys downward. And down it came. By the time the multinational, multi-departmental Bonn flag incident was finished, the company commander suffered through more shit-storms than was his fair share.

THE CORD JUST KEPT GETTING SHORTER

Lee and a linguist who bunked in the same eight-man room had worked the midnight shift. They came back to the Kaserne, ate breakfast, and climbed into their racks to get some sleep. An FDL buck sergeant who didn't have enough rank to rate a private room also bunked there. His only duty as far as anyone could tell was to lie in his bunk during daytime duty hours and listen to his 240-volt German *BLAUPUNKT* radio that came complete with a long power cord. Shortly after they dozed off, the sergeant came in, took his radio from his footlocker and plugged it in. Turning the volume quite loud, he laid down fully dressed on his bed. Lee awakened in a fog, having just fallen asleep. When he came to his senses, he climbed down out of his rack and approached the FDL, saying, "Vern and I have just come off duty and need to get some sleep. Would you please turn that thing off, or at least turn it down?"

"Glory, boy," said the sergeant. "Look at your sleeve and then look at mine. We are both E-5s, but I have hard stripes, and you don't. So, tough titty! I'll play my radio whenever I want and as loud as I want. Now piss off!" as he turned the radio on full blast, and climbed back onto his rack.

Lee had a Class B uniform being tailored and waiting for pickup across the compound. Because he wasn't going to get any sleep, went to retrieve it, and while paying asked for a few pins. The tailor gave him a small handful, many more than he was going to need. He stopped by the armory and asked the gun guy if he could borrow a pair of nippers with which to cut small wire. The sergeant found them, slid them across the counter, saying, "Don't forget where they came from."

Lee waited until the sergeant left for his nightly binge at the EM club. He took the long power cable for the radio, inserted a pin every foot or so up the length of the cord. Using the nippers, he cut off the pins, then worked them in until the hot and ground wires were connected while painstakingly making sure there was no sign of tampering. The next morning, Vern and Lee, asleep after their midnight shift, were not awakened by the blaring radio. Their wake-up call was a bright flash of light accompanied by what sounded like a small explosion. The sound and light were followed by a string of basic, banal profanity from the FDL.

Whoo! Those 240-volt short circuits are impressive!

Lee and Vern could sleep in for the next few days while it took the sergeant time to splice the cord. Occasionally it was *déjà-vu* with the light, sound, and profanity whenever the slow-witted FDL again spliced the power cord and plugged it in.

A QUICK STOP ON THE REEPERBAHN

Lee and Reese were in Hamburg taking the mandatory nighttime stroll down the Reeperbahn, the street known worldwide for its whores behind glass. Lee didn't believe in paying for sex, at least not directly. The indirect method was more expensive but left him with a somewhat clearer conscience. Reese, on the other hand, was inclined to sample prostitutes as he traveled around Europe—sometimes with dubious results.

About halfway down the street Reese stopped, nodded at the window front and declared, "I'm going to do her." Lee glanced about and saw a *Bierhaus* (beer house) behind them across the street. He pointed, saying, "I'll meet you back there." He went across the street and sat at the bar. After a couple of minutes, the bartender came by, and Lee ordered a draft beer. As the barkeep started to draw the beer, Reese climbed onto the next bar stool.

"I thought you were going to get laid."

"I did."

Oh, this is going to be fun.

"Well, the sixty-minute man you ain't."

Reese's eyes narrowed a bit.

Lee continued, "As a positive, unlike that little peccadillo in Spain, at least you didn't come back butt-ass-naked like you did in Barcelona. Or was it Valencia? I forget." Reese's eyes narrowed even more. "Also on the positive, you likely weren't there long enough for those little crab buggers to climb aboard and hang on, as in Amsterdam." Reese's eyes were now a narrow slit. The bartender sat Lee's beer down in front of him, and Lee responded, "*Vielen Dank, und ein Bier fur meinen Freund Speedy.*" (Thank you, and a beer for my friend Speedy.)

Slowly enunciating every syllable, Reese growled, "You say one more fucking word, and you are going to be wearing that beer."

Lee realized the fun time was over and silently threw up his hands in mock surrender.

ONE CHRISTMAS EVE IN THE 251st

Beau came from the South—where playing football bordered on righteousness—and he was an ardent disciple. He had been a running back for one of the Southeastern Conference universities before ending up in the army. Beau could best be described as an outgoing and personable fire hydrant with a southern drawl.

Lee and his Jewish friend Eli spent Christmas Eve at the EM club knocking back some nickel beers. For Eli, it was just another evening out. Lee realized his parents would look askance at where he chose to celebrate. He rationalized it was his only option because he was neither Lutheran, Jewish, nor Catholic—the only church possibilities in Frankfurt.

When they entered the barracks, the door's small window was broken. Visible were little splatters of blood on the floors and walls. They followed the splatter trail down the long first-floor hallway, up the stairs, and down the second-floor hall. There they encountered about ten GIs, in various stages of undress, surrounding the door to Beau's room.

Beau had also been at the EM club and was somewhat under the influence when he returned to the barracks. He pushed hard enough on the door's window to break it and received a cut on his wrist, just enough to draw a small flow of blood. His companions were themselves somewhat under the influence, and despite having no medical training, correctly deemed Beau needed a bandage to stop the flow of blood. Beau wasn't cooperative, and they chased him up and down the halls in a vain attempt to contain him, not cognizant of the amount of blood he was pumping out during the chase. They eventually cornered him in his room. However, all the hounds judiciously kept their distance from the fox.

When Lee's face appeared among the guardians, Beau recognized him. "Hey Lee, come on in." Lee sat down beside Beau on the bunk and said, "Let me see your wrist." After a quick look, he took out a handkerchief, laid it on the wrist saying, "Keep some pressure on it. You need a couple of stitches. I'm going to get my car and take you to the dispensary to get it done. You okay with that?"

Beau agreed.

Now entered two monosyllabic MPs someone had called. They appeared to be creatures evolving backward to the Cro-Magnon era. These MPs were perhaps good at directing traffic, but little else, and likely pissed off at having to be out picking up drunks rather than getting drunk themselves. Lee explained that he was going to take Beau to the dispensary and have the wrist stitched up. Instead of using common sense for a situation already resolved, one of the MPs, while unfurling a straitjacket, uttered, "He ain't goin' nowheres but in this."

Beau had calmed down. However, but when he saw the straitjacket, he bolted out of the room, knocking over the MPs and his fellow GIs like pins in a bowling alley.

Lee, having no desire to be trampled by his bleeding friend, went to bed.

Someone must have finally tackled Beau. The next morning, he awakened in a padded cell with an IV in one wrist and stitches in the other.

A few days later the walls were repainted, and the floors scrubbed.

That was quick. I guess the army can't have blood spatters lying about—it's probably bad for morale.

SHE WASN'T THE COMPANY COMMANDER'S WIFE

It was bound to happen. Lee was out after curfew at a Fasching party when who should he encounter but his company commander? The captain, with his arm around a very attractive German lass several years younger than himself, barked, "Wolfe, what the hell are you doing here? I don't remember signing a pass for you. Schedule yourself for an Article 15 tomorrow morning. Now get your ass out of here!" Lee had met the captain's wife. This gorgeous female accompanying the captain, however, was not her.

"To answer your question, Sir, I'm out soaking up some German culture, just as are you and Mrs. Shipman."

The young woman extended her hand, saying, "Oh, I'm not Mrs. Shipman, my name is Ilse."

Bless you, Ilse. You just saved my ass.

Lee bowed slightly, took her hand, saying for the captain's benefit as to its ramifications, *"Es ist mein Vergnügen, Fräulein."* (It is my pleasure, Miss.) With an emphasis on *Fräulein.*

The UCMJ defined adultery by an officer as a felony. In most cases, when found guilty of *conduct unbecoming an officer*, he usually ended up with a verbal slap on the wrist. If it was embarrassing to the army, a letter of reprimand went into his 201 Personnel File. However, if an officer held a high-level security clearance—as did this captain—and was convicted of adultery with a foreign national, he was unquestionably looking at jail time and a dishonorable discharge. Not to mention a divorce.

The captain realizing his situation, pragmatically said, "Wolfe, why don't we both just forget this ever happened? Do what we came here to do and have a good time."

"Great idea, Sir!"

At work, the next day Lee related to Mac what transpired the night before at the Fasching party. Mac, somewhat aghast, asked, "You mean you blackmailed your company commander?"

"Oh, nothing of the sort. No threat. He figured it out himself. If he gave me an Article 15, I could demand a court-martial. The last thing he wanted was being up before a bunch of senior officers testifying about the circumstances under which he brought charges. After that, I would be up testifying. For him, that would assuredly be career-and-marriage ending. Besides, he's not an asshole. I would guess by his age and only being a captain that he was probably an enlisted soldier before he became an officer. No harm, no foul, but I wouldn't be too keen on going through that drill again."

Later in the day, Mac walked by and threw down on Lee's desk a small laminated document saying, "Put that in your wallet."

Lee did put it in his wallet. It was an indefinite-term twenty-four-hour pass issued to SP5 Leland R. Wolfe, RA 18594199.

Some people end up with a 'Get Out of Jail Free' card. Mine is even better ... A 'Get Out of an Article 15 For Violating Curfew' card. I will use it only when I must.

Lee would later meet the captain at after-curfew Fasching events, always with Ilse at his side. They would nod to each other in passing, their unwritten compact intact.

Well, at least he's monogamous in his philandering.

STANDING FORMATION

In the two years that Lee was with the 251st Processing Company, he had *stood in formation* only twice. Standing formation is military speak for—among other things—GIs getting up at the crack of dawn to stand in ranks out in the cold to be counted. For most units, roll call was a daily occurrence. Not so in the 251st. As noted earlier, keeping track of the ASAers was akin to herding cats, and the simple arithmetic involved was likely beyond the capabilities of the FDLs.

The first formation was held to celebrate the reenlistment of an ASA draftee/recruit. This was such a rare happening that the company command structure decided it needed to be specially noted. In fact, he was the only such soldier to reenlist during Lee's tenure.

The second formation occurred when personnel from Fort Rucker arrived to recruit helicopter pilot trainees—Their offer was tempting! They announced to the assembled troops that the ASAers possessed the necessary skills to become helicopter pilot trainees because their high induction aptitude and IQ scores precluded further testing. The major enticement was they would immediately become warrant officers with the accompanying jump in pay. To GI grunts, warrant officer status was considered the best of all worlds. They held the privileges and respect accorded to commissioned officers but without the command responsibilities. They were, for the most part, considered first-rate technicians. The negative for the assembled troops was they would owe Uncle Sam another four years of service.

The officer giving the recruitment spiel, thinking the hook firmly set, boomed out, "All you have to do to take advantage of this once-in-a-lifetime offer is take a step forward."

Not a single soldier moved.

Remember, these GIs were smarter than the average bear.

Little did they realize how prudent their decision had been. The war in Southeast Asia was just beginning to fire up, and this recruitment was likely in anticipation of the future personnel needs in that conflict.

WHERE IS THAT GIANT SUCKING SOUND COMING FROM?

Raatz was one of those young men given a judicial choice between going to jail or enlisting in the army. He chose the latter. When undergoing his medical induction process, Raatz had both temperature and pulse—which in the 1960s—were the only prerequisites for acceptance into military service. What he didn't have were his kneecaps, which were lost in a motorcycle accident. The medics overlooked that little detail when he entered service. Raatz scored high on the entrance questionnaire, survived basic training with the bad knees, went through advanced training, and ended up in the 251st Processing Company.

Raatz was somewhat of an oddball. He insisted on being called by his surname rather than his given name, which he never revealed. That caused one GI to comment, "His parents must have given him a Gawd-awful first name for him to prefer being called Raatz." His nickname was a foregone conclusion—Rat's Ass. As in, 'Who gives a rat's ass?' He was married but did not bring his wife to Germany. Perhaps it was a matter of money. Maybe she held a lucrative job. Possibly it was just as well there was an ocean separating them

He had a salacious fascination about female genitalia, almost to the point of an obsession. Despite this exasperating fixation, Lee occasionally hit the Strasse with Raatz.

The EM club frequently brought in a singer by the name of Babalu. She possessed an attractive face, a great voice, and on a scale of one to sexy—She was an absolute ten! She didn't just walk onto the stage. She undulated into the spotlight. The GIs loved her, and when she was scheduled to appear, it was standing room only. The fire code for occupants allowed was violated beyond recognition.

Babalu's finale was something along the lines of Piaf's Milord: sing at a normal tempo, then drop the cadence and the volume to absolute silence. During this time, Babalu would sink slowly into a leg split on the glass stage floor. Using only leg strength, she slowly rose from the floor as tempo and volume increased until she was fully standing, her voice belting out the last words of the song. A dazzling performance!

Babalu was scheduled to appear again. Raatz approached Lee with the proposal that they arrive early to ensure getting a seat next to the stage. It meant they would be standing at the door at the crack of dawn—reluctantly Lee agreed.

When the club doors opened, Raatz and Lee were second in line. Raatz selected a two-seat table at the front of the stage. When he sat down, he opened his jacket and removed a sink plunger and set it on the floor. They nursed beers and ate pizza until the show began.

As Babalu started her finale and descended to the glass floor, Raatz took his beer and poured it on the floor under the table. He set the plunger in the middle of the liquid and waited. The room went totally silent, and completely dark except for the spotlight on Babalu, as she began her ascent. The instant her pudendum cleared the glass, Raatz pushed the plunger down and pulled it back up. A giant sucking sound ensued. Pandemonium reigned. GIs were laughing hysterically. Even the gig-hardened band members broke out laughing but somehow managed to carry somewhat of the tune.

Babalu never booked the Gutleut EM Club again.

The next morning Raatz, knowing the statute of limitations had expired on whatever he was charged with before enlistment, went on sick call. He complained of his knees hurting. For once, the army was expedient.

Raatz disappeared, never to be seen again by his fellow GIs.

BE SURE TO WEAR WHITE SOCKS

Late in his tour, Lee was sought out by newbies about where to go and what to do. His advice was, "Don't go to Kaiser Strasse, which is nothing but a sleazy red-light district, the same as you find along the Mexican border, say, Juarez or Tijuana. Instead, go over to the apfelwein stubes in Sachsenhausen. The fräuleins are friendly and looking for long-term relationships. Don't expect to get laid anytime soon. They're like the girls back home. They keep their knees together until they are good and ready. And, if you do happen to get lucky you don't have to worry about getting a case of the clap, which you might catch on Kaiser Strasse."

He and other GIs, who already had time on the ground, also gave some devious advice to the newbies saying, "Whenever you go out on the Strasse, make sure you wear white socks. And see to it that the guys with you also wear white socks. The fräuleins pay attention to that." What they neglected to say was this: the fräuleins paid attention to white socks because German males who had come out of the closet wore them as their signal to other men. The Germans subtly referred to them as *warmer brüders* (hot brothers). Over time, this scam became almost a rite of passage for newbies. Those conned, licking their macho image wounds, became the next generation of *old-timers* who advised the new guys to wear white socks.

Lee also advised new troops about English soldiers, "Wherever you are, if British troops come in, drink up, pay up, and get the hell out of there. Before the evening is over, the place will be crawling with Politzei and MPs. All those damned Limeys want to do is get into a brawl. If they can't pick a fight with the Krauts or us, they start pounding on each other."

WHO HAS AN EXTRA EAR TO DONATE?

The usual night-on-the-town suspects decided to forgo Dault's and try a gasthaus on the far west side of Frankfurt that came recommended by a cohort known to be a connoisseur of both beer and babes.

Lee rode in Eli's new Volkswagen to their destination. As it turned out, the beer assessment was accurate, but there wasn't a damsel in sight. Whenever the 251st Jewish troops didn't have members of the opposite sex available to hustle, they turned to their next priorities: consuming large volumes of the hops-and-malt beverages while debating amongst themselves about religion. Eli and Matt argued vociferously throughout the evening. As they left to return to the Kaserne, Matt followed Lee and Eli out to Eli's car. Wanting to have the last word, he stuck his head into the car just as Lee shut the door, which resulted in Matt missing a piece of scalp about the size of a silver dollar above his right ear. They tossed Matt into the back of the Volkswagen and the entourage headed for the army's dispensary in midtown Frankfurt.

The medic who examined Matt commented, "Well, there's enough room to graft on another ear. Which of you is the donor?" When none seemed amused, he inquired about what had happened.

Once he learned the offending vehicle was in the parking lot, he grabbed a flashlight and led them out into the night. Still stuck to the door, despite the high-speed run to the dispensary, was the missing piece of Matt's scalp. The medic retrieved and carefully unfolded it while someone held a flashlight as he worked. It appeared to be a pink, hairy, and a somewhat bloody prop from a horror movie. Gagging could be heard in the background.

A month later, Matt's head and hair appeared unscathed. Whether he learned to not stick his head into closing car doors was yet to be determined.

You know, Mac was a walking history encyclopedia, I probably learned more from him about happenings and events than most history majors would ever pick up in college. Berlin for instance.

THE BERLIN AIRLIFT

Shortly after the Checkpoint Charlie situation died down, Lee was leafing through the seemingly endless yellow sheets. Mac was sitting at the next desk, musing. "You know, Lee, I believe the last couple of months would not have happened if Gary Powers hadn't been shot out of the sky over Russia. The Paris Summit was coming up, and both Eisenhower and Khrushchev were looking for some so-called detente. The arms race was taking its toll on both economies, especially the Soviets. Khrushchev had seen the Allies' resolve during the Berlin airlift and had reservations about getting too froggy over Berlin. To save face over the U-2 incident, he wanted Eisenhower to apologize. There was no way Eisenhower was going to do that. The summit went to hell in a handbasket, and Khrushchev dug in his heels. This most recent goat-rope and the wall going up in August was just a spinoff from an event three years ago. The Soviets were again trying to take over Berlin and then West Germany. What do you know about the Berlin airlift back in fifty-eight?"

"Just that it happened, and it saved Berlin."

"Oh, it did much more than that. Not quite as dicey as what we've just been through, but it lasted for about a year."

When he first arrived, Lee had been dubious of Mac getting going on about historical events. Over time, he came to realize that his in-depth knowledge of the past was well worth listening to, and said, "Tell me all about it."

Mac proceeded. "Keep in mind that the West Berliners were already on near-starvation rations. The Soviets cut the highway, railway, and waterway access to and from West Germany, which brought in the critical necessities of life. The only route left was through the air. The Soviets offered the West Berliners the option of signing up for the East German ration card, which would afford them plenty to eat and to keep warm. The intent was to put them under the control of East Germany. Few signed on … they would rather starve and freeze than submit to the Soviets. The Soviets also cut electricity into West Berlin to only a few hours a day. The Berliners never knew when or if they were going to have power. The airlift was a phenomenon that in one short year drastically changed the attitude of people of two very different cultures. The Germans, who had despised the Americans, came to respect them, and vice versa. Not only did it change their attitudes … it also changed the views of the world toward both."

"I can see how that starve-and-freeze-rather-than-submit attitude changed people's minds. It's difficult to comprehend what they must've gone through."

"General Lucius Clay was a hard-nosed piece of humanity, but he also believed in doing what was right. He started off with an unorganized bunch of old cargo planes flying from Rhine-Main here in Frankfurt to Tempelhof in the American sector and Gatow in the British sector of Berlin. They carried in food and coal for the Berliners."

"Food I understand, but coal?"

"Yeah, Berlin depended on it for many things. The most important requirement, other than food to keep the Berliners from starving was to supply enough coal to keep them from freezing to death as they had the two winters before. World War II Generals Bradley, Marshall, and LeMay didn't believe Berlin was worth the trouble. By this time, Marshall was Secretary of State, Bradley was Army Chief of Staff, and LeMay oversaw the US Air Force in Europe. They were content to flush the two-million-plus Berliners down the Soviet toilet. Clay felt otherwise. A high-level pissing contest ensued. The volume and velocity were something to behold."

"What was Clay's situation to be able to take on those heavyweights?"

"He was a four-star who hadn't gained the hero status of the other generals during the war. But, he was an expert in logistics, and, at that time, commanded the Allied military in the Western sector. He frankly did not much like the Germans, but thought it unconscionable to abandon them."

"Good for him!"

"Clay brought on board a guy named Tunner who was an organizational genius. During the war, Tunner was in Asia and orchestrated the supply effort over the Himalayas. Soon after he came on board, the airlift was running like a Swiss watch. Clay went to Truman and said, in effect, 'Look what we can do,' and asked for more cargo planes. In due course, Truman dedicated nigh unto every cargo plane in the military inventory to the operation, much to the consternation of the mentioned generals. The airlift was a total victory, and the Soviets lifted the blockade. LeMay … with his boundless ego … tried, with some success, to claim credit for the endeavor. He didn't have a damned thing to do with it other than being an obstacle."

"Hey, thanks. I'd love to hear the rest of it, but my mind can absorb only what my butt can endure. Let's take a break."

Lee left the SCIF, caught the paternoster to the ground floor, bought two coffees and two pastries from the little German-run snack bar, and returned.

"What do I owe you?"

"Forget it. Spending Deutsche Marks is akin to spending Monopoly money. Let's hear the rest."

"After Tunner worked his magic, it became evident that another runway was needed in addition to Tempelhof and Gatow to handle the traffic volume. Tegel in the French sector was selected. Concrete for the runway would have been nice, but all that was necessary would have to be flown into Berlin. Some engineer suggested that if they laid crushed brick to a certain depth, it would handle the weight of the cargo planes. There was undoubtedly enough brick debris in Berlin for the job. Now all that remained to do was to scavenge an estimated ten million bricks, get them to Tegel, crush them, and lay the runway. The word went out to the Berliners that help was needed. Something on the order of seventeen thousand, mostly women, showed up for the task. They were paid a pittance but were fed a daily meal … a godsend for them at the time. There was no construction equipment in Berlin with which to crush the bricks, move the material, spread it out, and pack it down. The individual pieces of construction equipment in West Germany were too big and too heavy to load onto the cargo planes, so our Corps of Engineers took cutting torches to them, flew the pieces into Berlin and welded them back together again. When the outside world heard about the Berliners' involvement in building the airstrip, their attitude towards the Germans began to change."

"I can certainly see why. Help those who help themselves."

"The outside world hearing about this massive undertaking began with an airlift pilot named Halvorsen. He noticed large groups of children gathered near the end of the Tempelhof runway to watch the planes land. He went out to meet them behind the runway barricade and was impressed with how well the children behaved, despite their obvious need for food. He only had two sticks of chewing gum with him. He tore them into small pieces and handed them out. Halvorsen got this wild hair up his ass that it would be nice to give the kids candy and chewing gum as he flew over the next day. He couldn't just toss it out the window for fear of hurting the children and came up with the idea of dropping the candy and gum in handkerchief-sized parachutes. The following day, his limited supply of candy and gum, complete with their little parachutes, was tossed out as he flew over. The idea caught on with his crew and then also with the other airmen making flights into Berlin. It's a long story, but the bottom line was, it was successful beyond his wildest dreams. Tunner and Clay, realizing the public relations importance of this humanitarian effort, sent him back to the States on a promotional tour. Halvorsen appeared on television shows, met with civic groups, and caught the attention of candy and fabric manufacturers. He became a national hero. Providing candy and gum for the Berlin children became an American national endeavor. Soon, goodies were being dropped throughout Berlin before the cargo planes landed. By the end of the airlift eleven months later, boxcars full of candy, gum and little pre-made parachutes had arrived at Rhine-Main for distribution over Berlin."

"Great balls of fire! I had no idea."

"Spare me the rock-n-roll drivel."

"There's more … 1948 was a presidential election year. Truman was running for reelection on the Democratic ticket. New York Governor Dewey was running as a Republican. Henry Wallace, a Democrat, who had been dumped in the last election by Roosevelt from the VP slot in favor of Truman, was running as a third-party candidate. The only reason he was running, it seemed, was to keep Truman from being reelected. Everyone, even the Democratic faithful, expected Truman to get trounced. The candy for Berlin kids caused the American electorate to pay more attention to what was going on in Berlin. It resonated with the voters and Truman won the election. In my biased opinion, the candy bombers won it for Truman."

"How do you know all this stuff? Were you involved?"

"Let's just say I was sitting on the sidelines, listening."

Lee gave Mac a questioning look.

"This may come as a surprise. We sometimes intercept our own traffic. It's a good source of info."

"Uh-huh," Lee muttered.

Not to mention your little gaggle of super spooks that you traipse off to meet every month or so.

"By the way, you never heard the last part of this conversation."

"What conversation?"

BACK TO THE OLD NAZI BAR

A few months later, when Frankfurt mist turned to drizzle, Lee and Jimmy Joe were headed for a night on the town and picked up a trailer. They stopped at the old Nazi hangout with their usual salute to the former Reich faithful when entering.

As they finished their first beer, Jimmy Joe opined, "We need to lose our following friend. So, just for shits and grins, why don't we have another beer and let him soak up more rain while he ponders why we are hanging out with these old Nazi geezers?"

"Good idea," Lee said. Then to the bartender, "*Noch Zwei, bitte.*" (Two more, please.)

The bartender set the beers in front of them saying, "*Keine Kosten für Ami wie Sie.*" (No cost for GIs like you.) They raised their mugs to him in a mock salute saying, "*Prost!*" (Cheers!)

"This rapport stuff is working out just dandy," Jimmy Joe said, with a satisfied smile as he slugged down a healthy swallow of the great beer. "We oughta do this more often."

When they left, the trailer already had enough of the rain and was long gone.

BACK ABOARD THE USS GORDON IN NEW YORK HARBOR

A helicopter flew close overhead, and Lee and Isaac stood to watch. Isaac commented, "It's beyond me how those things manage to fly."

"I don't know how they do it, but they do. I've flown in one." Lee settled back down on his duffel bag and reflected about that event along with other temporary duty trips he experienced.

ROTHWESTEN

The ASA intercept station at Rothwesten—originally a Luftwaffe airfield, built in the 1930s— appeared to be anything but a military installation. From the air, it seemed like a small, quaint, rural village tucked away high on the mountain above Kassel. It escaped the war almost unscathed. On the ground, the only things that revealed its identity were signs such as Post Exchange instead of *Kaufhaus* (department store).

The mountaintop was reasonably flat, which made it ideal as an airfield for Germans fighters and other small aircraft during World War II. A matrix of rebar had been welded together and laid on the grassy field to provide a camouflaged runway. Old-timers claimed the Luftwaffe maintained a herd of sheep on the mountain to keep the grass down. A rumor persisted of underground hangars containing abandoned aircraft the Luftwaffe left behind. This story was given credence by the fact that the Luftwaffe exited the front gate as American tanks came in the back entrance. The rumor will likely remain forever unsubstantiated because the army dynamited and closed all the entries to the underground facilities.

During the war, it also served as a German camp for Russian POWs. After the war, it functioned as an Allied camp for German POWs. Turnabout was fair play.

Years later, the mountaintop provided the ASA an ideal place to erect antennas to gather Soviet and East German emissions coming from the East.

DEAR DAD

At times, the army and its allies performed war game exercises. Typically, they involved bringing in additional troops—or at least pretending to—from the United States and England to repel the Soviets if they invaded Western Europe. Those units already in place in Berlin were expected to hold for a week, whereas those manning the border were intended to sustain for forty-eight hours.

Anyone with half a brain—who knew the Soviet strength, armor, and firepower and how fast they planned to advance—were sure they would either be dead or marching eastward toward some Siberian gulag by the time replacement troops arrived. The realistic survival rate for Allied troops in rear-echelon positions was slim; however, for those poor bastards in Berlin and on the border, it was none. It would take an act of God for those in Berlin and those in the Fulda, Hof, and Coburg Gaps to see the sun come up the next morning once the Soviets started moving west.

Part of these exercises was to see if troops within the European theater could also be redeployed promptly. As part of one such drill, Lee and three other Spec/5 analysts from the 251st were ordered to Rothwesten with only enough time to return to the barracks—where they threw an extra fatigue uniform, some underwear and a few toiletries into a duffel bag—before being hustled off.

They made it to Rothwesten in an acceptable time. However, once there, there was almost nothing to do other than looking through a few local intercepts. That consumed no more than a half an hour a day but were required to remain at the exercise headquarters. To kill time, they sat around exchanging the usual GI stories of sexual conquests and other fictions.

Also, deployed to Rothwesten was a combat arms first lieutenant with the unfortunate last name of Chekenski. He was a ROTC product and had just replaced his *butter bar* with a silver one. Most likely, his only command experience was parading reluctant cadets around a state university drill field somewhere in the Midwest. He also had nothing to do. Being a young officer needing to impress his superiors, he took it upon himself to *shape-up* that bunch of ragtag Spec/5s from the 251st.

After two years in the army, those smarter-than-the-average-bear ASAers were not shape-up-able.

The exercise headquarters had been declared an operational work area where military courtesies were minimal. At first, this didn't seem to resonate with the young officer, and he was piqued that the GIs didn't come to attention when he approached. Over time, he accepted the situation, but it didn't diminish his enthusiasm when dressing-down an individual 251st soldier or all four as a group. This officer was one of those creatures whose voice functioned before his brain engaged. His criticisms were trivial, mundane, or unnecessary and quickly earned him the nickname Lieutenant Chicken-shit-ski.

The lieutenant found some fault with a GI, however inconsequential, and asked for an explanation. He repeated the GI's words, concluding with "is no excuse."

For example, in the first encounter, the lieutenant decided the haircut of one of the newly arrived GIs needed a trim. He asked, "Soldier, why isn't your hair cut to army regulation?"

The GIs replied, "Sir. I arrived on-post last night and this morning had to report for duty."

"Arriving last night and reporting for duty this morning is no excuse. Get a haircut, soldier!"

The young officer again showed up later in the day saying, "I told you earlier today to get a haircut. Why haven't you done so?"

"I've been on duty, Sir."

"Being on duty is no excuse. Get a haircut, soldier!"

After a few iterations of the aspiring officer's modus operandi, Lee waited for his *no excuse* turn. The lieutenant berated him for—in his opinion—Lee's fatigues not being properly bloused, saying, "What do you have to say for yourself, soldier?"

"No excuse, Sir."

"Well, no excuse is no excuse!"

"Sir, you are exactly right. No excuse is no excuse."

This guy will go far in the army, with his simpleminded stubbornness and inability to comprehend reality.

Matt was from Long Island and typical of those residing in the New York area—brash, vocal, and generally obnoxious. Matt had a lot of things going for him—knowing when to keep his mouth shut wasn't one of them. For several reasons, he became the ambitious officer's prime target. The most evident being his propensity to utter the not-so-polite acronym FTA in the presence of the lieutenant.

During his encounters with the officer, Matt repeatedly stated, "Sir, if you don't get off my case, I'm going to write my congressman about how I'm being treated."

On one occasion, anticipating Matt's response to his criticism, the lieutenant came prepared. He threw down a pad of paper, a pen, and a stamped envelope, saying with as much authority as he could muster, "Since you won't do it on your own initiative, I'm giving you a direct order to write your congressman about how you are being treated."

Matt responded, "Sir, I will need your name, rank, and unit, to tell him who gave me the direct order."

The lieutenant gave him the info.

Matt began his letter —

To the Honorable Matthew J. Gutnick, Sr.

Chairman of the House Armed Services Committee

United States Congress

Dear Dad:

I have just been given a direct order by an officer to write you regarding his treatment of me. The officer's name is Lieutenant ...

The lieutenant immediately informed the GIs that his presence was required elsewhere.

Matt said, "I'm going to finish this letter, and if Lieutenant Chicken-shit-ski ever shows up again, I'm going to make sure he reads it before I drop it in the mail. Otherwise, I'll put it in file thirteen. My old man has better things to do with his time than hearing about this pathetic piece of S*cheisse*."

THE HILO FLIGHT

A couple of days into the exercise, Lee and his three TDY companions reported for duty. As usual, there was little for them to do besides looking through a few intercepts. Their understanding supervisor told them to take a walk, get some air, whatever. He wanted them to check back in around noontime.

It was a beautiful, warm, bright, clear day with the sun ablaze. They decided to walk around the flat mountain top—first, to soak up some of the rare sunshine, but also to put as much distance between themselves and Lieutenant Chicken-shit-ski as possible. However, by now the lieutenant had made a career-saving decision. He was not about to hassle the non-shape-up-able 251st troops again because one of them was the son of one of the most influential men in America!

During the walk, a helicopter landed, and the GIs came closer to have a look at the strange new bird. A moment later the two chief warrant officer pilots accompanied by a civilian with an oversized box camera came out of the craft. As they saluted the warrant officers, one of the pilots said, "Hey guys, we're headed out to the Bahrdorf station on the border and back. We only have one passenger. Want to come along?" The offer was too good to be true.

For the GIs to see a helicopter up close was extraordinary. However, to get to ride in one was beyond imagination, and couldn't wait to clamber aboard. The GIs should have remembered the adage, 'If it's too good to be true—Beware!'

There was a row of canvas bucket seats with safety harnesses along one side with an open sliding door along the other. A gruff crew chief strapped the camera guy into to the middle position with an open seat on each side. He then strapped in the ASAers, two each on the sides of the photographer. As he pulled the straps painfully tight, he warned, "Don't even think about touching those straps."

Off eastward they went—*whup-whup-whup*. The view from the open side door at the helicopter's low flight altitude was spectacular.

There are as many shades of green in rural Germany as there are shades of gray in the cities.

After about an hour, the crew chief came back, taking a hard look at the safety harnesses—not saying a word—before returning to the front of the craft. Shortly after he disappeared, the pilot turned the bird over on its side. Well, not ninety degrees, but certainly more than a sixty-degree bank, the maximum supposedly allowed. Nevertheless, the only thing between the passengers and Mother Earth were the harness straps. The camera guy, clicking away as fast as possible, appeared to be ecstatic—The other four were scared shit-less!

The return to Rothwesten was blessedly uneventful. Once they had landed and were off the copter, one of the warrants, with a demonic chuckle, said, "Hope you guys enjoyed the ride, especially the turn at the border." All saluted, then, to maintain an iota of their macho images, the GIs mumbled something to the effect that it was an experience to remember. Undeniably, it was.

Memories of this flight triggered another remembrance.

THE FLIGHT TO AUGSBURG

Mac approached Lee, asking, "Could you do me a big favor? I have a bunch of documents I need to get down to Augsburg ASAP. You're the only guy I have available who has the security clearance to be a courier. There's a pilot out at Hanau who has done me a bunch of favors, and I owe him one. He needs some air time to keep his flight pay. If he flew you down to Augsburg with those documents, we would kill two birds in one fell swoop."

Stifling a disparaging comment about Mac's mixed metaphors Lee said instead, "A favor for you? Flying over Germany on a cloudless day like this would be a favor to me!" Little did Lee realize what was in store for him.

Lee arrived at the Hanau airfield with an inch-thick bundle of double-wrapped top secret documents and found the pilot. The airplane was an old, World War II propeller-driven trainer. The pilot strapped Lee into his seat, affixed a helmet on his head and handed him a half-dozen barf-bags saying, "You're most likely going to need these. Gonna be lots of turbulence today." Off they went into the wild blue yonder. The sky was blue, but the *wild yonder* excerpt must have been a euphemism for a near-death experience. As far as Lee could tell, the aircraft went every direction except forward. Periods of zero gravity followed by bone-jarring drops at the bottom of air pockets. The helmet on his head was a godsend.

One fell swoop turned into one swell foop.

Much to Lee's surprise, the aircraft managed to land and throttled to a stop at the Augsburg airfield. As he deplaned, he handed the pilot the unused barf-bags, to which the pilot responded, "I'm impressed. With most folks, the ground crew would need to take a fire hose to clean out your section of the cockpit. So, what's your secret?"

"No secret, Sir. I grew up on a cattle ranch and spent untold hours in a saddle atop a horse. I have this theory that those who often rode horses in early life don't suffer from motion sickness."

"You oughta consider aviation as a career. Whaddya think?"

"Not only no, but hell no!" A belated "Sir." ended their conversation.

Lee delivered the classified documents and caught the next train back to Frankfurt. The returning locomotive didn't encounter any air pockets, and Lee caught up on his sleep.

THE LÜBECK MESS HALL

Lee was lost. He was in his POV on TDY to Lübeck. He had missed the autobahn entrance and was now on a minor road somewhere in a forest, somewhere in Germany, with no landmarks in sight.

Well, that ought to narrow it down to about a thousand square miles.

Lee needed to look at a map. He pulled the station wagon off the road. The hood of the vehicle encroached into the adjacent walking and bicycle pathway that was twenty to thirty yards across. Lee retrieved a map and was studying it when a bicyclist approached down the path.

The bicyclist was a scrawny little guy wearing work garments with an Afrika Korps forage cap on his head. The bicycle bordered on antique with original hard rubber tires. The bicyclist stopped in front of the station wagon when he realized it belonged to a GI. He glared at Lee, backed up the bicycle about forty yards and came pedaling as fast as he could.

He hit the chunk-of-iron Pontiac at the front fender well. As might be expected, he flew over the hood ending up in a tangled clump of body parts. When he arose, he seemed none the worse for the wear aside from a mouthful of pine needles and his forage cap askew.

The bicycle was a different story: the fork was bent, the front wheel now positioned under the seat and nowhere close to being round and useable.

What the hell was that all about?

Lee folded the map and backed onto the roadway. He rolled down the window yelling, "Auf-fucking-Wiedersehen!" as he drove away.

He found his way onto the autobahn and arrived at the ASA Lübeck outstation late that evening and was shown a bunk to spend the night. The next morning, he awakened, cleaned up, put on a fresh uniform, and went to the mess hall.

The breakfast *menu du jour* was steak and eggs cooked to order. At lunch, it was steak cooked to order with—unlike other army mess halls—a recognizable veggie. And at the evening meal, it was steak cooked to order with yet another identifiable side dish.

The next morning, as he sat down with his cooked-to-order steak and eggs, Lee struck up a conversation with a GI across the table, commenting, "The food here is unbelievable. All I've been exposed to are the consolidated mess halls at Devens and Frankfurt. For those morons, quantity comes first, and quality is a rare afterthought. You know what I'm talking about, having gone through Devens. I think the scrambled eggs I had yesterday morning were the first in two years that were edible. This morning I ordered three sunny-side up. Lo and behold, guess what showed up on my tray along with this great steak?"

The GI chuckled and said, "*Bon appétit.*"

"This must be a great duty station. You're close to Lübeck for good nightlife. The Germans don't seem to have the same animosity towards occupation troops here in the British Zone that we have further south." Lee recounted the episode with the bicyclist the previous day.

The GI nodded saying, "Yep, only these dumb Dubs would take a few pounds of a bicycle up against a ton of station wagon. We get a little of that here ... and they wonder why they lost the war."

Lee was in cholesterol rapture with his flawlessly prepared steak and eggs when the GI said, "Being here in the Brits' zone, we are not constrained by the army's idea of what a mess hall should serve. We have our separate budget and can buy whatever we want to eat. We hire our own cook, not a GI. The nightlife is good, and the Germans, for the most part, are friendly. However, this is not the great duty station you make it out to be. We have a miserable climate. You have no idea what it's like here in the winter when storms, and there are a bunch of them that come in off the Baltic."

"That may be, but you ... for sure ... eat better than any soldiers in the whole damned army."

THE GOOD, THE BAD, AND THE SKUNKY

Sometime back in the early 1500s, whoever specified beer brewing standards in Germany, *ordiniert und verordnet* (ordained and decreed), the only ingredients to be utilized in beer brewing were malted barley, yeast, hops, and water. Ordained indeed. Beer, after all, was considered by most Germans to be holy water.

After four hundred years, the Germans brought this mix of ingredients to an art form. One couldn't buy a nasty-tasting or foul-smelling beer anywhere in Germany unless the brewer decided otherwise.

If one puts freshly brewed beer into a clear glass container and exposes it to sunlight, the beer becomes skunky. The adjective is self-defining. The longer it sits in this condition, the skunkier the odor and taste become. Maggot-gagging is a good analogy for a well-aged beer receiving lots of sunshine. To date, no solution had been discovered to negate the stench. Dousing the area with tomato juice helped somewhat, but it made one hell of a mess to clean up.

Lee was again on TDY, near Helmstadt, on the way to give a briefing at the nearby ASA outstation at Bahrdorf. He stopped at a local bierhaus and ordered a beer. Because he was an obvious GI, the beer served was utterly skunktified.

You bastard! The war has been over for fifteen years. Accept the reality that you lost it.

When no one was looking, he splashed some of the beer on the wall behind him and poured it into every nook and cranny he could find.

He took out a Deutsche Mark, and, on its back inscribed a large swastika with a marker pen intended to be used at the briefing. Thus, rendering the note worthless.

Whew! I've got to get out of here. It's already starting to stink to high heaven.

Lee stood, got the bartender's attention from a distance, showed him the front side of the Mark, which was twice the cost of the beer, and placed it on the table next to the mug. He departed, saying, "*Sehr Gut Mein Herr.*" (Very good, Sir.)

Once outside, Lee muttered to himself, "Why can't some of these sniveling Krauts admit the war is over? In the meantime, they can kiss my Ami ass!"

IN THE 5K ZONE

Lee was on TDY to Mt. Meissner, an ASA outstation just inside the west side of the East German border. It was a glorious day, but Lee considered any day when the sun was shining in Germany to be glorious. He was driving his POV—the trusty old Pontiac station wagon—in his Class B uniform with his arm out the rolled-down window. Relaxed and enjoying the scenery, but nevertheless mindful he was within the 5K border zone.

As he drove along, he came upon a crew stringing communications wire alongside the road. He recognized the individual supervising the work.

I'll be! That's Master Sergeant Baker from Devens.

Lee screeched to a halt, backed up, and exited the station wagon.

Baker met him. They placed their hands on each other's shoulders, which was as close to a hug as the army permitted.

"Sarge! Damn, but it's so good to see you!"

"You too, Lee! And look at you. All squared away in that tailored Class B uniform, and a Spec/5 already. You must have paid some attention to me back at Devens."

"More than you'll ever know, Sarge," he responded, as they disengaged.

They chatted about what had transpired since they last saw each other, including the death in Vietnam of Tom Davis, their classmate at Fort Devens.

Sergeant Baker admitted, "I didn't graduate from the class, which is just as well. At least out here, I know what the hell I'm doing. How about yourself?"

Lee gave him a brief synopsis and inquired about the sergeant's family. His wife was with him here in Germany and his children, of whom there were several, had either graduated from major universities in the States or were currently enrolled.

"So, Lee, how's your love life here in Germany?" "Busy enough, and at times, a little bit too chaotic ... there's a bunch to choose from ... but, as of yet, none quite fit the bill to be a keeper."

As Lee departed, the sergeant warned, "Pay attention up here. Sometimes it gets downright scary."

A few miles down the road the sergeant's advice came true.

The American fifty caliber machine gun makes a distinct sound— *whomp, whomp, whomp*—when fired. Lee heard *whomps, whomps, whomps*, which meant multiples of those deadly buggers were being discharged.

Verdammte Scheisse! What the fuck is this?

Abruptly he came upon a type of vehicle he had never seen before with quad-mounted fifty caliber machine guns firing intermittently. Lee had come upon an escape attempt by folks from the proletarian-promised-land of East Germany. They were putting their lives on the line to get to the West, as the American soldiers provided covering fire. It was strictly against army orders to fire live rounds into East Germany. These guys ostensibly hadn't gotten the memo. They weren't shooting at the East German border guards, just putting enough shots in the air to keep the bad guys across the line hunkered down.

A master sergeant in full combat gear, looking as if he ate Gila lizards for breakfast, stopped him, yelling, "What the fuck are you doing here?"

Lee shoved his travel orders out the window.

After a quick glance, the sergeant pointed down the road and bellowed, "Get your ass out of here. Now!"

Lee put the pedal to the metal.

I doubt he ran me out of there for my safety, but rather to cover up that hail of lead he is raining down across the border.

A few miles down the road, Lee said to himself, "It's time to get the hell and gone out of Germany. I'm starting to think and swear like a Kraut."

BACK ABOARD THE USS GORDON IN NEW YORK HARBOR

Lee and Isaac eventually got around to the inevitable discussion GIs have—girlfriends, trysts, and other self-proclaimed female conquests.

"Heidelberg was a great place to meet girls," said Isaac. Not only were there the local fräuleins, but it appeared as if every American tour through Europe made a stop in Heidelberg." After the requisite amount of bragging, Isaac asked about Frankfurt.

"The social nightlife in Frankfurt is fantastic. At times, it seemed as if I took on one too many," Lee responded.

"Let me guess. You ended up with a case of the clap?"

"Oh, no! Though … when you're burning the candle at both ends, you tend to run out of wax, if you know what I mean." With that, Lee began to reminisce about some of the most memorable ones.

THE POLISH GIRL

Fasching is to Germany as Carnival is to Rio or Mardi Gras is to New Orleans.

It begins at the eleventh minute of the eleventh hour of the eleventh day of November and ends at midnight on Fat Tuesday preceding the start of Lent beginning on Ash Wednesday. It is a Catholic celebration. As best as Lee could determine, there were few practicing Catholics in Frankfurt, but all denominations turned out in droves to observe this event

It must be like St. Patrick's Day when everyone loves beer and anything green ... even green beer. Or like Cinco de Mayo, when everyone commemorates the single battle the Mexicans won in a war they lost.

There were Fasching parties throughout the time, with an abundance of celebrations as Ash Wednesday approached. Lee soon learned that some couples put their marital vows on hold during Fasching, notably toward the end of the festival season.

Lee met Anna at an early Fasching outing in the Römer Ratskeller. They had a strong physical attraction. The animal magnetism or whatever that phenomenon is called, was overwhelming. Anna was Lee's epitome of what a woman should be. Beautiful face, long of the leg, boobs, and butt resolutely resisting gravity, and hazel eyes that changed color depending on her mood.

She had been an orphan growing up in Poland. Considering her age, her father might well have been Polish, German, or Russian, considering the recent conquering armies. She made her way out of Poland and through East Germany before the wall went up, ending her arduous trek in Frankfurt. Somewhere along the line, Anna learned to speak English quite well. Lee was so enamored that he avoided making inquiries. Anna undoubtedly appreciated his lack of questioning.

Lee could only speculate what Anna liked about him. He was tall, trim, broad-shouldered, and wore glasses. He remembered an overheard comment from a former girlfriend, "When he stands sideways, you can't see him. When he faces you, all you can see is your reflection in his glasses."

Lee considered himself a good dancer. He could swing and sway to anything involving a two-step, and he jitterbugged with the best. Regrettably, about the only Fasching dance offering was the waltz— *boom-trap-trap, boom-trap-trap.*

How in the hell is someone with two legs expected to dance a tune in three-quarter time?

Lee managed to fake it. Replacing quick up-and-down foot movement with long gliding steps, he and Anna swirled around the dance floor as if they had danced together for years. When tired of dancing, they found one of the many dark and secluded corners in the Ratskeller. There, they kissed and fondled until some German came by saying, "*Nehmen Sie ein Zimmer.*" (Get a room.)

At the end of the evening, Lee asked if he could perhaps see her home. Anna declined. He then offered a dinner date sometime in the future. Anna again demurred but suggested they meet each other at a future Fasching event being held at a different locale. Lee began to suspect that Anna was on a marital-vow sabbatical.

And so, it went: Lee and Anna met at Fasching parties and had wonderful times together, but Anna refused to see Lee elsewhere.

Lee ultimately had enough and confronted her, saying, "You're married, aren't you? That's why you won't go out with me."

"No, I'm not married. But, believe me, my naive Ami, I have seen more than my share of reality. And our reality is ... if we date, we will become intimate and fall in love. You hold a high-security clearance. If we were to be a couple, there is no way my background can be checked, and you would lose your clearance. But that is trivial compared to this ... the day will come when you are on the train to Bremerhaven, and I will be left standing at the station. We will be waving goodbye forever. So, let's enjoy our time together now and let the future take care of itself."

THE NICE GERMAN GIRL

At one of Lee's first outings during Fasching, a fräulein asked him to dance. She didn't meet Lee's rigorous definition of a keeper. She was a bit thick of ankle and a touch heavy of the thigh, topped off with an ample, gravity-prone bosom—but she did have an attractive face and a full head of blond hair. Obviously, no part of her body had ever experienced a razor. She could have been the poster picture of the *Nice German Girl* anywhere in Deutschland. Her name was Renate. She lived with her parents in a village in the Taunus Mountains above Frankfurt and commuted to work as a secretary in downtown Frankfurt via the streetcar system.

What's going on here? A 'nice' German girl is hitting on an Ami. Let's play this out and see where it goes.

Lee continued to dance with her throughout the evening and suggested a future dinner date at an upscale restaurant in downtown Frankfurt. She accepted and thus began a long-term, albeit platonic, relationship. Renate spoke English well, and from a cultural point of view, she was great to have around.

Later in their get-togethers, Lee suggested, "Why don't I take the strassenbahn up close to where you live and meet you? We could have a good schnitzel meal at a local gasthaus. I'm sure you know which one is the best."

Renate unexpectedly demurred.

A-ha, now I get it! The 'nice' German girl doesn't want to be seen by neighbors, much less her parents, in the company of a detested Ami.

After that, Lee played a game where the ball was always in Renate's court, and frequently suggested he come up to see her in her village. Eventually, she agreed to a picnic lunch at a nearby deserted castle that was in near-total ruin. She met him as he departed the streetcar with a picnic basket on her arm and led him through back streets and alleys to the castle ruins. The picnic lunch, complete with flip-top beers, was typical good German fare. Lee, however, was going to drop Renate off his screen—enough deceit already.

What he wasn't going to forget were the castle ruins.

These ruins are a perfect place to go for someone on the run, which I might well be if the Soviets decide to shoot their way west. A high vantage point, a nearby village in which to buy or steal food and drink. No one seems to come here. Shelter from the elements. A small campfire lit without being seen. Perfect, indeed.

THE BELGIAN GIRL

Lee met Irene at a Fasching party. She was a petite and alluring woman. At the end of the evening, she invited Lee to her quarters. As Lee later observed, "In keeping with the graces of a perfect hostess, she proceeded to boink my brains out."

Irene was from Belgium and about ten years older than Lee. It soon became apparent that she was one of the young Belgian women who had fraternized (slept with) the German occupiers during the war. At the end of the war, they were run out of the country after their heads were shaved and being publicly humiliated.

Despite the age difference, they were a perfect sexual match. Irene was Lee's libido mentor and appreciated his staying power.

She was often on Lee's arm despite the digs from fellow GIs about their age difference, such as, "It's so sweet your mother came to visit you in Germany," or "Doesn't she know it's not socially acceptable to cuddle up in the cradle with the likes of you? Huh, Baby boy?"

Yeah, right. At the end of the evening, I have a romp or two in the hay while all you have is your hand and imagination.

THE CASUAL GIRLFRIEND

Lee was a regular at Dault's, as were a couple consisting of a GI and his schatzi. The young woman, unlike most German females, was long of leg, trim of ankle, and slim of hip. Her breasts were high and resisting the pull of gravity. Along with being tall and having a lovely face, a slender body, and an outgoing personality, Lee rated her a near-ten on his potential keeper scale. However, there was a problem—she was always accompanied by the same GI. When they sat nearby, Lee tried to flirt with her. She moved her eyes toward the boyfriend, smiled and slightly shook her head, as if to say, "Don't bother, you'll be wasting your time."

She was also within hearing distance when Lee ran off the first trailer with his pseudo 'I'm the badass counterintelligence agent looking for assholes like you' spiel. A couple of evenings later, when Lee and his drinking buddies were seated and sucking down their apfelwein, the fräulein came up behind Lee. She placed her breasts on his shoulders, ran her hands through his hair, thoroughly mussing it up saying, "*Guten Abend, meine eigenen lieblings Spion.*" (Good evening, my own favorite spy.) Then she went back and joined her boyfriend.

One of the other GIs was a German linguist. He grinned, saying, "Wolfe, do you realize she announced … to anyone within hearing … that you belong to her? *Meine eigenen* in German translates to *my own* in English, in case you didn't know."

"That broad is a definite keeper," Lee declared, after taking a hearty swig of the cider, "I wish she were my own, but that's regrettably not the case."

Every night afterward when she entered, and Lee was there, she performed the same routine and then went back to her boyfriend. It drove Lee crazy.

WOLFE, YOU DUMB . . .

After duty, Lee and his friends were sitting in the EM club drinking their nickel Lowenbrau while deciding whether to go out on the Strasse. Their conversations were the usual GI banter—sexual conquests and other fabrications.

A group of linguists entered and sat at an adjoining table where they ordered drinks from the always accommodating German waitress. When their drinks were delivered, Reese commented, "Those guys almost never come in here, and wouldn't you know it

... they ordered martinis. I guess the beer we drink is too low-brow for their sophisticated tastes."

With that, he rose and walked to their table asking, "You were all trained at the Defense Language Institute in Monterey, right?

They, as a group, nodded with indifference.

"I heard the rumor that the DLI is going to go co-ed."

This got their attention.

"Yeah, they are now going to allow in male students, can you believe that?"

One of the linguists pushed back his chair as if prepared to come up swinging. There stood the athletic, muscular Reese with his ever-present shit-eating grin on his face. Discretion being the better of valor, the troop returned his attention to the martini.

The Monterey Marys promptly finished their drinks and departed.

At the table on the other side, a soldier named Al said, "I'm so horny that light socket over there is starting to look good."

Another GI turned to the fellow sitting next to him, saying, "Hey, Joe, why don't you get that hairy Nazi Schatzi you're diddling, you know, Sasquatch's sister, to shave under her arms and Al could use all that hair to create a muff around that socket."

Then another chimed in, "Yeah, Joe, maybe persuade Betty Yeti also to snip off a big handful of her short-and-curlies, which she would never miss, to make it look authentic?"

"Up both of yours! Stick it where the sun never shines! At least I don't keep a five-pound bag of flour handy ... so I can roll her in it and then go for the wet spot ... as you do with your fat little fräulein," came back the GI named Joe. And to the other heckler, "My schatzi doesn't have a fifteen-minutes-for-fifty-pfennig parking meter installed alongside her bed, as does yours."

Yet another GI went trilingual. "Someone needs to remind Al that, with this fabricated *muschi*, he doesn't need to strap a board across his ass to keep from falling in as he did with that last *schlampe* he was *schtupping.*

That conversation regarding the more endearing attributes and behaviors of their respective girlfriends continued further downward. As if that was conceivable.

At his table, Lee said, "You know that girl who comes up behind me every time we go into Dault's?"

Eric knew precisely which girl Lee was talking about but wanted to yank Lee's chain and rub a little salt into his wounded ego. He asked, "You mean that good looking schatzi who drops her boobs on your shoulders before she makes a rat's nest of your hair? That one? Must feel good, huh? What's the matter, don't have the *cojones* to take on her steady boyfriend?"

"Yeah, that one," replied a miffed Lee. "I can't figure her out. Is she hitting on me? Is she trying to make her boyfriend jealous? She's been around when I've run off trailers, so is she warning the nearby Germans to be careful about what they say? Drives me up the wall with what she's doing."

"Wolfe, you dumb shit," pronounced Reese, getting right to the point. "You're nothing but her backup plan to get her to the land of the big PX. She already has you on her boat. The next time she sticks her nipples in your ears and the boyfriend isn't there, she'll row you ashore and won't miss a stroke."

The other GIs grinned and nodded their heads while Lee glared at Reese.

"Double entendre intended," chortled Reese.

Everyone except Lee broke out in laughter.

A TRAVES DE ESPANA, THRU SPAIN

Lee and his cohorts were on leave. Behind them was all the dreary gray of Germany. They were headed to sunny Spain. They traveled south through France in Lee's station wagon, surrounded by vineyards as far as the eye could see. Somewhere near Lyon, out of the blue, Reese commented, "You know, southern France would be a great place to live if it weren't for all the fucking Frogs." All concurred with a nod of the head.

They arrived in Barcelona, found a place to stay, and mapped out their extensive travel plans. Well, in fact, their usual predictable pursuits—drink plenty of *cerveza y vino*, spend as much time at the beach as possible, and captivate the *senoritas*. Preferably all at the same time. Seeing the sights would be incidental—eating was deemed optional.

Without delay, they headed for the Kit Kat Klub just off the tree-lined Ramblas. It was without a doubt the best little whorehouse in all of Europe. It was a mandatory stop for the 251st troops when they went to Spain, for various reasons. The girls were young and fresh with a positive outlook on life, unlike the prostitutes elsewhere in Europe with their ridden-hard-and-put-away-wet looks and survivalist attitudes. Whenever a GI went into a house of ill repute, he expected to be hustled for drinks and a quick stay in the hay. Not so at the Kit Kat Klub. The girls liked to socialize with the GIs and improve their English skills. They didn't hustle drinks or tricks and drank whatever the guys were drinking.

This is the same as a sorority-fraternity get-together back at Podunk U. But the girls here are a damn sight better looking than those I remember back at that cow-college.

The girls were indeed hookers and would turn a trick, but they were much more. They were enterprising capitalists in Franco's fascist Spain. For starters, they carried gold-embossed business cards explaining their fees as consorts or mistresses or whatever you wanted to call them. It was a long-term plan. The first of eight days in the john's employ was quite expensive. However, with each day's progression, their price dropped an eighth, until, after eight days, their service was on the house. 'If he keeps me that long, he might decide to keep me forever, and I would be on my way out of whoring and this godforsaken country,' appeared to be their rationalized logic. "*Con un poco de suerte y la gracia de Dios.*" (With a little luck and the grace of God.)

After a couple of days in Barcelona, they headed south to Valencia and found a room close to the beach. It was culinary sacrilege to go to Valencia and not partake of *Paella Valenciana*. After consuming a family-sized platter of seafood and curry-laden rice, they returned to their room. There they undertook yet another Spanish tradition, *una siesta de medio día* (a midday nap). They were getting the hang of the Spanish lifestyle—eat and sleep.

When they awoke, Reese was missing. Lee had some experience with Reese's free-range roaming. "Shit! No telling what he is up to … trust me … it won't be good."

Levi responded, "He's a big boy. He can take care of himself."

"He is indeed a big guy, but whether he can take care of himself is a known unknown."

About an hour later, in staggered Reese, utterly sloshed and stark naked. He carried his wallet in one hand and a rag about the size of a washcloth over his genitals in the other. Everyone broke out laughing. Lee asked, "Where the fuck have you been?"

Reese slurred, "That wash a great piesh of assh," before collapsing semi-comatose onto the nearest bed with the usual huge grin on his face. Someone tossed a blanket over him. Not out of compassion, rather to spare them the sight of his bare derriere.

The next day they were off to Madrid. In a little village, somewhere between Valencia and Madrid, the muffler and tailpipe on the station wagon came loose and began dragging on the street. Lee pulled to the side of the road and stopped. There was a nearby *tienda* (store) where the travelers bought and drank multiple cervezas until the exhaust system cooled enough to be reattached. Lee grabbed a pair of pliers and his essential toolkit item—a small roll of baling wire—out of the toolbox. He and Reese climbed underneath the car. They wired the loose parts back into place. When they emerged, dusting off the road debris, they found themselves surrounded by a gaggle of senoritas. There were exclamations of, "*¡Que Guapo!*" (how handsome). Lee from New Mexico knew the translation and Reese from Oregon had no clue, but they both bowed low at the waist, with their right arms swinging in front of them as if acknowledging the applause of a dramatic performance. They climbed back into the station wagon and headed toward Madrid, leaving the heart-throbbed maidens in the dust.

As they approached Madrid, Lee was amazed by how much the area resembled northeastern New Mexico—mesas surrounded by prairie.

Madrid wasn't a major stop on their agenda, rather more of a junction point, where they spent the rest of the day and night. That afternoon they went to the Plaza de Toros to observe the bullfights. Sitting in the hot sun, they watched two world-class matadors— whose names Lee immediately forgot—do their thing. None of the GIs were favorably impressed. They later discussed what they experienced.

"Downright barbaric," said Levi. "It's no wonder these people put Franco in charge."

"The bull doesn't have a chance," added Eric. "Those guys on horses with lances make hamburger out of the bull's neck and back muscles. Not to mention the prissy little dudes that stick pins into its back. Then, after the prima-donna matador gets around to finally killing the poor creature, they cut off parts to give to him."

"Yeah, if I were in charge, they would cut out the bull's asshole and give it to him," Lee asserted. "It would take one to know and appreciate one."

"Too bad the bull didn't gore the guy under the chin and carry him around on his horn for a while," Reese suggested. "That would dampen their enthusiasm for this so-called sport."

They spent the night in Madrid with the station wagon parked on a narrow street. The next morning, they found it had been sideswiped—most likely by a garbage truck—during the night. There was a gouge the entire length of the vehicle about a half-inch wide and a half-inch deep. Lee was angry, yet pragmatic. "Well it certainly ain't a Mercedes, but it bends," he grumbled.

They made their way to an American military airbase on the outskirts of Madrid to catch an R&R flight to the island of Majorca.

Along with their luggage, they were loaded onto a twin-engine puddle-jumper for the short hop to the island. After quite some time on the runway, a crew member announced, "This baby ain't gonna fly, but we've got a standby all ready to go." They loaded onto the standby and without delay became airborne.

When they landed on Majorca, they discovered their luggage had not been transferred when they changed planes. They inquired if their luggage might perhaps be sent on the next flight. After some time on the radio, the agent came back, saying, "I've got good news and bad news. The bad news ... After you departed, they fixed the problem with the plane, and your luggage is now on a tour of North Africa. The good news ... When you get back to Madrid, your stuff will be waiting for you."

The guys made the best of it. They found a place to stay, drank beer, and worked on their tans while enjoying the balmy Mediterranean breezes. Without toiletries and changes of clothes, the social scene was out of the question.

They were a grungy lot when they returned to Madrid, but their luggage was waiting for them.

The terminal contained a restroom with running water and mirrors. After a liberal application of soap, razors, toothpaste, combs, and changes of clothes, they headed north toward Pamplona, where they planned to spend the night. Before leaving Madrid—as they often did—they stopped and bought wine, cheese, bread, and hard sausage. They found a roadside park and consumed a tasty meal.

About halfway to Pamplona, Lee became nauseous, pulled to the side and proceeded to barf out everything in his abdomen except his appendix. When he, at long last, came up for air, Lee discovered all three of his companions were performing the same ritual. Purged and now exhausted, they unrolled their sleeping bags and bunked down for the night by the side of the road in the always accommodating station wagon.

It was mid-morning when they arrived at Pamplona. It was a quiet, picturesque community tucked away in the Pyrenees. The streets were deserted, unlike when the masses of people attended the running of the bulls.

"I'm hungry," said Eric. "Let's try to find someplace to get breakfast."

"You gotta be frigging kidding!" exclaimed Reese. "You have the attention span of a gnat. Does, what happened last night, ring a bell? Sheeze!" Reese was in the majority. They left Pamplona and headed to San Sebastian, arriving early in the afternoon.

Christopher Columbus had lived in and sailed from San Sebastian. Most of the city celebrations centered around good ole Chris. Today happened to be one of them. It included an enormous parade down the main thoroughfare through the city blocking off both ends of the route. Escape out of town was out of the question until the parade ended.

"This is kinda like Dobermans," offered Levi. "They'll let you in the yard, but won't let you out."

"I'm a little concerned time-wise," said Lee. "We're stuck here in Spain, like ugly on an ape, with all of France and half of Germany to go across to get back to Frankfurt. If we don't make Paris by tonight, we won't make Frankfurt by the time our leave runs out. We've been AWOL using phony paper on a bunch of occasions and never been caught. Now we have this off-the-wall clusterfuck! Someone once said words to this effect, 'When the guillotine falls, it falls for all sins.' Wouldn't it be a tad ironic if we, at long last, got nailed because of this parade?"

Sometime around dusk, the seemingly endless parade ended. The travelers made their way toward Paris, where they arrived around midnight. It was too late to book a room, so Lee pulled to the curb. They unrolled their sleeping bags and for the second consecutive night bedded down in the station wagon.

Lee awoke at first light. There were gendarmes everywhere, including two leaning against the sides of the station wagon smoking cigarettes. The GIs had spent the night outside of the Paris central police station, unquestionably the safest place in the entire city to have spent the night. Lee awakened the others, expecting the worst from the French police. The policemen at the hood, realizing the occupants were awake, stepped away. One of them bowed slightly at the waist and gave a hand signal to proceed. He then gave a short, sharp salute.

"I'll be dipped in shit," Lee muttered. "After all those raunchy, and demeaning things I've said about the Frogs, along come the gendarmes, both civil and polite. Who would've guessed?"

Maybe some apology is in order? Nah. I've got enough on my plate worrying about the conniving Soviets.

Happiness was seeing Paris fade in the rearview mirror. The guillotine didn't fall on the nonchalant travelers after all. They made it back to Frankfurt in time.

THE CORNISH GAME HEN

Mac was in an uncommonly grumpy mood when he returned from a late lunch at the officers' club. He sat down at Lee's desk, saying, "We had Cornish game hen for the meal today. How in the hell do they expect someone with only one hand to eat a whole fucking uncut chicken?"

"All chefs have an ego," said Lee, as he scanned an intercept and dropped it into the burn bag. "I'll bet he comes out with his funny hat and wanders around waiting for the diners to congratulate him on his culinary artistry. The next time they serve that meal, why don't you call the chef over and pick up the bird by one leg and chew out a couple of chunks, commenting as to how good it is. He'll get the message."

"By damn! I'm going to do just that!"

A month later Mac came in from his noon meal at the officers' club in high spirits. As he sat down near Lee's desk, he related, "We've had two Cornish game hen meals since we last talked about this. At the first one, I did just as you suggested. It embarrassed the shit out of the chef in front of a bunch of people. Today, it all came out boned and thinly sliced ... and I got a dessert on the house. Excellent meal! By the way, how does a country boy like you know about chefs and their egos?"

"My chef was Tito, who ran a Mexican restaurant in downtown Albuquerque. He would come out of the kitchen in his dirty and greasy apron to mingle with the diners while looking for approval of his green chile meals. They were so hot and spicy it brought tears to your eyes, and you dreaded the next morning on the pot. Their egos are always the same, whether it's greasy Mexican food or officers-club fare."

PETE THE LEFT-HANDED CRYPTANALYST

Lee and Mac were taking a break after Lee had gone down to the first floor and brought back some bad German coffee offset by good German pastries.

Lee asked, "That civilian guy, Pete, a super decent fellow. What does he do here?"

"An absolute gentleman. He's a cryptanalyst."

"Okay ... my question still stands, what does he do here?"

Mac smiled, saying, "You're a perceptive little shit. Pete broke the codes the Soviets were using when they invaded Hungary in fifty-six. As it turned out, this breakthrough in knowing what the Soviets were doing was invaluable at the time. He claims, being left-handed, he could break the code because whoever developed the enciphering system was also left-handed.

"You're kidding me. I received some rudimentary cryptanalyst training at Devens. I was quite good at it, but it had nothing to do with whether I was right or left handed. And, you are now exclusively left handed. Has that changed your analytical processes?"

"No. However, Pete was the one who broke the code. I have to go with what he claims."

"All our encrypted stuff goes back to NSA. Why isn't he back there working with the supercomputers?"

"He has been offered numerous jobs back at Fort Meade but likes to live here in Germany. The powers that be, realizing his contribution during the Hungary invasion, are content to let him run out his time here until retirement as a reward for a job well done."

MAC'S HOT-BUTTON

Mac had a hot-button—his pencils. He would break off a new pencil, saving only about three inches on the eraser end. He inserted it into a crank pencil sharpener, using two fingers to hold it steady while using his thumb to turn the crank. Lee saw this was agonizingly difficult for Mac to do—not to mention a waste of pencils. He offered, "Why don't you let me do the sharpening?"

Big mistake.

Mac erupted. "I may only have one arm and hand, but I'm not a helpless paraplegic. I can sharpen my own damned pencils, thank you! Get your scrawny ass out of my sight!"

Lee never went down that road again. Whenever a newbie showed up, he advised him, "Whatever you do, don't offer to sharpen Mac's pencils."

AMID THE FAMOUS?

One day, while thumbing through the seemingly bottomless pit of intercepts, Lee overheard the following conversation between Mac and the civilian cryptanalyst Pete.

"Do you remember David Cornwell, the Brit we worked with?" asked Mac.

"Of course, I do. How could anyone possibly forget that guy?"

"I ran into him in London on my last trip. He's now out of the SIS and in the process of writing a book that he's going to call *The Spy*

Who Came in from the Cold. It will be published shortly. I think that's great. Maybe we can identify some of his characters. Hopefully, none of them are you and me. Regrettably, he is going to use the pseudonym John le Carré. With that faggoty Frog name, the book will never sell."

"Well, we'll see …"

Holy crap! Am I spending each day with two renowned Cold Warriors? I don't even begin to have a clue about what they may have done.

THE BERLIN TUNNEL

"Do you know anything about the CIA's Berlin tunnel a few years back?" Lee asked as he and Mac were sitting at their desks leafing through intercepts.

"Just a little bit. What most people don't know is that it was a joint venture with the Brits' SIS. When it was discovered, Khrushchev was trying to *make nice* with the Brits and decreed no finger be pointed at them. In fact, all the comm equipment, of which there was a bunch, came from England. Thus, the CIA got all the credit, or all the blame, depending upon how one remembers that fiasco. The CIA came in and built a large warehouse with a huge basement in the American sector just across from the Soviet sector. In the fall of fifty-four, they began digging a tunnel, almost fifteen hundred feet long, to three telephone trunks that serviced the GSFG military headquarters. The basement size had been predetermined to accommodate all the earth that would be coming out of the tunnel. A humongous amount of dirt, something around three thousand tons, if I remember correctly."

"So, who did all the digging? That's a hell of a lot of dirt to move."

"For the most part, GIs with top secret clearances like you. The Brits brought in professional miners when they got close to the trunks."

"I'll bet the recruiters didn't mention anything about shovels when those poor bastards signed on for an ASA assignment."

"Once there, they tapped into those trunks and recorded the traffic. Analysts and linguists worked their way through what turned out to be miles of magnetic tape recordings."

Oh, he knows just a little bit about the tunnel, does he? How about every excruciating detail? Sit back, listen and pay attention. There is no doubt more to come.

And indeed, there was.

"It was a hell of a good idea. Just one problem. The Soviets had a mole high up in the SIS who was on the tunnel's planning or approving committee. They had known about it before the first shovelful of dirt came out of the tunnel. The mole turned out to be a fellow named George Blake. The Soviets considered him such a high-level asset ... he was providing them with the names of a multitude of British agents within the Soviet Union ... they permitted the taps to operate for almost a year so as not to compromise him with the Brits. He was eventually exposed, tried, and sentenced to forty-two years in prison. At least he didn't show up at an international press conference in Moscow like some of the earlier Brit spies. Our cousins have a bad reputation of their high-level intelligence agents showing up at press conferences in Moscow. Burgess and Maclean, for example. Well, perhaps I shouldn't be too critical ... it's not been so long ago that we experienced our own Martin and Mitchell doing that very same thing."

"Did we get any good intel from the tunnel?" Lee asked.

"A lot of order of battle stuff. Unit identifications, locations, commanders, and so on. But not much else. It's, by and large, out of date now."

Lee inquired. "If the Soviets knew about it beforehand, why didn't they use it as a disinformation tool?"

"A lot of people wondered. The press media and individual authors espoused that point. Although, when all was said and done, that didn't appear to be the case."

BACK FROM LONDON

Lee drove to Calais with his usual traveling partners. Leaving the station wagon behind, they took the ferry to London. Once there, they set about seeing the favorite tourist sites: the changing of the guard at Buckingham Palace, St. Paul's Cathedral, the Tower of London, Trafalgar Square, and so on. When he returned from the trip, Mac, as he frequently did, asked for Lee's impressions of the places and people he had seen. "What did you think of the Brits and London? And don't pound sand up my ass, because I often go there. So, how was your trip?"

"Jolly good, old chap," replied Lee in a weak attempt at the English voice, then reverting to Americanized English, giving Mac a litany about his opinion of the Londoners, saying, "Well, to begin with, they drive on the wrong side of the road.

"Don't even think about stepping out into a street before looking in all directions, including up. Twice, I damn near got run over by a double-decker bus.

"Their monetary system is beyond comprehension. Pounds, shillings, guineas, half-crowns, pence, quids, farthings, bobs. No two of which are divisible by a common denominator.

"On the other hand, they seem to be scrupulously honest. When we bought something, we would pull out a handful of whatever money we possessed, and they picked through it and returned change in yet another coin or two that we hadn't seen before.

"They speak a language that is vaguely familiar but appear to be unable to pronounce the letter H. I was somewhat in awe of the Brits' ability to utter an off-the-wall word that made perfect sense when spoken. Then there are the Cockneys, who most likely don't even understand each other.

"The food was atrocious. It's either boiled beyond recognition or made into so-called pies ... out of God-knows-what ... so one doesn't know what he's eating. We mostly lived on fish and chips since it seemed to be the only meal fit for human consumption.

"They brew great dark beers, porters, and stouts. Much better than anything you can find here in Germany. But be prepared to drink them warm. Refrigeration is a foreign concept to the Limeys.

"The bars in pubs have no bar stools. They stand and lean, or as they would say, 'A bevy of bloody blokes propping up the bar, with one hand around their pint of mild, and the other scratching their bollocks.' I suppose the lack of stools shortens the distance to the floor when they get falling-down drunk.

"They love their inbred monarchy for some inexplicable reason. A considerate bloke warned us to never use the words bloody and Queen in the same sentence.

"For the most part, are polite, friendly, and orderly, especially when it comes to getting on and off public transportation ... unlike these fucking Krauts.

"The women are all short and dumpy. And in need of a tan. But then, likely, it's impossible for them to remedy either condition. While there, I don't think I saw even one attractive woman.

"When we went into a pub, I thought about bringing up all the kings named George and the kindhearted things those guys did for the Irish and Americans throughout the centuries. I decided not to. They probably didn't want to talk about their Georges.

"Most females and a few of the men referred to me as *Luv*. It was okay for the women to say it. However, I regarded all the *Luv-ly* males ... in their own vernacular ... as bloody buggers.

"Lastly, and most conspicuously, they need to give some thoughtful attention to their oral hygiene."

Mac took a moment thinking about Lee's comments before saying, "That's a pretty good summary of our cousins. I see you picked right up on their anglicized vocabulary, especially their overuse of *bloody*.

You were astute to not bring up the King Georges ... they can get downright hostile when it comes to certain aspects of their history. And, you are correct, England does have more than its fair share of male homosexuals."

Lee later encountered a GI friend interested in going to London and gave him the same line of gab he gave Mac. The only difference was the issue of the Brits' oral hygiene, saying, "If you go, whatever you do, don't get a blow job unless you want your dick to rot off in about three days. However ... now that I think about it ... in your case, it would undeniably be a good idea."

The GI asked, "You grew up on a ranch, didn't you?"

Lee nodded.

"Let me put this into a context your feeble mind can comprehend: "Fuck you *and* the horse you rode in on! But thanks anyway for the info."

Lee thought about suggesting that his friend also go fuck himself as part of this fuck-fest, but instead said, "Glad I could be of service."

Enough of the pleasant memories for now. We were involved in some serious shit ... a bunch of which we can never tell anyone.

THE CUBAN MISSILE CRISIS AS HISTORY RECORDED IT

THE BACKGROUND

The United States placed Juniper nuclear-armed ballistic missiles in Italy and Turkey in 1959. They were outdated technology but within striking distance of Moscow. This got Soviet Premier Khrushchev's attention. Khrushchev regarded President Kennedy as a wimp and believed he could be maneuvered about in the international arena. Nikita's perception seemed well-founded, considering John F's performance (or nonperformance) at the Bay of Pigs, the Vienna conference, and the start-up of the Berlin Wall.

The Bay of Pigs was a blatant breach of international law and an unmitigated disaster. After changing the invasion site, Kennedy okayed the invasion of Cuba, using Cuban exiles. The invaders foundered once ashore in an environment for which they had not been trained. Kennedy withheld the desperately needed and expected air and naval support. The invading forces either died on the beach or were taken captive.

At the summit meeting held in early June 1961 in Vienna between Kennedy and Khrushchev, the ill-prepared Kennedy was devastated by the aggressive and demeaning Soviet. The net result can best be summarized by Kennedy's own statement, "Khrushchev just beat the hell out of me."

From the time, the Berlin Wall started to go up, nary a peep was heard for three or four days from the Kennedy administration. This inaction only strengthened Khrushchev's opinion about the President's lack of fortitude.

Compounding this situation was the Eisenhower and the Kennedy administrations' attempts to assassinate Castro and overthrow the Castro regime under the guise of a covert CIA operation called Operation Mongoose. Brothers Jack and Robert Kennedy purportedly micromanaged the plans to overthrow the Cuban government and assassinate Castro. Now, we have the second violation of international ethics—It's in extremely poor taste for heads of state to try to *snuff out* other heads of state! In this undertaking, Kennedy received numerous CIA inputs, along with suggestions from nonexperts. He even met with author Ian Fleming, the James Bond fiction writer, who added his two cents worth. The proposed ways to kill Castro included poisoned fountain pens, ice cream, and cigars. Perhaps exploding cigars and seashells would do the trick. The most auspicious plan was to have a mistress slip him a lethal Cuba Libre. This almost happened, but the senorita chickened out at the last moment.

Aside from helping a Soviet-leaning country on the other side of the world, Khrushchev had an equally pressing agenda closer to home. East Germany—and especially the Soviet sector of Berlin— were to be the keystones in his architecture for the building of the East European Soviet bloc.

The Cold War was also happening halfway around the world. Khrushchev and Castro entered an agreement to place Soviet missiles with nuclear warheads in Cuba. The construction began around mid-year 1962. By September, Soviet intermediate-range nuclear missiles were being positioned in Cuba.

Khrushchev's logic appeared to be this: if Kennedy wimped out and didn't take a stand about Soviet nukes being deployed ninety miles from Miami, Khrushchev could militarily run the Allies out of Berlin without fear of reprisal. Or, if Kennedy grew a pair of balls and resisted, Khrushchev might then bargain for taking the missiles out of Cuba if the Allies abandoned Berlin. Or he could negotiate removing the missiles from Cuba if the United States withdrew their missiles from Turkey. Or perhaps all three—It was potentially a win-win-win situation for the shoe-pounding Russian!

AS IT HAPPENED

A long history made short. Well, somewhat shorter.

There was confusion during the crisis itself and the historical accounts that followed as to what categories of missiles were involved. The Soviets were installing two types of weapons. The first was surface-to-air missiles (SAMs), defensive weapons. The other was surface-to-surface missiles (SSMs), offensive weapons, specifically medium and long-range. The Soviet's obvious intent was first the placement of defensive SAMs throughout Cuba, to protect the offensive SSMs when they were installed later.

Starting in July 1962, unusually large numbers of Russian cargo and passenger ships began docking in Cuba. The number of these arriving vessels increased markedly in August and September.

On 20 August, the concerned CIA director informed the White House of the abnormally large volume of cargo being offloaded from Soviet ships arriving in Cuba, together with the reported presence in Cuba of a significant number of Russian soldiers; and, the sightings of possible missile components being moved under cover of darkness. These reports and sightings suggested offensive weapons were being installed. This information was also passed to those within the intelligence community with the need to know. (The 251st was among that select group because part of their mission was to locate those same missiles within Eastern Europe.) The President's advisors blew off the increased docking as nothing more than an increase in trade between the two nations. They opined that the Soviets would not place offensive weapons outside the Soviet bloc. The CIA director's suspicion had been confirmed by reports from the Cuban people themselves—an unexpected, but largely ignored and overlooked source. The Soviets moved their unassembled missile and launch components only between midnight and dawn. The missile transport vehicles were quite long, and whenever a turn was required, any home, building or obstruction in the way was bulldozed away. Since mid-summer, there had been hundreds of reports about missiles arriving, sent from family members in Cuba to those who had fled to Miami. To this point in time, the Kennedy administration's response prompted by this information was underwhelming: no reaction noted.

The construction of the SAM sites, which began in July, was well underway, with several nearing completion; and, assembly of the SSM sites had started.

Three days later, a significant number of Soviet passenger and freighter vessels en route to Cuba were observed and photographed. Among the latter was one that had what appeared to be poorly concealed medium or long-range missile weapon components lashed on its deck. Mac circulated a picture of the vessel with its shrouded cargo, saying, "No question about what is beneath that cover. The shit is about to hit the fan."

From what they experienced in their own area of responsibilities within the Soviet bloc—combined with Mac's input about what was happening elsewhere around the world, the troops in the 251st seemed to have a front row seat on the fifty-yard line throughout the crisis. It was not known where Mac was getting his information, but as usual, the old-boy-network proved to be a credible source. Mac limited the most sensitive information to a select few—Lee was one of those.

On 29 August, a U-2 overflight was finally allowed by the White House, and it verified the SAMs in Cuba were now operational. Analysts concluded that the SAM sites in Cuba were being placed in the same pattern as those providing air protection for long-range missile sites in the Soviet Union. Mac commented, "Those steel-toothed bastards have their SAMs geared up. Now we can expect to see long-range surface-to-surface weapons put in place. Trust me, they wouldn't have gone to all this trouble just to protect Castro's worthless ass."

Long-range missiles fired from the Soviet Union had the range to target American allies in Europe, but they could barely reach Alaska. The lower forty-eight was out of range. However, by mid-September, intermediate-range missiles (SS-4s) and their launchers had arrived in Cuba. The Soviets intended to build nine missile complexes, six of which had an intermediate range of up to twelve hundred miles and three long-range missiles with a range up to twenty-eight hundred miles. The only part of the United States out of range of the Cuban-based Soviet SSMs were parts of Alaska and Hawaii. Nikita was about to have the entire continental United States in his sights.

While this was going on, intercepts revealed Soviet Air Force personnel throughout Eastern Europe were being recruited for duty in Cuba.

Also, in early October, Cuban radar and air surveillance systems were up and operational; and, Cuban MIG fighters began confronting US reconnaissance aircraft flying off the coast of Cuba.

That little blob of land just off the Florida coast was about to get the Kennedy administration's full attention and scrutiny. However, to date, the American public had been kept in the dark about what was happening in Cuba. Perhaps, because the incumbent party was not expected to fare well in the upcoming midterm election if voters learned what loomed just off the coastline of Florida?

Things continued to muddle along until U-2 aerial photos of the Cuban SSM sites were taken on 14 October, examined by photo analysts the next day, and delivered to the White House the following morning. The Kennedy administration and its historians insisted that 16 October was the earliest they were aware of Soviet missiles in Cuba.

The proverbial shit hit the fan. There was now indisputable evidence of SSM sites already in place, or soon to be operational. Armageddon was on the horizon with the unpredictable and aggressive Khrushchev aiming at the seemingly feckless Kennedy.

On 15 October, Mac gathered everyone and passed around copies of the U-2 photographs taken over Cuba, complete with source-and-method-of-collection code words. It appeared to be chaparral-covered terrain, some of which was bulldozed away. On them were banners and lines indicating things such as tents, erectors, launchers, and missile transports. "There it is guys, our worst nightmare confirmed. Katie bar the door!"

For the next few days, similar photos circulated through the 251st SCIF personnel, to their considerable unease and consternation.

On 19 October, U-2 flights confirmed there were now four operational SSM sites. What the cameras did not show were forty thousand-plus Soviet troops in Cuba. Sneaky, those Marxists.

Throughout this disconcerting and at times unnerving episode, the Soviet diplomatic corps insisted the missiles were only in Cuba for defensive purposes, even after the Kennedy administration had conclusively informed the rest of the world otherwise.

The hawkish Joint Chiefs of Staff, General LeMay most of all, argued fervently for an immediate full-scale air assault on Cuba with a land invasion to follow. To his credit, Kennedy realized such action would give the Soviets an open invitation to take Berlin. He squelched that idea. But what was he to do?

They came up with the idea of a blockade. Just one problem. Per international law, a *blockade* is an act of war. So, they came up with the term *quarantine* to subvert the legal language and were prepared to put warships at sea around Cuba to enforce the quarantine/blockade. However, the word quarantine abruptly dropped from usage. The term blockade endured. All these semantic machinations, when the word they were looking for was *embargo*.

Within the military are various levels of danger flags. For the Department of Defense, DEFCON is the Pentagon's alphabet soup for defense readiness conditions, ascending from 5 to 1 as things get progressively more perilous. Roughly, they signify: DEFCON 5—All is well; DEFCON 4—Pay attention; DEFCON 3—Increased force readiness; DEFCON 2—Nuclear war is possible; and DEFCON 1—Nuclear war is imminent.

On 19 October, another U-2 flight verified four of the SSMs were operational. Mac gathered the troops saying, "Well, shit! The Soviets have operational surface-to-air and surface-to-surface missiles scattered all over Cuba. The muckety-mucks running this show can't find their dicks with both hands. Some of them want to bomb Cuba back into the dark ages, others want a full-scale invasion, and others don't want to do much of anything for fear of pissing off Khrushchev. Your guess is as good as mine, but get ready for some long days."

On 21 October, a Defense Readiness Condition BRAVO was declared within the SIGINT community; this was the second highest level of alert and the equivalent of DEFCON 2. The SIGINT BRAVO alert meant that intelligence troops throughout the world were expected to be on duty twenty-four hours a day, seven days a week. Halfway around the world, this included the warm bodies within the 251st.

And indeed, the days got longer. Mac informed the troops of the Readiness Condition BRAVO. (It would still be a week before the rest of the world went to the DEFCON 2 alert level.) "Guys, we're going to a twelve-hour-on, twelve-hour-off schedule. I'm restricting you to the Kaserne when off duty. And please, stay off the booze!"

On 22 October, Kennedy informed congressional leaders of the missiles in Cuba and the planned blockade. They were alarmed and concerned, and for the most part didn't believe a blockade alone was a strong enough response.

Later that day, the president went on television to inform the nation what was happening only ninety miles off the Florida coast. He further told the world he was placing the military on DEFCON 3 alert. Now, it was not just members of Congress who were distraught, but also the rest of the nation. Their distress was conspicuously greater on 26 October, when the alert level was raised to DEFCON 2.

Had the Kennedy administration been inattentive? Or, was there a political motive regarding the upcoming midterm elections? Was it to wait until the last minute to confront Khrushchev and make a big to-do about the situation—all to further the Democrats' chances in Congress? If politics was the motivation, it turned out to be the election *October Surprise* of all time.

The Republicans, with gusto, accused the Kennedy administration with dereliction of duty for ignoring the Soviet threat less than one hundred miles offshore. There were leaks from the spook community to their political allies and the flood of family reports now being made public by the Miami Cuban population about missiles in Cuba, which only added to the general discontent and unease.

While addressing the nation on 22 October, President Kennedy showed aerial photographs of the SSM sites and released them to the press. Clearly labeled were the locations of erectors, launchers, missile transports, and even the tents the Soviet troops were living in. Those throughout the intelligence community had already seen them. The first photos shown and given to the print media were complete with the highly-classified source-and-method-of-collection code word emblazoned upon them. Revealing this sensitive and restricted material to the world at large was a definite need-to-know *no-no*! The next iteration of site photos had the code word removed, but it was too late—the train had left the station—and the keepers of code words were miffed. On the other hand, the U-2 hierarchy was aghast—Now the Soviets knew the sophistication and capability of our imagery!

The Kennedy administration ordered one armored division deployed to Georgia, which wasn't all that far from Cuba. Five other army divisions were ordered to prepare for combat. Shorter range strategic air command bombers, the B-47s, were scattered at civilian airports around the country and B-52 heavy bombers were sent to roam around the wild blue yonder near Soviet territory.

By this time, there was various and sundry posturing, threatening and waffling on both sides, politically, diplomatically, and militarily. The net result was the pucker-factor of the world, in general, was going up exponentially!

Then on 23 October, intercepts revealed a drastic change in Soviet radio transmissions. Soviet military commands in Cuba were now overtly passing unusually large volumes of traffic within Cuba itself and between Cuba and Moscow; and, a dedicated enciphered link was established between the commander of Soviet forces in Cuba and Moscow. No more pretense of radio silence.

To top it all off, the ASA intercept stations were picking up large numbers of high-precedence traffic throughout the Soviet bloc. Not a good omen!

When the U-2 photos of the Cuban missile sites the president released to the print media the previous day appeared in newspapers—complete with the source-and-method-of-collection code word—the security-conscious GIs came unglued. 'How could that possibly happen? If we had done that, we would now be grabbing our ankles at Leavenworth,' was the general sentiment of the grousing GIs.

On 24 October, Khrushchev, via the news agency Tass, informed Kennedy that the embargo would lead to war. This warning was followed by a telegram to Kennedy stating that the blockade was an act of aggression and that his ships heading toward Cuba would be ordered to ignore any threatened action.

Then things got confusing. On that same day, twenty-two Soviet ships on their way to Cuba received orders from their command in Odessa to turn around. 'Does the Soviet left hand in Odessa know what the hell the Soviet right hand in Moscow is doing?' was a question on everyone's minds.

All except one Soviet ship turned around. The ship's captain evidently didn't get the memo and continued sailing toward Cuba. Those within the intelligence community were entertained by the ship's captain—who, after having shots fired across his bow by an American destroyer—was frantically trying to communicate in the clear with Odessa. After several failed attempts, he gave up and made a command decision. He turned his ship around.

Until 25 October, the troops were permitted to return to the Kaserne for a meal, clean up, and catch up on some much-needed sleep. That day, the Farben Building—the seventh-floor SCIF, in particular—became their twenty-four-seven home away from home, when Mac announced, "Pay attention, all you swinging dicks. As of this moment, you are to man your stations twenty-four hours a day. Nothing, but nothing, is to fall through the cracks. Do you hear me loud and clear?"

On 26 October, Soviet units in East Germany began leaving their garrisons and moving toward the West German border. Soviet tactical aircraft, such as they were, were placed on five-minute alert status. On the other side of the world, a U-2 mistakenly strayed into Soviet territory. The Soviets sent up MIG fighters to try to bring it down. The Americans sent up F-102s to try to bring them down. As luck, would have it, neither side was successful. The alert level for American forces was raised to DEFCON 2.

Kennedy throughout had resisted his hawkish advisers' insistence for a full-scale invasion of Cuba. However, on 26 October, he wavered and informed his advisory staff that he believed an invasion was the only way to remove the missiles from Cuba. Then he vacillated again and did not order the attack, leaving only an air assault campaign or a blockade as options.

Blockade it was.

Things turned chaotic within the intelligence community. ASA intercept stations were monitoring enormous volumes of GSFG traffic and passing it to the 251st for analysis. They, in turn, promptly forwarded pertinent alerts and reports as Soviet units within East Germany hurriedly left their garrisons, deployed tanks to rail yards for shipment, and headed for the border.

On 27 October, Murphy's Law was once again proven in what came to be known as Black Saturday. A U-2 was shot down over Cuba, and low-level reconnaissance planes were fired upon. The Soviets took total control of the Cuban Air Force and the Cuban air defense system, suggesting they had no confidence in the Cubans' decision-making. The Soviets also moved nuclear-armed cruise missiles to just outside Guantanamo Naval Base in Cuba, and nuclear warheads for SSMs were transported to launch sites. While all this was going on, a Soviet submarine commander patrolling the Cuban coast was seriously thinking of using a nuclear torpedo on an American destroyer that was making half-assed attempts to bring him to the surface. The Americans were alleged to have tossed hand grenades overboard—not the best of depth charges. To top off all that, Castro insisted that Khrushchev initiate the first nuclear strike against the United States. Apparently, Castro had the inside scoop, because the CIA had reported that very morning—all missile sites in Cuba were operational.

Abruptly, it all came to an end. Only later would the world learn that Kennedy and Khrushchev—both having decided mutually assured destruction wasn't the answer—negotiated a truce.

During the night of 27 October, Kennedy sent his brother Robert to meet with the Soviet Ambassador to the United States. He offered to remove the missiles from Turkey within five months of the Soviets doing the same in Cuba. However, this agreement was to be kept a secret to allow the Kennedy administration some face-saving in the world's opinion. To sweeten the deal, the United States pledged never to invade Cuba. A deal was struck—much to the relief of the world at large—the details of which, would be publicly forthcoming at a later date.

Khrushchev didn't hit his win-win-win trifecta, but he at least won one. Cuban missiles were traded for missiles in Turkey.

Most of the GIs had been on the job for at least seventy-two hours without the benefit of showering or shaving, and they had only been able to eat German junk foods and pastries available at the small stand on the first floor. They caught occasional cat-naps wherever they could, using classified burn bags as pillows.

On the morning of 28 October, Mac gathered the analysts and linguists who had been on the job since early in the crisis. He said, "Well, it looks as if Kennedy and Khrushchev decided not to blow the world to smithereens. You guys have done a hell of a good job!

Go back to the Kaserne and get some rest and something to eat. And, for God's sake, take a shower! I've arranged for transportation to pick you up out front, so you don't have to wait for the shuttle bus. I'll see you here tomorrow morning ... back to our usual shifts."

IF THE WORLD HAD KNOWN WHAT OLEG PROVIDED

A little-known but critical player in this tense world event was a colonel in the Soviet GRU who was a double or triple agent because he worked for both the British MI6 and the CIA. Before the Cuban crisis, he provided these intelligence agencies with invaluable information regarding the number, reliability, and placement of Soviet nuclear weapons throughout the USSR, including their targets. His name was Oleg Penkovsky.

To protect this agent and other intelligence sources, President Eisenhower left the world uninformed as to the American missile balance-of-power dominance at that time. Kennedy was apprised of the United States' advantage in nuclear warhead delivery systems over the Soviets, but nevertheless, while campaigning for president, he advocated how woefully unprepared we were. Khrushchev was content to let this misrepresentation persist. The actual disparity in nuclear delivery balance could, and should, have influenced Khrushchev's posturing and the American responses.

In addition, this mole provided the Allies with the names and responsibilities of more than a thousand GRU and KGB officers and agents. He also revealed that rocket delivery systems had been delivered to all the Soviet Bloc countries sans nuclear warheads and that the warheads for those systems were under Soviet control and held in the GDR. Aside from being an egotistical and philandering fellow, his input was priceless.

The Soviets began to suspect Penkovsky by the time the Cuban missile crisis came along. However, he was permitted to continue to pass plans and information regarding the launch sites in Cuba in order to protect another high-level mole they had embedded within British intelligence. In May 1963, he was charged with espionage and treason. After a short and highly publicized trial, he was sentenced to death. The sentence was carried out immediately; and, most likely with a bullet, at point-blank range, to the back of his head. A firing squad would have been too honorable an end for this traitor.

THE APPROPRIATE SALUTE

It was mid-morning that beautiful late October sun-shining day when the mangy and dog-tired troops exited the Farben Building to await their transportation back to the Kaserne. Once out on the front steps, were off their feet and on their butts in an exhausted stupor. Before long, a chauffeured staff car with three stars on the rank flags pulled up. The driver jumped out and opened the door for the general who, considering his late arrival time, had enjoyed—unlike the soldiers sprawled about on the steps—a good night of sleep, a leisure bath, and a bountiful hot breakfast. As the general bounded up the steps, the GIs came to attention and prepared to salute. As he approached, oblivious to the stand-down in Cuba because of his late arrival for duty, bellowed, "Good morning men! Isn't this a beautiful day to go to war?"

The GIs saluted. When the general was out of hearing range, Lee said, "That asshole is going to be big time disappointed when he finds out there isn't going to be a war. Did you give him the appropriate salute?" The responses came back, "Yep," "You bet," and, "Too bad it wasn't a full colonel. That way we all would have given a Bird the bird. But a three-star general was even better."

SOME AFTERTHOUGHTS ABOUT THE CUBAN CRISIS

Shortly after the crisis ended and the Soviet ships steaming toward Cuba had turned around and headed back across the Atlantic, Lee waited until he and Mac were alone to ask, "What do you think broke the deadlock in Cuba?"

Mac replied, "The Brits and we have a mole in the Soviet's hierarchy. I've never been told the mole's name, for obvious reasons, but know that he is high up in the GRU. He was passing along all there is to know about their missile capabilities. The bottom line is that if the Russians get into a nuclear exchange with us, they will come up a day late and a ruble short. When things turned to shit in Cuba, Kennedy … despite all his campaign blather about how weak we are … finally realized the credibility of the intel the mole had provided and garnered up enough balls to confront those steel-toothed bastards and get them to pull their missiles out of Cuba.

"There's a rumor that as part of the deal we will take our missiles out of Turkey and never invade Cuba. Likely, it will be years before the world learns what was really agreed on."

Now all of Mac's interactions with the super-spooks make sense. Heaven knows what else he was told throughout this confrontation that left the entire world scared shitless?

"Kennedy has a midterm election coming up, and the Democrats in Congress are not projected to do well. I think he decided to sit on the missiles until just before the election and then make a big show of it to strengthen their chances in November. In the process, the sorry SOB almost turned us all into radioactive dust."

Lee nodded.

"I, however, do give Kennedy credit. For as badly as he fucked things up, he did a good job of unfucking them. At the same time, he's trying to rewrite history. You and I knew the Soviets had missiles in Cuba in mid-August. I'm sure that if a couple of nobodies like us halfway around the world knew about those missiles, they also told the president. He claims he didn't know about them until 16 October. Give the world a break!"

GO FORTH

Unlike Oleg Penkovsky, Lee thought Baby Huey—who was near the top of his shit list—deserved to be shot. Huey spent his off-duty time in his rack and was always asking others leaving the barracks and going to the EM club to bring back something for him to eat. At first, a few complied. After a while, the response was something along the lines of, "Goober, get your fat, worthless ass out of the rack and do it yourself."

He eventually got around to asking Lee, who asked him, "You're from Alabama, which is part of the Bible Belt, right? Do you believe every word in the Good Book applies to you?"

"I am, and o' course I do."

"The Brits have a unique interpretation of Genesis 1:28. They use it all the time. I think it's applicable in your case."

"Huh?"

"What they say is, 'Go forth and multiply within!'"

"Huh? Whatzit mean?"

"Go fuck yourself!"

THE BURN BAG DETAIL

The 251st generated an inordinate amount of paper trash—most of it top secret code word material—the destruction of which was a logistical nightmare.

The individual classified burn bags were gathered, loaded into carts like those used for room cleaning in hotels, transported in a freight elevator down six floors of the Farben Building, rolled a hundred yards or so to a nearby incinerator, tossed in, and burned. At times, as many as six carts were involved.

In charge of this detail was the senior enlisted soldier who was issued an AR-15 rifle with one round of chambered ammunition.

Christ on a crutch! One bullet to safeguard as many as six soldiers and thousands of highly classified documents.

The fellow with the rifle, after returning to the sixth floor, was supposed to unchamber the round. To confirm the weapon was no longer lethal, he would pull the trigger after positioning the barrel into a box of sand.

By and large, the destruction of classified waste went well. But, as expected, Mr. Murphy was destined to once again prove his law. Without paying attention to detail, the soldier with the rifle neglected to unchamber the round, pointed at that sandbox, and pulled the trigger—*BLAM!*

The results were predictable. Those nearby briefly lost their hearing and were enveloped in a cloud of dust. Those not so close immediately dove under their desks. The trigger-pulling GI was never again issued a weapon.

HEIDELBERG

Eli was about as laid-back as they came. The only time he ever became agitated was when he and his Jewish brethren argued about some point of their faith. He was studying to be a pharmacist when he was drafted. Eli finished at the top of the class in their training at Fort Devens; Lee was a close second. They subsequently became Mac's two primary analysts. As such, he did not permit them to take leave at the same time. Nevertheless, they became good friends and often were together when off-duty in the evenings and on weekends.

Traveling in Eli's recently purchased new VW, they made their way to Heidelberg on the Neckar river. Heidelberg had escaped the ravages of the war, unlike the massive *Schloss* (castle) on the mountain above Heidelberg, which, between lightning strikes and invaders, experienced a rather tough time throughout the centuries. However, structurally it was mostly intact. Within it was housed the *Apotheke* (pharmacy) Museum.

They came to Heidelberg to hustle American babes on tour. However, once Eli was in the museum, he became enraptured with pill-making history. The museum displayed artifacts dating back to the time of Christ and was undoubtedly the best of its kind in the world.

No way in hell I'm ever going to get Eli out of here. And I want to go out and try my new pick-up lines.

Tugging at Eli's shoulder to get his attention, Lee said, "I'll meet you at four o'clock where we came in."

Eli, in ancient chemical euphoria, just nodded.

Lee's new pick-up lines turned out to be an unadulterated catastrophe. The reaction of one young American female was, "Dweeb, you are one pathetic piece of … whatever." And that was the most positive, polite, and non-profane response Lee heard that afternoon.

On the trip back to Frankfurt, Lee was in a funk and Eli continually recalled what he observed in the museum.

Well, Eli surely enjoyed a better day than I did. Snotty American bitches. Live and learn … no more preplanned pick-up lines. And, I wish Eli would just shut the fuck up.

THEY DECIDED TO ~~GET~~ LEAVE EARLY

Jimmy Joe had met a new fräulein. He considered his chances were fair-to-middling of getting into her *höschen* (knickers). The problem was, the young lady wouldn't go out with Jimmy Joe unless he brought another GI along to double date a female friend. Lee had met this girlfriend who, while she wasn't coyote ugly, wasn't anywhere close to being rated a keeper. Jimmy Joe approached Lee about the double date, and Lee resisted. Jimmy Joe persisted, and Lee eventually condescended, saying, "Only because you are an asshole, buddy. You will owe me one!"

The double date was in the far north of Frankfurt and turned out to be a non-event for Lee and his companion. On the other hand, Jimmy Joe and his girl were getting it on. It was well after curfew when they climbed aboard a streetcar and headed south, the only passengers aboard. Lee and his date went into the passenger compartment, sat down facing backward, watching their friends while ignoring each other. Jimmy Joe and his fräulein remained on the open-air loading platform at the rear of the streetcar and began to kiss and fondle. The conductor came back, collected fares, then went back up to continue his chat with the driver.

At the next stop, three black GIs, unquestionably under the influence and feeling their oats, came aboard on the rear platform. Straight away they began to hassle Jimmy Joe and his girl. Jimmy Joe grabbed one, then another and threw them off the streetcar onto the cobblestone street. The third interloper was an elusive little bugger, hopping about in a crouched stance while fending off Jimmy Joe. By now the streetcar was up to its top speed of about thirty miles an hour. The evasive one had his back to the steps onto the platform when Jimmy Joe rushed forward. The black GI made a horrific decision. He jumped backward. It was about three feet down to the cobblestones where he landed, still in a crouch—for about a ten-thousandth of a second—before becoming a blur of arms, legs, and head tumbling sideways down the cobblestone street.

Ooooh! That had to hurt.

Jimmy Joe, his rat-killing done, went back to devoting all his attention to the fräulein. Kissing and caressing—a minimum of action with lips but an unfettered use of hands.

The conductor had noticed the black soldiers when they boarded the streetcar. Now they were unseen. He came back slowly and warily, looking behind each seat as he continued down the aisle. When he came alongside, Lee said, *"Sie beschlossen, zu früh verlassen."* (They decided to leave early.)

Lee's reminiscences returned to the serious stuff.

THE SOVIETS' PLAN FOR TAKING BERLIN

Mac put together a separate analytical team consisting of Sergeant First Class (SFC) Ramsey, Greg Howser who was one of the rare Spec/7s in the entire Army, Spec/5 Leland Wolfe, and himself. Lee appreciated the Spec/7 being included. The guy was, without a doubt, an expert analyst. Lee's ego justified his own inclusion. SFC Ramsey was somewhat of a mystery in that his analytical skills weren't all that great. He, however, had handled the cleanup of the burlap bag fiasco very well. Perhaps Mac had him on board for no reason other than to ride herd on the off-the-job loose cannon named Lee.

Mac took them off the SCIF floor and into a vacant side room saying, "Whatever you're working on now, put it aside. I want all your attention focused on what I'm about to tell you. We all understand the importance of the order of battle. What if we could determine the Soviets' planned invasion of Berlin and West Germany based on the traffic we intercept during their war games exercises? We know the frequencies they use doing those drills, so we can screen that traffic off from the rest. My guess is … that during the exercises, they likely use maps where the grid coordinates have been altered. So, we need Soviet maps of Europe showing different scales to try to figure out the alterations."

"And I suppose these maps are going to fall out of the sky like manna from heaven," said Greg.

"Trust me, I work for the government," chortled Mac with a grin. "I'm off to London for a couple of days. Clean up whatever you're working on, or hand it to someone else. For all I care, you can shit-can it. Have your asses geared up and ready for some long days. When I get back, we're going to be balls to the wall."

When Mac came back into the SCIF three days later, he was carrying a large roll of something enclosed in what resembled butcher paper. After removing the double wrapped outside coverings and revealing top secret material, Mac said to the Spec/7, "Okay smartass, here's your manna from heaven."

There were maps of all scales, notated in Cyrillic, showing bits and pieces of Europe. They ranged from small-scale maps in excruciating detail to one that presented almost all Western Europe. When Lee saw the latter, he exclaimed, "Holy shit!"

"What does Lee see on that map?" Mac asked, looking at the other two. Receiving no response, "Tell them, Lee."

"This map shows almost all of Western Europe, from Denmark down to Spain and all the way to the English Channel … but it shows only about the west one-third of the GDR. Meaning, the Soviets don't intend to defend East Germany. Those bastards are only planning and training for the invasion of Western Europe."

"Dead on! Now let's get organized. Get some help and move your desks over here. I want you facing and surrounding me, so all I have to do is scoot and not have to get out of my chair."

Considerable bitching and moaning ensued from the other GIs as they were interrupted and put to manual labor. The loudest complaints came from those whose turf was taken.

"Go into the small conference room. The rest of the floor doesn't need to hear this." Once settled in Mac continued, "We're going to begin by concentrating on Berlin, for a couple of reasons. First ... Teufelsberg is the ideal intercept location since it sits in the middle of our target area. Second ... I have a gut feeling that this is going to be the easiest one to break because they almost certainly do this war game exercise multiple times a year. The large-scale war game drills only occur once or maybe twice a year. I see it's time for lunch. Reconvene back here."

Lee took the long shuttle ride across town to the dingy, odoriferous mess hall. Mac took a short walk to the opulent officer's club. The other two went home to eat with their families.

After they had returned, Mac continued, "As you know, the Russians don't keep any troops, armor, or artillery within Berlin itself. However, they are literally and abundantly available next door under the command of the Twentieth Guards Army. One motorized rifle and three tank divisions. If the balloon goes up over Berlin, portions of these units will be dancing the Russian two-step down the Kurfurstendamm."

"FYI, for those of you who haven't had the opportunity to go to Monterey and forever be labeled a Mary, the Russian two-step is called *Devochka Nadya*," said the linguist Greg.

"Thank you for that enlightening bit of trivia ... now back to the real world. My guess as to what they do regarding passing grid coordinates during war games is put a transparent sheet over the map, then realign the base grid coordinates on the overlay. For example, what was the grid for Magdeburg is now the grid for Potsdam. This alteration no doubt confuses the shit out of most of the Soviet troops who are a few cards short of a full deck."

"So, what do we do until the Twentieth Guards have their next exercise?" Lee asked.

"What if I told you that you could cut and run, drink beer, and chase broads to your little heart's content?"

"That'd make me happier than a pig in shit. My guess is ... that's not going to happen ... is it?"

"I don't mean to rain on your libido parade. However, your chances are simply slim, and none. And Slim just rode off into the sunset. Instead, you're going to get your scrawny butt to work."

"Who said that the army isn't full of fun, travel, and adventure?" Lee muttered.

"Here's what we're going to do," Mac pronounced while plopping down an enormous stack of the yellow intercept sheets. "I rat-holed these beginning some time into the last exercise. I'm not sure how far into the drill they were at the time. First, we only need to look at the Twentieth Guards war games traffic. Set aside anything that has a grid coordinate or a physical location in it. Highlight the time of intercept and the frequency so we can determine who was where and how far into the exercise they were at that point. Treat anything that has both grid coordinates and a physical location, as if your family jewels are wrapped around it! That's the way we're going to break this open. Once we get a compromise ... more than one would be nice ... tying a grid to a location, we move our map to its proper location and plot out the rest of the coordinates we've intercepted. We then have a rough draft of their planned order of battle. Also, set aside anything that refers to map scale and be on the lookout for any unit identification or commanding officer as you normally would."

This challenge resonated with the team members. They couldn't wait to start scanning those little yellow sheets.

"We are all going to be looking at each piece of the intercepted traffic. I'm going to put a little buck-slip on each batch with me at the bottom. Meaning I'm the only one allowed to drop the intercepts into a burn bag."

The team wasn't thrilled with Mac's edict. It was as if their analytical competence was being questioned, but they remained silent.

"During this exercise, I came across some operator chatter that had a compromise between a grid coordinate and a physical location. It's the one on the top of the stack with a big red star on it. One of the operators was confused, not only because of the grid change but also the scale of the map being used. His buddy helped him out, tying a grid to a location and, in the process, he made a huge COMSEC screw-up. I have a feeling that this will continue to happen. I saved all the traffic from that point forward. At the time, I didn't have manna from heaven on which to lay it out. What we are going to do is see how much of the exercise we can reconstruct and be prepared for the next one."

The intercept sheets were separated into three stacks, complete with buck-slips. The GIs began their screening and old habits die hard. When an intercept didn't contain any pertinent information, the viewer routinely dropped it to his side without looking and put it in his burn bag rather than placing it aside for Mac to examine later. Upon seeing this, Mac commanded, "Stop what you're doing right now and put your burn bags in front of your feet under your desk."

"Give us a break, Boss," said the Spec/7. "When you've done this a million times, it's a hard habit to break."

"Amen," added Lee as the SFC nodded vigorously.

The GIs dutifully highlighted time and frequency on anything with a grid, which were set aside from the pile deemed not to be saved. They came across a few, but not many, potentially related to the order of battle Their batch was passed on to the next on the buck slip. No other sheets had been set aside by the time the other two pair of eyes had seen them. They brought this to Mac's attention with the SFC saying, "Three scans are a waste of our time."

"We'll see how thorough you were after I look at them. Then I'll decide." After Mac scanned the sheets and found nothing amiss, he allowed the burn bags to come out from underneath the desks.

They took the intercepts, placed them in chronological time order and proceeded to plot them on the overlay. The results were impressive. It became apparent that Mac had begun collecting the intercepts while the exercise was well underway. What was also evident from the time frame was that the Soviets were moving from the outskirts of Berlin toward the center, which was no big surprise. What *was* a *big* surprise—The Soviets planned to take Berlin in one day! Frequency analysis revealed several units under different commands subordinate to the Twentieth Guards were involved.

After some thought, Mac opened with, "Okay. What is it that we know and what do we know about what we don't know?"

"And," chimed in Lee, "what we don't know about what we don't know."

Ooooh! Shouldn't have said that. One of these days, my alligator mouth is going to overload my hummingbird ass.

Mac's eyes hooded. It had been a long day. He had suffered enough of his smart-mouthed protégé, but let it pass, saying, "I'm not sure about how they change the grid coordinates. Do they mark an X on the overlay from the standard map and then move the overlay and report that coordinate? Or do they take pluses and minuses of the longitude and latitude and have operators do the arithmetic before they transmit the grid? I think the latter is much too sophisticated for those low-level troops ... but if we get a compromise ... it doesn't matter. What else?"

"I think they will continue to use the same scale map for the Berlin exercises and may or may not use the same grid offset," offered Greg.

"Excellent, what else?"

"From the grids, we know where they planned to place their units, but we don't know whether they were tanks or motorized rifle," said Lee. "Our order of battle knowledge sucks at that level for those units around Berlin. Would it be possible to have the radio-direction-finding folks on standby whenever they start another exercise, so we could at least identify the transmission locations? Perhaps with the help of the Potsdam missions, we might determine the units involved."

"My thoughts exactly. However, you're still high on my shit list for that don't know, don't know utterance."

Mac was gone for a couple days to coordinate with the radio-direction-finding units and with the American and British military liaisons in Potsdam. He didn't bother to talk to the French equivalent.

Shortly after that, the Soviets decided once again to plan to take Berlin—at least on paper. The duffers came on board, identified the locations of the transmissions and passed that information to the so-called liaisons. The liaisons already had some of the order of battle data in hand and immediately reported to the team. They then sent out their two-man overt spy teams to try to fill in the blanks.

It became apparent, after processing and plotting the captured data, that the grid change from the previous exercise was not used this time. A totally frustrated Mac grumbled, "Well, shit! Everything went according to plan. We got a ton of grids. The duffers were Johnny-on-the-spot. The mission guys came through as they usually do. The only thing we didn't get was a grid to a location compromise."

Lee offered, "We have the overlay from the first exercise with a grid versus location breach and the overlay from this one. Why don't we overlay the overlay and see if we get any matches? If we do, we can use the compromise from the first exercise for the second drill." After some jiggling of the transparencies—except for a couple of outliers—it was a perfect match.

"Christ all-fucking-mighty, why didn't I think of that!" exclaimed Mac. "Lee, you are now completely off my shit list."

By the time the next Soviet *taking of Berlin* exercise was done, again with the help of the duffers and the American and British liaison missions, it was evident which Soviet units would travel which routes as they conquered Berlin. The team prepared a report that went to the powers that be. It was enthusiastically received, except for those commanders whose preconception was that the Allied garrison would hold out for a week rather than one day.

Now the team was prepared to undertake the Soviet plans for the conquest of Western Europe.

Enough already about this serious shit! Which of my experiences was the most fun?

ATTRAVERSO L'ITALIA—THRU ITALY

Lee and his travel friends were looking at the company bulletin board on which was an advertisement for a ten-day tour through Italy during the Easter holiday break, with stops in Austria and Switzerland. The highlight of the trip was a guided excursion through the Sistine Chapel on Easter Sunday. The tour was sponsored by whoever ran the GI schools for dependent students in Europe. Military personnel were also welcome.

Lee said, "You know that my station wagon isn't in the best shape … broken into in Paris and sideswiped by a garbage truck in Madrid. And, to be honest, it doesn't always fire on all eight cylinders. Besides, we are now pulling down E-5 pay along with the MOS supplement. Why don't we sign up?"

"Works for me," responded Reese and Eric concurred.

Everyone had agreed, except Levi, who was Jewish, and seeing the Sistine Chapel, particularly on Easter Sunday, wasn't high on his agenda.

They recruited Gus, an unsullied kid from the Great Lakes area, to be their fellow traveler to replace Levi. Gus was outgoing, at times gregarious, with his glass always more than half full. However, he was a funny-looking little dude. He was short in stature, prematurely balding and—although an above-average athlete—possessed a belly paunch. That and protruding ears and nose gave him the appearance of a smiling gargoyle. A decent fellow, even if he looked like he had been put together by a committee. He was also annoyingly innocent and naïve.

This foursome boarded the tour bus in Frankfurt at about midnight. The only open seats were the four directly behind a middle-aged couple in the front two seats on the bus, who turned out to be the bus's chaperones. They slept as best they could the rest of the night, awakening as they arrived in Vienna.

Vienna

After debarking, they gazed about and saw that their bus was one of three on this tour. When everyone departed the coaches, the tour's manifest included three bus drivers—two of them middle-aged and a young, handsome European in his mid-twenties. Three middle-aged couples—one couple per bus—who were school administrators ostensibly acting as chaperones. Their mission for the next ten days was to keep their charges on their feet, off their backs, and out of the clutches of predatory males—in particular, any low-life enlisted men who somehow finagled their way aboard this exclusive tour. The priggish female chaperone was overheard to say, "If we had to have the military on this tour, why couldn't they have been captains and majors, or at least lieutenants. But no, we end up with those enlisted ... whatever." Added to the tour buses entourage were four finagling, lowlife—and very horny—GIs, along with the 150 young women with whom the GIs would spend the next ten days.

Eric exclaimed, "Fan-fucking-tastic, we've done died and gone to poontang heaven!"

The enthusiasm of the GIs waned precipitously as they surveyed their potential targets. Reese commented, "There ain't a keeper in the bunch." He appeared to be correct. A few were downright homely—most were merely plain.

Eric conjectured, "There must be a conspiracy among universities and colleges, that the first thing they do is to run incoming female freshmen through a one to ten attractiveness screening. Only those falling between three and seven can study to become a school teacher."

Reese, while scrutinizing the group, "Those girls spent four or maybe five years in the prime mating grounds of America. Let me put this into horse-racing vernacular. There are winners, close seconds, and distant thirds. What we have here are three busloads of also-rans."

Eric suggested, "Why don't we each pick out one of those also-rans and treat her like she's the homecoming queen. *Voila*! It's beddy-bye time!"

"Give us a break!" Lee said. "Even I have some scruples when it comes to getting laid. Truth be told, I won't bed down a married woman ... unless she begs. Then, I do it only out of pity."

"Yeah, right," responded Reese. "The only pity involved would be for poor, pathetic you after she turned you every way but loose."

"What's pitiful, after seeing what's available to choose from, are the possibilities of getting a decent lay on this tour. So, let's buy a bottle of wine each time we stop, suck it down as we go, and just play tourist," concluded Lee. And that's pretty much the way it went, along with a few experiences not part of a tour's usual agenda.

The female chaperone in the front seat again began making disparaging comments about the soldiers behind her, while ensuring that the GIs would hear her. At the next stop, Reese pulled the others aside and said, "Let's mess with that bitch's mind."

All agreed.

Reese proposed to nonspecifically identify a girl by her features, geographic origin, or whatever and fabricate a sexual liaison for the night before. Then, throughout the next morning's conversations, they would present their fabrications for the benefit of the woman seated in front of them.

The first morning's bits and pieces of conversation included some of the following:

"That shy girl with the beautiful blue eyes isn't at all shy in bed. She damn near broke my dick off. I'm lucky I survived the night."

"Those three girls from Massachusetts or somewhere in New England like a foursome. It was demeaning. I was a human dildo, just a piece of meat, being passed around among them. And it was confusing as hell. I never knew which one had dibs on my Johnson at any given time. They did, however, keep it occupied throughout. It was a bit messy, but I guess someone had to do it."

"The two roommates with the southern drawl like to share. They flipped a coin to see who would go first. I was sloppy seconds for the one that lost the toss."

"The girl with the ugly sandals swallowed it all the first time. She does like her throat strokes."

The next morning's feed to the front seat regarded orgasms, intermixed with comments like these:

"Little Miss Priss screams like a banshee."

"The Yellow Rose of Texas sounds like a siren going off."

"Georgia Peach chatters like a chipmunk."

"Miss New Jersey must have screamed 'Yes' a hundred times."

Indeed, none of the utterances were anything but a fantasy; but, by the time the tour reached Rome the chaperone heard of sexual escapades far beyond her own experiences and references to body parts she did not know existed. No doubt she was now convinced she was watching over a bunch of kinky nymphomaniacs, including some inclined toward lesbianism.

Venezia

Throughout Venice—slowly and inexorably sinking into the lagoon—almost every canal was spanned by a banner advocating *Vota Communista*. Lee was in awe of Venice and its Byzantine elegance. The tour gave the expected exposure to the Doge's Palace, the Bridge of Sighs, and Piazza San Marcos (aka St. Mark's Square), as well as the Basilica itself. Walking through St. Mark's Square, provided one took care to not step in pigeon poop or ankle-deep in water, was breathtaking.

Lee was particularly intrigued by the replicas of four massive copper horses outside the Basilica and the original four horses and a *quadriga* (chariot drawn by four horses abreast) inside the Basilica. They were at least a millennium old. The horses and quadriga were taken from Constantinople during a Crusade almost eight hundred years before and brought to Venice. Napoleon later took the horses to Paris and placed them atop the Arch of Triumph, but they ultimately ended back in Venice.

Well, certainly well-traveled. As we say about ponies and nags that are properly cared for … they've been ridden hard, but never put away wet.

Across Tuscany

Among the gaggle of school teachers on the bus tour was a young woman from the Bronx. She dressed and walked a bit more like a hooker than a schoolteacher. She was big-bosomed, big-butted, and a bit brazen and always carried a big bag. The GIs immediately gave her the nickname of the Bronx Babe, or BB for short, due to the bunch of Bs she had in her bio. Overheard from one of the other school teachers was a snide, "I'll bet she keeps a gross of condoms tucked away in that bag."

Since the beginning of the tour, she made uncomplimentary statements to Gus about his physical appearance. Somewhere across Tuscany, she made yet another. Lee had enough. He got in her face saying, "One more like that and I'm going to slap your fat ass all the way to Rome!"

Big mistake.

BB had found the man of her dreams—someone who wouldn't put up with her shit. She returned to her seat and about a half hour later came back up the aisle, tapped Lee on the shoulder with a thumb up, indicating that she wanted to sit beside Gus. Lee was completely surprised at the sincere and emotional apology she offered to Gus.

He was again surprised at the next stop, after getting off the bus, when BB took Lee's hand, saying, "Thanks for what you did back there. I needed that."

I threatened her with physical violence. Now she's thanking me?

She said, "I've got to get my head on straight. I've always been insecure about my physical appearance. To compensate for my anxieties and to get them before they get me, at times I make observations about others, tactlessly voicing those views."

Lee had yet another big surprise coming. BB continued to hold his hand as they walked along. As far as she was concerned, they were now a couple. As it turned out, she was fun to be around. BB was well read and articulate, even with her Bronx accent. Lee did not intend to become intimate—she just wasn't his type. Heaven knows what her intentions were. However, because of his dubious relationship with BB, Lee, without further ado, was deemed *persona non grata* by the other one hundred forty-nine single women on tour.

Firenze

Florence begins with a consonant and ends with a vowel. Renaissance starts with a consonant and concludes with a vowel. All the men who made the Renaissance happen in Florence had names that began with a consonant and ended with a vowel. After two hours into the tour of Florence, all those names starting with a consonant and ending with a vowel—of which the guide spoke in almost reverent terms—started to run together.

The traveling GIs discovered the upscale tour booked rooms that appeared to have two toilets in each bathroom. They had no clue of the purpose of one of the devices. To put it bluntly, they didn't know a bidet from a bidarka. Being practical, they learned that—whenever ice was available, which was infrequent—the fixture was a handy place for chilling a bottle of wine. On one occasion, they iced down some Italian beer, only to discover it possessed even less flavor, aroma, and head foam than its American equivalent. So, vino it was for the rest of the tour.

Lee left Florence with a couple of distinct impressions. Renaissance paintings—whether on the wall, a ceiling or canvas—weren't his bag. The sculptures were a different story. Michelangelo's David and his other sculptures were huge and well done.

If one likes Renaissance art, you could spend a lifetime here. I think I'll pass.

Roma

The tour made two stops in Rome, one going south, the other coming north. The first stop accomplished most of the tourist requisites—St. Peter's, the Coliseum, Trevi Fountain, the Pantheon and so on. The second time through was mostly reserved for the highly-touted Easter Sunday guided tour of the Sistine Chapel.

The tour booked rooms at a hotel on the Via Veneto, one of the busiest streets in Rome. Lee had run out of toothpaste. It was mid-afternoon when in search of a *farmacia* (drug store) he stepped out onto the *strata* (street). He found it practically deserted. As he passed a darkened portico, out came a voice, "Hey GI, wanna fuck?"

Lee startled, responded, "No, I just want to brush my teeth," as he kept walking.

I'll bet that that's the first time she's heard that turn-down.

Somewhere around Rome, BB realized Lee's interest in her was only as a friend and not as a lover. She began to spend less time with him and more time with the handsome European bus driver. This change in BB's focus released Lee from the stigma of being her *boy-toy* and allowed him to look for other targets of opportunity. At the top of his list was a young woman of Eastern Mediterranean ethnicity who went unnoticed in Vienna when all the school teachers were lumped together as also-rans. Her name was Alisha. She unquestionably had keeper potential.

Alisha and Lee shared a mutual physical attraction and found opportunities to spend time together. She was a devout Eastern Orthodox faithful. Learning that Lee was a Methodist, which Alisha regarded as a cult, almost brought any possible relationship to a halt. Lee persisted, and over time Alisha acquiesced, thinking perhaps that she could convert this heretic. By the time the tour got to Sorrento, they were spending considerable time together.

Sorrento

High above the Bay of Naples, Sorrento was a pleasant place to spend an evening. At nighttime, the overlook of Naples was spectacular. However, as the GIs discovered during the daytime, Naples at the street level was disgustingly ugly and dirty.

Naples is to Italy as Newark is to America, the absolute two last places on earth anyone would want to live.

Capri

The next day, on the boat ride to Capri, Alisha and Lee were together. When they entered the Blue Grotto in a small boat, they put their heads between their knees to get below the low-hanging entrance. The grotto with its blue waters and acoustics was an out-of-this-world experience.

I'll regret this for the rest of my life if I don't do it. On the other hand, I may drown in these beautiful clear blue waters.

Lee took Alisha's head in both hands and planted a kiss on her lips. Lee didn't drown—Alisha returned his kiss.

Roma again

Back to Rome for a second time and the much-anticipated visit to the Sistine Chapel on Easter.

A small glitch arose regarding the tour agenda. The Pope closed the Sistine Chapel to the public to hold a private Mass. All the travelers were disappointed. The female chaperone on Lee's bus was livid and vocal. She vented to her husband, saying, "I didn't want to come. But you talked me into it! The only reason I came on this damned trip … and babysit all these trollops … was that I would get to see the Sistine Chapel. We've had this visit scheduled for months, and along comes some guy who, at the last minute, kicks us out because he wants to use it for himself. Who the hell does he think he is?"

She assuredly wasn't a Catholic.

I'd bet she's a Presbyterian, who mistakenly believe all Popes vanished after Luther got done nailing his stuff to the church doors in Wittenberg.

Pompeii

Visiting Pompeii is like going back into a time warp. As they walked through the ruins, Reese commented, "Clever, those old Romans. They certainly knew how to move water from one point to another. I suppose it had something to do with all the baths they took."

Sex, as illustrated in many of the frescoes, was conspicuously high on the long-dead Pompeii males' agenda. They also seemed to be obsessed with—and often, much exaggerated—the size of their genitalia. The tour passed a couple of frescoes. One mural depicted the Vestal Virgins, the other portrayed a man holding a balance scale with his enormous penis on one side of the scale, being balanced by a sizable pile of gold coins on the other. Lee noted that the school teachers barely glanced at the chaste Keepers of the Hearth as they went by, but lingered for a time—some to the point of loitering—observing the fellow holding the scale.

Well, not all that much has changed in two thousand years.

Torre di Pisa

Lee and the Bronx Babe—who was, as always, carrying the large, ever-present handbag—were climbing the tower of Pisa. It was a near-vertigo experience. Circling upward, the wall nearest you would lean in, go vertical, lean out, and go vertical again. The climb was made even more difficult by the deep grooves worn into the stone steps after centuries of traffic.

Three young Italian men came up from behind. One of them caressed BB's ample buttocks. Up came her purse in a mighty roundhouse swing, catching the offender full in the face with a resounding thud. The molester—while yelping what were no doubt Italian expletives—performed an ungraceful back-flip down three steps, landing on all fours.

Holy shit! She must have a brick in there along with all those alleged condoms.

The Lothario-wannabe arose while attempting to orient himself to the leaning wall space. Here came the handbag again. This time he ricocheted off an in-leaning wall down a couple more steps. He attempted to again get to his feet, but his companions were holding him down while jabbering away in Italian. They were presumably telling him it wasn't in his best interest to stand up again.

BB, satisfied that the *ragazzaccio* (naughty boy) had been taught his lesson regarding groping females with large handbags, rejoined Lee. They continued to the top of the tower overlooking the multitude of terracotta roof tiles adorning the roofs of Pisa.

Milan

The tour came up the west coast of the peninsula and stopped at Milan to allow their travelers the opportunity to see da Vinci's Last Supper and to attend the historical and famous La Scala opera. Almost all the tour had already signed-on for the opera. There were four stragglers. Guess who?

"Any of you want to go listen to the fat lady sing?" asked Reese.

The responses that came back were all negative. "Wasn't the opera Dante's seventh level of Hell?" and, "I'd rather have a root canal." Eric opined the most pragmatically, "If the CID ever finds out we went to an opera, we will be no different in the eyes of those goons than are our limp-wristed Marys."

Instead of the opera, they enjoyed a leisurely evening meal along with a couple of bottles of fine wine. They were in bed long before the opera attendees heard the diva sing her elaborate—and for most of the tour listeners, incomprehensible—aria.

Somewhere along the way to Geneva, the tour buses pulled into an overlook stop of the Alps for the picture takers.

Lee met up with Alisha, asking, "So, how was the opera last night?"

"Pfft. Excruciating. I'd rather have all my molars removed."

"That's essentially the excuse I gave for not going."

A woman after my own heart.

Geneva

Shortly before leaving for the evening meal, Lee advised his roommate Gus, "I think I'm going to get lucky tonight."

Gus gave a knowing nod.

As the evening meal was winding down, in came one of the bus drivers carrying on his shoulder the largest bottle of whiskey Lee had ever seen, at least two gallons. He announced for all to hear, "Party in my room. Everyone's invited." The diners followed him like lemmings to the cliff. The party was soon in full swing. The room was crowded with those already drunk or soon to be so.

Lee and Alisha met up. He suggested, "Why don't we get out of this bedlam and go for a walk along the lake?" She agreed. They walked hand in hand along the waterway with an enormous geyser of water spouting in the distance, occasionally stopping for a kiss.

Well, here goes nothing.

Lee summoned the courage to say, "Would you like to come up to my room?"

"I thought you were never going to ask."

Keeping the tradition of first-time lovers, they kissed and fondled while gently undressing, piece by piece, their soon-to-be-intimate partner. As if on cue, the instant Alisha's brassiere hit the floor, in came Gus in all his gnome-like splendor. He was only wearing a grin befitting a horny gargoyle and a pair of boxer shorts. Quicker than one could say *ménage à trois*, Alisha was dressed and gone. Likely forever.

Lee sat down on the bed, elbows on knees with head in hands, waiting for blood to flow from one brain to the other. "Gus, what did you think I meant, when I said, I might get lucky tonight?"

"Well, I know you're a good poker player. I figured you had a game going."

All Lee could manage to do was shake his head—the one to which blood had recently returned.

Back to Frankfurt

The next morning, an extremely hung-over, bleary, red-eyed, bunch of folks wobbled their way onto the three buses for the trip back to Frankfurt. As they traveled, Lee reminisced about his experiences.

Well, that was some fun ten days ... although utterly chaste ... thanks to Gus. Now back to worrying about the fucking Russians.

BACK ABOARD THE USS GORDON IN NEW YORK HARBOR

As Lee reflected on the incident in the 5K zone and the flight to Augsburg he remembered what beautiful weather it had been, a couple of those rare days with the sun shining. Another such memory came to mind.

GERMAN HORSE RACING

It was a beautiful sunshiny day. Lee didn't want to waste it without being somewhere outside.

He grew up in northeastern New Mexico where, as in all New Mexico, horse racing was a way of life. He was a better-than-average handicapper and almost always left the track with more money in his pocket than when he went in.

Frankfurt featured a horse racetrack, and Lee decided to give it a try. He took the long streetcar ride to the outskirts of the city where the racecourse was located. It was a different world from the one he knew. Rather than a tote board, there were poles scattered about with paper tacked to them indicating odds on the horses for the next race. A guy took your money and issued a slip of paper instead of a tote machine popping out a ticket.

Along with the usual riffraff expected at a racetrack, some of the clientele were attired like American cowboys straight out of a county fair, with boots, buckles, and Stetsons. They mingled with folks dressed as if attending the English Ascot, where there had been horse racing since the 1700s. When it came to the racing dress code, the Ascot is to the English what the Kentucky Derby is for Americans. Some Germans in Frankfurt gave their best trying to emulate both the aristocratic English and the wild American west.

The races themselves were little more than an equine demolition derby. Many of the races were steeplechases, complete with hedges to clear and small hidden ponds of water on the other side of the barriers. Some horses refused to jump, at times dumping their jockeys on the dry side of the obstacle. Others almost cleared the hurdle, depositing their riders into the pond on the far side. It was entertaining to watch. But, the return on Lee's short-term investments was dismal.

One race was unusually long. The field of horses disappeared for some time before reappearing, prompting an American to comment, "It must have been the time for the jockeys' afternoon beer break."

Lee didn't cash a single ticket. Nonetheless, he still had enough change in his pocket to pay for the lengthy streetcar ride back to the barracks.

It was fun, but it's the last time I'm going to bet on horses in Germany.

GOLFING IN BERLIN

Berlin was known for its historical significance. And, because of their involvement in recent events in or involving Berlin, such as the Wall going up and the Checkpoint Charlie face-off—not to mention the Cuban Missile crisis which precariously affected Berlin—Lee and most of the 251st troops held an overwhelming desire to see the city. However, because of their high-level security clearances, were prohibited from traveling behind the Iron Curtain unless on official orders.

Lee and others were dutifully reading the Company bulletin board. The Army Security Agency-Europe was holding its annual golf tournament in Berlin this year.

Lee and two conspiring companions, Brett and Sam, schemed to see Berlin under the pretext of being golfers, even though the only golf clubs ever held in their hands were putters at miniature putt-putt courses. Realizing they needed at least one golfer in the foursome, they recruited a guy named Derek, who had been on the golf team at a major Midwestern university.

They presented themselves to the company commander, announcing they were the contingency representing the 251st. The captain seemed delighted, commending them for their esprit de corps.

They needed to prepare themselves for the tournament. The army maintained a golf course high above the Rhine down near Cologne. They made the trip, rented clubs, paid the minimal greens fee and, under Derek's tutelage, proceeded to hack their way around the course. By the sixth hole, they were almost always hitting the ball with the first swing. A week later, they made the trip again. After the second time around the course, they would be rated as *duffers*, which was someone content to have a score of 120 strokes on his card.

The following weekend, complete with orders, they were on the night duty train from Frankfurt to Berlin. At times, this journey was an experience for travelers that might be haunting and remain unforgettable as they made their way to that little island in the communist sea called Berlin! They sped along the well-maintained West German tracks until they reached Helmstadt. There, the West German locomotive was replaced by an East German engine and an East German crew. Three engine changes would occur before arriving in Berlin. The train and its passengers made their way to Marienborn for inspection by the Soviets.

The Soviets and the East Germans were not allowed into Allied passenger cars of the duty trains. To make up for this alleged indignity, they turned to state-sponsored harassment. The train would be stopped for quite some time. The paperwork for the trainload of GIs was meticulously examined by a single Soviet inspector, looking for any little anomaly to deny an individual GI access to Berlin. The train was bathed in light from massive searchlights. Stationed every ten feet or so was a uniformed East

German guard with a rifle in one hand while the other held the leash of a vicious-looking dog. Guards with mirrors on long poles inspected underneath the train. When their passage was finally approved by the Soviet inspector, the duty train slowly made its way toward Potsdam. The rail line was pre-WWII and received barely enough maintenance by the East Germans to keep the cars upright and on the tracks. The locomotive was likely of the same era, considering the volume of coal smoke that made its way into the compartments. Somewhere along the line, the train was shuttled onto a railway siding to allow a freight train to slowly pass. Dawn was breaking when they, at long last, arrived in Potsdam, with yet another locomotive change. The outgoing Russian's inspection was almost as rapid as the incoming inspection had been slow. The Soviet inspector at this end would save his chickenshit harassment routine for GIs when they tried to leave Berlin.

Eventually, they made it to the end of the line at Babelsberg, where an army bus was waiting to transport the arriving golfers. The 251st contingent watched other golfers climb down from the train, appearing as if the PGA Tour had arrived. All the other golfers owned a set of clubs, undoubtedly with more than the maximum thirteen clubs allowed in competition. Most of those guys boasted a handicap in the single digits and would be disgraced if they shot bogey golf. All other units except for 251st had held playoff tournaments to determine who would go to Berlin.

The golfers were transported to the Berlin Golf and Country Club in the Wannsee District. It was a beautiful resort, open to all military personnel stationed in Berlin except the Soviets. But then, pasture pool wasn't the Ruskies strong suit anyway. The 251st visitors masquerading as golfers spent the night, arose, ate breakfast, and headed for the course. It was one of those rare days in Germany where the sky was clear and the sun shining. It was a beautiful day to play golf, but that wasn't the reason they had made their way to Berlin.

Fortunately, since arriving sans golfing paraphernalia, the 251st contingent was able to rent clubs and buy balls before teeing off a little after ten. By the fifth hole, there were at least three other foursomes backed up behind them. Likewise, open fairways were in front of them as far as the eye could see. The course marshal took off in a golf cart to unplug the delay in his smooth flow of Arnold Palmer wannabes. It didn't take long to find the problem. As he approached the choke-point foursome, he anticipated a confrontation when he suggested to the duffers they should withdraw from the tournament. The marshal thought he might even have to forcibly eject them. Much to his surprise, they slammed their clubs into their golf bags and did not bother to pick up their balls as they headed off the course. Little did he know they came to see Berlin—not to play golf.

Sometimes, the well-laid plans of mice and men ... even if they are lowly GIs ... do work out.

The 251st foursome immediately set off for central Berlin. Area-wise, Berlin is a huge city. It took all their considerable analytical skills to decipher the streetcar system to get where they wanted to go. By the time they got to their destination, it was well into the afternoon. They were starving and decided to try the *Knackwurst mit pommes frites* (currywurst with French fries) and *Weizenbier* (wheat beer), all for which Berlin was well known. They were handed a paper plate with the fries and a wurst slathered with what appeared to be tomato paste.

"My Gawd," exclaimed Derek after taking a bite. "This is atrocious. The wurst tastes like a whole head of garlic mixed with a little bit of pork. And the ketchup shit on top is not only messy but disgusting."

"This wheat beer reminds me of the watered-down piss they serve back in the States," added Lee. "Barley is the only grain that should go into beer."

All agreed with both assessments.

They ate the fries, found a trash can for the wursts and went back and ordered a civilized bratwurst. They did drink the beer.

They made their way to Potsdamer Platz, where an observation platform was constructed to allow a look over the wall. The visual difference between East and West Berlin was dramatic. To the east, remained piles of rubble and windowless, roofless, soot-stained structures poking their way out of the debris. In the west, it wasn't quite yet a vibrant community, though obviously, it was working its way there.

Lee observed, "Look at the people in the east, then those in the west. In the east, they are plodding along with their heads down. On this side, they have their shoulders back and heads up, with a pep in their step."

"That tells it all, doesn't it?" said Brett.

They made their way to Checkpoint Charlie on Friedrichstrasse. Silently and individually, they recalled those intercepts, read and analyzed, as they viewed the cobblestone streets where it occurred. They had made the pilgrimage to their revered Cold War Mecca.

It was now time to be a tourist. The Reichstag was visible east of the Wall in the not-too-far distance, and the remnants of the *Gedächtniskirche* (Kaiser Wilhelm Memorial Church) was on the west side. They walked past the upscale shops on Kurfüstendamm, the street commonly known as Ku'damm, and then to Brandenburg Gate.

The Reichstag was in the process of an on-again-off-again restoration by the East Germans. Brett said, "I'm disappointed. I hoped to see it all totally shot to shit, just as the Russians left it." The Brandenburg Gate barely inside the Soviet sector sat in the middle of a large square, walled off on both sides between East and West Berlin. It had also been riddled with gunfire during the war. The Soviets or whoever had performed an amateurish job of repair. Atop the Gate sat a magnificent bronze four-horse quadriga. As had happened in Venice, Napoleon had also taken this one to Paris for a brief visit, but it ended up back in Berlin. Then sometime after the war the Soviets decided that it should be facing the east rather than west, and went to considerable trouble and effort to turn it around.

Old Bonaparte sure had a discerning eye for horseflesh, even if they are metal.

The bombed-out memorial church referred to by the Germans as the *hohle zahn* (hollow tooth) remained much as it was following the war. Lee remarked, "It's interesting, isn't it? In downtown Frankfurt, they left the ruins of the old Opera House. Here in downtown Berlin, they left the ruins of the Kaiser Wilhelm. And both are about the way they were at the end of the war. Do you think someone high-up may have a hidden agenda to remind the Germans of the perils of war?"

They wandered the Ku'damm, marveling at how upscale it appeared, prompting Derek to say, "Except for the German instead of the English, this looks like Rodeo Drive."

"Yeah? You wouldn't know Rodeo Drive if it bit you in the ass," countered Lee.

"Cowboy, not everyone grew up on a cattle ranch in Nuevo-No-Sabe-Nada-Mexico. My mother regularly shops on Rodeo."

They stopped outside one of the ritzy hotels to look at the unbelievably expensive *la carte*. Brett opined, "At those prices, the appetizer must include a blow job while you're drinking Dom Perignon and eating beluga caviar." The others shook their heads and continued down the street.

They found a bierstube and settled in. Unlike Frankfurt, the beer was expensive, and very unlike Frankfurt, the Germans were downright cordial. After their third beer, the bartender set down another round saying, "*Auf den haus.*" (On the house.)

Lee asked, "*Was gibt?*" (What gives?)

"*Hier in Berlin wissen wir, dass Sie Amis bei uns sind.*" (Here in Berlin, we appreciate that you Amis are with us.)

"I didn't get all of that, but it was something like, 'We value you being here steadfast with us,'" said Lee.

The bartender, who was no doubt fluent in English nodded, smiled, and walked away saying, "*Geniessen!*" (Enjoy!)

It was well into the early morning when the foursome made their way back to the golf resort. They slept in and had a late breakfast.

Brett noted, "The tournament ends around four this afternoon. We must catch the night duty train back to Frankfurt. Berlin is one damn big city. No way are we going to be able to get anywhere and back in time."

"Well then, let's go get ourselves some beers and go out to the eighteenth hole and watch them come in," said Lee. "Since we came for a golf tournament, knowing which unit won might be a good idea when we get back."

As they lounged around near the eighteenth green, the course marshal came up and inquired, "Hey, aren't you the guys that dropped out early?" They all nodded. "I appreciate what you did rather than give me a ration of shit. However, not picking up your balls confused the living daylights out of the foursome that came up behind you. Don't do that again. Okay?"

Lee responded, "Not to worry … we are all short-timers and won't be back. It was fun and worth the trip." Then whispered to himself, "But the golf part sucked."

The tournament ended, and they headed back to the rail station to catch the night duty-train to Frankfurt. Getting travel orders verified by the outgoing Soviet inspector was again tedious.

Good old eloquent Yogi, he was spot on. Leaving Berlin is déjà-vu, all over again. Perhaps, the pissed on, pissed off Soviet major has been transferred from autobahn to train duty, so he doesn't have to line GIs up and count them.

Finally, as dawn was breaking, the train arrived in Helmstadt, then, without delay, returned to Frankfurt.

Looking at all those little yellow sheets now have more relevance after seeing the Soviets and East Germans up close and personal. Time well spent.

JIMMY JOE'S PAYBACK

Lee came in just before curfew and climbed into his bunk and immediately fell asleep. Soon after that, his bed was shaking, with Jimmy Joe saying, "Wake up Lee, wake up, wake up, wake up!"

"Huh?"

"Remember I told you I would pay you back for that blind date? I've met a couple of airline stewardesses, sisters from Georgia. They want to party. You know what that means, don't you? Wham! Bam! You don't even have to say, *Thank you, Ma'am*! So, cowboy, get your rear in gear and saddle up."

Lee splashed on something that resembled a deodorant and quickly dressed saying, "What's the situation?"

"They are waiting for us in the lobby of that swanky hotel next to the Hauptbahnhof. They have a layover until a flight out tomorrow afternoon. They claim they have stashed away in their room a bunch of those little bottles of booze that get served on the airplane."

Two very horny guys hustled down the long walk to the hotel. Waiting for them in the lobby were the two comely Georgia peaches.

The front desk was manned, but there was a sign informing potential clients, *Kein Zimmer Verfügbar* (no rooms available). Also, waiting was the *Poitier* (the German cross between a concierge and a night watchman). This upscale hotel was near enough the red-light district to get clients wanting to occupy a bed on an hourly basis, and also aware of folks who wanted to spend the night without themselves renting a room. The Portier was having none of that with this group.

When they stepped toward the elevator, he demanded to see their room keys. Only the girls had them, and the guys couldn't buy one because the hotel was fully booked. Neither attempts at bribery by the GIs nor flirting by the girls would change the Poitier's mind. After several such tries, one of the girls said, in a slow, double negative, southern drawl, "This asshole ain't never going to give. Sorry guys, it would've been fun."

As they walked back to the Kaserne, Jimmy Joe remarked, "I've never done sisters at the same time. Separately, yes. I would've liked to have put that notch on my belt."

"You perverted bastard! No way in hell was I going to be part of a foursome. Besides, after they'd seen the size of my dick it would have just been a threesome, with you sitting on the sidelines watching."

"Only in your dreams is your teeny-weeny weenie bigger than mine."

"Oh yeah? And regarding what happened or didn't happen tonight ... you win some, lose some, and some, like this evening, leave you with a boner that just won't go away. Thanks for thinking of me, but since I didn't get laid, you still owe me a payback."

Enough, for now, of remembering the good times. We did do some damned fine analytical work ... even if I must say so myself ... since the security gurus sure as hell won't let it ever be known.

THE SOVIETS' PLAN TO TAKE EUROPE

It was late in the year. As usual, the Soviets began their annual GSFG-wide war games exercise. Units moved out of their garrisons and into training areas. The Potsdam missions were having a field day with their snooping. Likewise, the ASA intercept stations throughout Germany were sucking copious numbers of Soviet transmissions out of the ether as the Soviets planned their conquest of Western Europe.

As usual, the Soviet grunts were confused and confounded by the map grid substitutions imposed upon them for the exercise. As such, it didn't take long for Mac's team to find a grid-to-location compromise resulting from confused operator chatter. In fact, they ended up with several such breaches. They plotted the Soviet advance as they started across Western Europe—rapid advances, with artillery, tank, and infantry units leapfrogging each other along autobahns and secondary roadways heading westward. The advances were consistently sixty kilometers per day, substantially more distance than the Allied defenders was expecting. "Perhaps they wouldn't plan on going quite so fast if they knew that all the roadways and bridges have been booby-trapped with huge amounts of explosives at chokepoints along the way," Mac said. Then he exclaimed, "Oh fuck! Forget you heard that. It's need-to-know *way above* your grade level. I'm serious. Do not … do not ever repeat that!"

The Soviets' primary goal was to split Western Europe in half by capturing the major bridge crossings over the Main and Rhine rivers, thereby separating the Allied armies—the Americans and the French to the south and the English and Germans along with other NATO forces to the north.

Their planning was to advance as a combined front into central West Germany, primarily through the Fulda Gap and the Coburg and Hof equivalents a little further to the south. Once within central West Germany, they split into three columns, with one heading straight for the English Channel, another toward the Iberian Peninsula, and the third toward Scandinavia.

Once Western Europe was in Soviet hands—at least on paper—and their tanks were done with the shooting and chewing up of the East German countryside, everything returned to normal.

With the *trial run* war games in preparation for the conquest of Western Europe now concluded, the Soviet units returned to garrison and the volume of signals passing through the airwaves markedly diminished.

Mac and his team began preparing what was going to be a mind-altering report for the powers that be.

THE SOVIETS' PLAN TO TAKE EUROPE USING NUKES

Soon after the first GSFG-wide war games drill, the Soviets fired up yet another GFSG-wide exercise. This time, the troops didn't go into the field, and the East German countryside didn't get mangled. Only an envisioned conquest of Western Europe via radio communications ensued. As before, it didn't take long for operator chatter to reveal a grid-to-location compromise. As before, rapidly leapfrogging artillery tank and infantry units headed west, splitting apart the Allied forces in Europe north and south of the Main and Rhine rivers in this communication-simulated war game.

Again, this was a major thrust into central Germany that then broke into three advancements as they moved westward, one curving south through France toward the Iberian Peninsula, the second straight toward the English Channel, and the third curving northward toward the low countries and Scandinavia. There was, however, one significant difference. In addition to the grid locations, as various units reported their intended advance early in the operation, there were also grid locations being passed throughout Western Europe as far west as the English Channel. After several of these were plotted, Mac, with his knowledge of the critical military, transportation, and communication placements throughout Europe, exclaimed, "Sweet Jesus! Those steel-toothed bastards are planning on using nukes!"

Shortly after the exercise concluded, the team prepared two detailed reports of the Soviet strategy to overtake Western Europe. One depicted conventional warfare, the other revealed their planned use of nuclear weapons.

Contained in the reports were maps showing the various routes the Soviet units would take as they moved westward. Mac plotted out the routes. All hunkered down over the map, he held the document with the stub of what remained of his right arm while drawing arrows, holding his self-sharpened pencils in his clenched left fist. The results were not aesthetically pleasing graphics.

I know better than to do this, but here goes.

"Mac, I had considerable drafting experience in college. These reports are going to get a wide distribution. I don't know how to say this other than ... your drawing sucks. So why don't you let me do the graphics?"

Yes, Lee should have known better.

Mac exploded, "Don't you ever learn? Does my saying to you that just because I only have one arm doesn't mean I'm a helpless paraplegic ring a bell?"

Lee discreetly withdrew from the area. The reports went out to the powers that be, complete with wobbly arrows drawn with a blunt lead pencil. These reports received undivided attention, and would—

for decades—remain the authoritative cornerstone of the planned Soviet conquest of Western Europe.

A FLEETING FIFTEEN MINUTES OF FAME

During that exercise, the team also benefited from another COMSEC breach. This transmission-compromise break again came from operator chatter. A Soviet troop at one end didn't know which frequency he was supposed to use. His helpful buddy at the other end told him that during war game exercises he was to use X, but when in garrison or on nearby maneuvers, to use Y.

Once the exercises were over and the Soviet units back in garrison, the team took the Y frequency, expanded the spectrum on the high and low side, then begin to pay careful attention to that band of electromagnetic wave transmissions coming through the ether from the east. Soviet tankers had their specialized jargon and vernacular, the motorized infantry had theirs, and these new guys spoke their own lingo. Without question, the parlance they heard was coming from missile troops.

The team couldn't wait to be the ones to first verify Soviet nukes in Europe. Once the Soviet troops were back in garrison or deployed on minor exercises, the team would get an intercepted coordinate grid and request a picture-taking overflight. About half of East Germany could be photographed by C-130 planes with side-looking cameras while flying through the three air corridor doors into and out of Berlin. The Soviets evidently knew this and tucked their missiles elsewhere, out of range of these reconnaissance flights. However, it hadn't been that long since Gary Powers had his ass shot out of the sky over Russia. As such, the request went way far up the chain of command before being approved. Tactical intelligence has a very short shelf life. Before deciding to authorize the flight, the decision-maker would see when the request was submitted to know how current it might be. By the time the team's requests made their way up the military's bureaucratic communication food chain, the information was stale and starting to mold. All their calls for an overflight were consistently denied.

Frustration replaced optimism. Mac was querulous, saying, "What the hell do we have to do to get the attention of those assholes leading from behind a desk? The only thing I see is twenty-four-hour coverage. That way, when we have an evening or nighttime compromise, we can send a request for an overflight out without delay rather than waiting until the next day. I was even desperate enough to send a request to the Potsdam liaisons to go look in East Germany at a location we detected."

"What came of that?" asked the Spec/7.

"It must have been passed off to the Brits because the response that came back was: 'The only thing we found at this bloody locale was a fog of mosquitoes, all big enough to bugger a turkey standing up.'"

Lee quipped, "Don't you just love their command of the language we share?"

Later, Mac approached Lee saying, "You're not going to like this … I'm putting you on the midnight shift to monitor the Soviet missile traffic. I have only three of you, and I want twenty-four-hour-a-day coverage. The Spec/7 and the E-6 hard-stripe outrank you. They picked the day and the swing shifts."

"It figures. Newton was right about gravity. Especially in the army. Shit does roll downhill."

"That's true … sorry."

Lee came to like the midnight shift. Get off duty, return to the Kaserne, catch some rack time, eat lunch at the mess hall if it wasn't downright disgusting or at the EM Club if it was. He had the whole afternoon and evening to carouse, and as such his social life didn't suffer. For the most part, the German girls didn't do one-night stands but were more than willing to arrange future dates. And, there was no one to notice if he happened to show up for duty a little under the influence after an evening out on the town.

Lee arrived one night, somewhat in that condition, and found an immediate compromise on a missile location. He thought about his options.

Why not? What's the worst thing they could do? Draft me and send me to Germany? They've already done that.

Lee proceeded to enter a date-time-group (DTG), which is the date and time a transmission is dispatched, on the request for an overflight. The DTG he entered was two days later than what showed on the calendar on the wall. Off went the request. By the time the request made its way up to whoever decided about the overflight, the DTG was recent. The flight flew. Sure enough, sitting in a clearing in an East German forest was what appeared to be a fat, ugly, dark gray toad. It was a Soviet SS3 missile system capable of nuclear warhead delivery. Lee was the first to verify the presence of those weapons in Europe and had his fleeting fifteen minutes of fame.

Lee received a Letter of Commendation. It read, in part, 'I commend you for the highly significant reporting you recently accomplished … blah, blah, blah. The data you provided the intelligence community was of such importance … blah, blah, blah. Your devotion to duty is exemplified in this act for which you are commended … blah, blah, blah.' It was signed by an infantry colonel instead of someone in the intelligence hierarchy, further diminishing Lee's one and only claim to fame.

Well, I guess that's vague and innocuous enough, so no one will ever know what the hell I did. He also failed to mention my devotion to duty was exemplified by the fact that I was half-sloshed when I postdated the DTG on the overflight request.

The day following receipt of photographic verification of the missile launch system, Mac was ecstatic but skeptical saying, "You didn't by chance happen to fudge a little on the request DTG, did you?"

"What DTG?"

Mac smiled, saying, "Okaaay! I know that you're not going to reenlist. However, I have something you might want to think about."

"What's that?"

"First, a little background. I've been frustrated over time. Whenever I come across someone, I can depend on and who thinks the way I do, he disappears off the screen. The career soldiers get rotated, and the conscripted like yourself can't wait to be the hell and gone. So, I put in for ... and was granted ... a civilian GS seven-slash-nine position to be my assistant, aid, gofer, whatever. I'm offering you that job."

Lee was stunned.

Holy whatever! The social life here is unbelievable. I would be working for the man I consider to be the smartest guy in the universe. My own bachelor's pad. And, my pay would be exponential to what I'm making now as a Spec/5 ... on which I'm living damned well.

"How much college credit do you have?"

"Two years, but my grade point was dismal. That's what ended me up in the army."

"With that much college, I might be able to start you at the nine level, if not, in a year I would promote you from the seven to the nine."

Please, don't make it any harder than it already is.

"When I was in advanced training I realized I had some analytical skills," said Lee. "At that point, I promised myself I was going to get my shit together and go back and finish college. Major in something analytical, perhaps economics. Then go on from there."

I've made some bad decisions in my life. This may turn out to be the worst of them all.

"Sorry, Mac, I must keep my promise to myself, and say no. But you have no concept of how much your offer means."

"Well, if you happen to change your mind, you know where to find me."

"Yeah, but considering my limited analytical abilities, it may be difficult since you sit at the desk directly in front of me."

"Perhaps you will have a rare lucid moment and be able to pull it off."

BACK ABOARD THE USS GORDON IN NEW YORK HARBOR

Both Lee and Isaac had traveled extensively throughout Europe. During their conversation, they discussed the pros and cons of their favorite destinations. Isaac's was Paris. Lee's was Amsterdam. Their exchange of experiences triggered Lee's remembrances of time spent in both Amsterdam and Paris.

THE HUNDRED-YEAR STORM

Late on a Thursday afternoon, Mac called Lee and some of the more senior analysts together, saying, "All is quiet on the Eastern front, so I'm going to head out to the War Office in London. Sergeant Ramsey and the newbies will hold down the fort. I'll see you guys on Monday."

Lee rounded up three of his usual traveling suspects. They headed for the Class VI store to stock up on cigarettes for bribing and bartering purposes. Back at the Kaserne, Lee retrieved a pad of blank leave forms from his footlocker—which he had earlier liberated from the first sergeant's office when the first-shirt happened to be absent. The soon-to-be traveling crew found a typewriter and typed up and signed their bogus leave documents, making sure *No travel permitted in the 5K zone* appeared, to give the false papers some authenticity. They passed through the Dutch border—after bribing the border guards with the usual two packs of cigarettes—and spent an inexpensive weekend hustling local females, drinking good Dutch beer, and eating in the diverse restaurants for which Amsterdam was famous.

When they went to bed Saturday night, the clouds over Amsterdam seemed more ominous than usual. They awoke the next morning to a so-called hundred-year storm. Eighteen inches of snow and a centigrade temperature below zero. Lee slogged out to the station wagon and knocked away enough snow to get in. When he tried to start the motor, the battery didn't have enough oomph to get the eight cylinders firing.

Back inside, Lee apprised the others about the situation, saying, "We've got to be back in Germany before midnight. Otherwise, we are AWOL. Not only will we be AWOL, but AWOL on bad paper. We may perhaps be up to our asses in alligators."

"No *shit*, Sherlock," responded Eric. "Do you *really* think so? What gave you your *first clue*?"

"So, keep your leave papers with you unless it looks like we're being taken in. In that case, I don't care what you do, stick them up your ass or swallow them ... or both ... just get rid of them."

Lee picked up his remaining stash of cigarette packs and headed back out. Shortly, along came what in the States would be called a tow truck with a blade in front. Lee bargained with the driver for the remaining cigarettes to jump-start their vehicle and plow a path to the nearby Dutch equivalent of the autobahn. The driver, seeing those beloved Camels, immediately agreed and hooked up jumper cables. The engine fired on the first turn of the key. Lee left it running and rushed inside to tell the others they were leaving.

The GIs loaded up and followed the snowplowing tow truck to the autobahn entrance. Theirs was the only vehicle on the road. Lee centered the station wagon in the two lanes and headed eastward, the car looking like a jury-rigged snowplow. Which it was.

Thank you, General Motors for a vehicle that weighs a ton and a V8 engine to push it through this snow.

After a few miles the snow level diminished, and by the time they reached the German border, the road was clear. Once safely into Germany, Reese quipped, "After you had told us to either stick our leave documents up our asses or eat them ...or both ... I think Eric gave a lot of thought as to which he would do first if he had to do both."

"Knowing him as well as I do, he almost certainly got it bass-ackwards," opined Levi.

Soon they were on the outskirts of Frankfurt.

Back to all the damned little yellow intercept sheets and what Ivan is up to.

AMSTERDAM YET AGAIN AND ON TO PARIS

Lee and the usual suspects were again back in Amsterdam—this time, carrying legitimate travel documents. Their itinerary: Frankfurt to Amsterdam, then to Paris, and back to Frankfurt.

They each bargained a carton of cigarettes for bed and breakfast and were ready for a night on the town. Everyone headed different ways. Reese, to the infamous red-light district. Lee set out by himself, having learned that *getting lucky* when pursuing young females with Eric and Levi along was basically impossible. He left them to fend for themselves.

Lee encountered four American college girls beginning their European tour in Amsterdam. Three of the girls were already glommed onto by American naval cadets who, after sailing the Atlantic as part of a so-called maritime training exercise, were now enjoying Amsterdam. The unclaimed female was perky, cute, and exhibited great legs. Lee staked his claim.

The group decided to eat at a restaurant with a dress code requiring males to wear a tie. The cadets met the standard, but Lee was the typically attired GI in civilian clothes. He only owned one tie, the military issue, and it was back in a locker in Frankfurt. His date, realizing the situation, hiked up her skirt—revealing legs to die for—unbuckled the snaps, stripped off a nylon and tied it around Lee's neck in a perfect Windsor knot. They entered the restaurant and enjoyed an outstanding meal.

After eating, Lee and Christie, his newly acquired girlfriend, broke off from the other group and began roaming Amsterdam, hand in hand. They had a strong physical and emotional attraction. However, tonight they realized that having met only hours before—and sensing a genuine affection that precluded a one-night stand—they would be friends and not lovers during the time they would spend together.

For the most part, Amsterdam was a vibrant and exotic city all twenty-four hours of the day and night. It possessed all the aura of *April in Paris* without the rain or some idiot singing and dancing in the street.

"Such an old city, and yet so progressive," Christie opined.

"Yep," was Lee's laconic, southwestern, all-encompassing response.

They wandered along the canals, over the seemingly innumerable bridges, admiring the architecture as they went. They ventured into the ill-reputed red-light district. Christie was appalled by the open prostitution, and Lee was afraid he might encounter Reese and be obliged to explain to her why he knew this voyeur.

When they tired, they stopped at sidewalk cafes and had a drink. At one stop, a middle-aged Dutchman took an uninvited seat at their table. He introduced himself and asked, "You are Americans, aren't you? We Dutch love Americans for what they did for us after the war. We are, how do you say, kindred people?" Somewhere in the lengthy conversation that followed, the Dutchman offered, "The only thing we Dutch are intolerant of is intolerance itself."

Right on. And, we are indeed akin!

Lee and Christie later ventured into a pot shop and downed a cup of coffee while observing the mellowed-out clients. Fearing too much of the secondhand smoke, they soon departed.

Dawn was breaking in the east when the late-night wanderers concluded they had enough of Amsterdam. It turned out that Amsterdam was a twenty-four-hour city, except for taxis, and they walked the long distance back to her hotel. There Lee took her in his arms and gave her a brief kiss on the lips, saying, "This was a night I will remember for a long time."

"Me too!" murmured Christie, with an emotional catch in her voice.

Lee left.

Two ships passing in the night. Why me? Under different circumstances ... if only we had more time to spend together, with me not in the army and her not traveling ... then she might be my keeper for all time.

Luckily, Lee's B&B wasn't that far distant. As he approached their one-dollar-and-fourteen-cents-carton-of-Camels room, he overheard the following conversation —

"Jeezus-fucking-Christ!" Levi bellowed as he paced the room.

I wonder if it's blasphemy when a Jew says that?

"Where is that *goy* Wolfe? I want to get to Paris. If I had the car keys, I would leave his ass right here in Amsterdam. Anybody have any idea where he might be?"

"The last time I saw him, he and this broad were going to a restaurant that required a tie. It goes without saying, he didn't have one," responded Eric. "She gave everyone a thrill when she took off a stocking and tied it around his neck. That guy is an absolute genius when it comes to picking pieces of ass with great legs."

Levi roared, "*Schtupp* you! Wolfe! And, especially his *shiksa* pieces of ass with great legs! I want to get to Paris!"

"Oh, chill out," said Reese, vigorously scratching his crotch. "My guess is that right about now she is wrapping that nylon around his dick to try to keep it up. If that works, we won't see him until noon."

Lee burst through the door saying, "What's keeping you guys? We're supposed to be on the way to Paris." Levi was miffed but silent as they loaded up and headed south.

Before leaving Amsterdam, Reese anxiously announced, "I need to stop at a pharmacy." When Lee saw an *apotheek*, he pulled over. Reese went in and quickly returned. Apparently, he had done this before. When Reese returned to the car and was again seated in the shotgun seat, he dropped his trousers and boxers to his knees while copiously dousing his genital area and clothing with the white powder he had purchased. Panic ensued among the other three. They hadn't experienced those little, biting, body lice—crabs—but were acquainted with those who had; and, who pronounced them as definitely not fun to have up close and personal.

Lee pulled to the side, demanding, "Get your gear all the way to the back, and you are restricted to the rear seat! Not negotiable! Or we will leave your bug-infested ass here on the edge of the road!"

Eric and Levi nodded in concurrence, but they realized it would take all three of them and a stroke of luck to evict the muscular Reese from their midst.

Reese complied. In the meantime, the other two moved forward—after a liberal application of Reese's powder to the area where they would sit—they squeezed in alongside Lee. He scarcely had enough space to steer. The front seat passengers often and nervously peered over their shoulders, expecting a swarm of creepy crawlies with lobster-sized pincers advancing from where Reese was sitting.

They made their way to Paris and checked into a hotel. The others insisted Reese leave the suspect garments he was wearing when he left Amsterdam in the station wagon.

They did in Paris what was expected of tourists. Notre Dame. The Winged Victory at the Louvre. Up the Eiffel Tower. And so on. Later, when having an evening meal at a restaurant, they learned why Francophiles, other than the Frogs themselves, were few and far between. The French—with their disdain for anyone or anything not French—were rude, arrogant, lived in the past, and were universally disliked.

Levi insisted on having escargot.

Eric said, "Have you ever seen a snail and the trail it leaves behind? They have constant diarrhea. You Yids won't eat pork, milk with meat, or shellfish. Nevertheless, you're going to dig a creature filled with shit out of its shell and eat it? Give Abraham and us a break!"

Their meals were so-so. The rating for the escargot offering went unknown because Levi refused to comment. However, the *Fromage* at the end of the meal was delectable, and they attacked it with gusto. What had been a fully laden tray of cheese was almost bare before the maître d' grabbed it off the table and walked away, saying words about Americans that were doubtless derogatory. The removal of the cheese and the disparaging verbiage caused Reese to comment, "That Frog can eat my snail. It'd be the biggest and juiciest thing he has ever had in his mouth."

Eric responded, "Yeah, but your snail also tends to leave a trail behind as it drags along."

The next morning, when they approached the vehicle, they discovered a little wing-window broke out, a door opened, and the things left behind the night before—Reese's likely crab-infested clothing—stolen.

"There is a just God," commented Eric, reflecting everyone's sentiment.

Lee pointed the station wagon in the direction of Frankfurt. Paris faded in the rear-view mirror.

Back to worrying about the damned Soviets.

IF THE BALLOON GOES UP

Lee was cognizant of the Soviet capabilities if they decided to invade West Germany. He was also aware of the unlikelihood that the Allies could hold them back if the balloon went up. The Soviets planned to advance sixty kilometers a day, which meant they might be in the Frankfurt area in about two days.

The 251st, like all units in Europe, frequently went on heightened alert. The ASA units were low on the alert notification priority list and was often called off before the 251st was notified. Perhaps this revealed the regular army's attitude toward the ASA: 'Those spooks don't report to us. Why should we care? Let them find their own way out.'

What happens if the balloon does go up? What then?

Lee approached Chief McDuff with those questions.

"Specialist, you and all of your ilk show up to assist in the destruction of classified documents and equipment."

"Then what?"

Not knowing the answer, the chief snapped, "Just follow orders!"

Lee then addressed a signal officer captain assigned to ASA who was working in the SCIF. He again posed his questions. The captain had evidently given a lot of thought to this possibility. "Well, we try to destroy the classified stuff as best we can. Considering what little lead time, we will have, I doubt we come anywhere close to getting the job done. As to the *then what?* My guess is we will all be on our own."

Lee went to Mac with those enigmas. Mac, being himself, got right to the point, saying, "Our retreat and evacuation plans are a total fiasco conjured up by some desk jockeys back at the Pentagon. Among other things, it calls for military dependents and civilians like myself to gather at a common location before being escorted to safety. In the time it will take before they are finally gathered together, all the Soviets will have to do is take them into custody, rape the women, shoot them all ... or send them off to Siberia. I've made plans and arrangements to get myself and my wife out. I strongly suggest you do the same."

Lee set about to do just that. There were issues to be resolved. When and where to travel? What to take with him? How to hide the obvious fact that he was a GI?

Which way to go? For sure I can't go east, and I don't want to go west where all the fighting will be. So, it is north or south. Going south where it's warmer would be nice. Let's face it, you don't much look Italian ... but you would pass for a Dane anytime. North, it is.

Lee remembered the incident when the former Afrika Korps troop riding a bicycle rammed his vehicle.

Perfect! Travel on the back roads and woods looking like a German laborer trying to escape the carnage. Need to get some used German duds.

Lee also remembered the castle ruins in the Taunus mountains where Renate took him on their last date. This was an ideal place for someone on the run to hide, and he would not just be running but running scared.

Great! I'll steal a bicycle before everyone realizes they are the only mode of transportation left available and go there. I need to lay low for a couple of reasons. First, to make sure the invasion troops have advanced and the occupation forces have not yet arrived, which is the window of opportunity to travel. Second, to allow time for my GI haircut to grow out and start a scraggly looking beard. Now, what to take with me?

Lee made a list that included a lightweight backpack, tinned edibles, a few toiletries, a couple changes of underwear and socks, matches and fine steel wool for starting fires, a small first aid kit, and water purification tablets. Also listed were a detailed map of central and northern Germany and a waterproof covering for his sleeping bag. The sleeping bag was the only military-issue item he planned to take with him. He purchased two large, lightweight wool shawls and inserted them into the sleeping bag, knowing that the only way to sleep in the cold was to keep both head and feet warm. The places where he could bed down when headed north would not be pleasant—likely under bridges, in culverts, under piles of leaves, or who knows where else. Completing his list were used German work garments.

He had a good map of Germany. Most of the needed items were easy to find and could be purchased at the PX. His one drawback was that he despised the only canned meats available—Spam and sardines. Despite that culinary bias, he bought a few of each, along with the other items on the list. His wallet took a hit.

Finding used German work garments was a different story. After much searching and frustration, Lee located a used clothing outlet far south in Sachsenhausen. The used work clothes were the right length, but the waist and hips were much larger than Lee's hummingbird ass. Still, he bought them, along with a pair of used work boots that would be comfortable if he wore a couple of pairs of socks. To top out his ensemble, he selected the shabbiest forage cap available. He hauled this garb back to the tailor shop in the Kaserne.

When the tailor saw the used, ill-fitting garments, he was appalled and inadvertently uttered, *"Hast du den Verstand verloren?"* (Have you lost your mind?)

Unoffended, Lee chuckled, saying, *"Tun Sie Ihr Bestes."* (Do the best you can.)

After the tailor had performed his magic, the pants didn't require a belt, and the upper garments fit perfectly. "What a total waste of talent," mused Lee.

He took his accumulation of stuff to the station wagon, packed the backpack, removed the spare tire from the well, and placed his gear into that space, leaving the spare topside.

Hopefully, I won't have to use them. But who knows, with a bit of luck, I might end up alive in Copenhagen amongst all those beautiful young women.

THE PEN PAL GIRL

An excellent way for GIs—who were not interested in German girls—to meet young women was to visit tourist meccas such as Heidelberg. A few years earlier, with the remembrance of the war still vivid, Germany wasn't high on traveler agendas of places to visit. Now, however, they came in droves.

Derek and Junior ventured to Heidelberg and encountered a couple of American girls on tour. They established a relationship with the young women. As the girls' tour moved south, Derek and Junior would meet them at the next stop. Junior's family had serious money, and he had a Porsche which allowed them to zoom down the autobahn, meet the girls, and get back to Frankfurt in time for their next shift of duty. However, somewhere in Austria or Switzerland, they ran out of time to get back and were declared AWOL. Their absence got the security folks' full-blown attention. They remembered all too well the recent defection to the Soviet Union by

NSA cryptographers Martin and Mitchell, who held the same security clearance as Derek and Junior. Those defectors showed up in Moscow at an international press conference. That embarrassment was not going to happen again—Every MP in Europe was looking for them!

Derek and Junior arrived back in Frankfurt of their own volition, but not without penalty. Derek's punishment was being restricted to barracks for a period of time. Junior, normally a conscientious and dedicated soldier, had allowed the organ he usually used for peeing to do the thinking for him; and, had missed a shift of duty when in charge of troops. He lost his security clearance, and immediately thereafter unceremoniously departed the 251st.

Derek and his girlfriend had become enamored. She was coming back to be near Derek and bringing with her a girl who had never been to Germany. To entice the young woman to travel with her, she wanted another GI to communicate with her friend to establish some rapport before they arrived. Derek approached Lee, explained the situation, and asked him to be a pen pal with this new girl. Lee was completely skeptical, saying, "You've got to be kidding. Being a pen pal will be no different than having a blind date, which I know about from bad experience. They all have great personalities, except when they show up, they have fallen out of the ugly tree and hit every branch on the way down."

Derek persisted, and Lee reluctantly consented to begin writing. When Lee's early-out notification came in, he approached Derek and told him that he would soon be history.

"Shit!" exploded Derek. "I don't have time to get somebody else writing. They already have their tickets and are going to be here in early September."

"You know this newbie McKay? He's a good-looking kid, and his name is also Lee. I never signed my letters with anything but Lee. Why don't you get with him and see if he's interested? If he is, just swap out the Lees. She'll never know the difference."

"You're a genius, albeit somewhat perverted!"

Oh, the tangled webs we weave.

President Kennedy was to tour and speak in Frankfurt on 25 June 1963, the day before visiting Berlin. At the start of the day of the president's visit, Mac got everyone's attention, saying, "The president is going to be in town today. I'm going to release anyone who wants to go see him. He's going to be out at Hanau to meet with the troops, then he's going to speak at Paulskirche downtown. I would suggest going to Hanau because the situation here in Frankfurt is going to be a madhouse. What doesn't get done today, we'll pick up tomorrow."

It was a perfect opportunity for the GIs to head to their favorite watering holes, snuggle with their schatzi, or perhaps return to the Kaserne and get some much-needed sleep. No one would know if they went to see Kennedy.

A couple of troops left, but most stayed.

At the end of the day, Mac approached Lee, saying, "I'm amazed. In any other unit, the place would empty out the instant I stopped talking. What gives?"

"Well, a few things. Most of us, myself included, who've been through the Berlin Wall going up and the way Kennedy handled it … definitely not our nation's finest hour … not to mention his bungling of the Checkpoint Charlie and Cuban fiascoes, just aren't that fond of the guy. Also, there's the fundamental commitment to duty. I think the real reason most of us stuck around was to provide support, if needed, to a boss … you … who treats us like human beings."

The big, gruff, profane hunk of a man turned his back on Lee and used his only hand to wipe at his eyes as he walked away.

The next day, President Kennedy was in Berlin. An estimated three-fourths of its population lined the streets to welcome him. A huge crowd gathered to hear him speak near the Brandenburg Gate. Never since Nuremberg in the 1930s had the German people been so enthused about a politician. Lee and Mac listened to the armed service's radio broadcast as events unfolded, prompting Lee to say, "You'd think this was the second coming of *Der Führer.*"

"Well put. These Krauts do have a short, selective memory, indeed. It hasn't been all that many months since Kennedy let the city be divided without anything more than a weak protest. And in the process, it killed off almost any prospect of Germany ever being reunited. Who knows what inspires these dumb Dubs?"

When it came to Kennedy's speech itself, Lee spouted, "Did you hear that? Our President just declared himself to be a jelly donut with his, *Ich bin ein Berliner* pronouncement."

"Not the case at all. I don't much like the guy, but that was brilliant. He was talking about free men everywhere being citizens of Berlin. The Krauts didn't hear any of that. Instead, all they heard was Kennedy ineptly declaring himself to be a Berliner. They didn't give a shit that he stuck *ein* into the phrase *Ich bin Berliner*, proclaiming himself to be a piece of pastry, instead of being a Berliner."

THE SPOOKS SHOW UP AT O-DARK-THIRTY

In the spring and summer of 1963, counterintelligence agents occasionally entered the Gutleut barracks in the early morning hours in a manner that would have made the Gestapo proud. They rousted Monterey Marys out of bed and took them to the outskirts of Frankfurt for interrogation. Lee had two Marys bunking in his room.

Lee and Reese were sucking down nickel beers at the EM club when Reese asked, "How about Peel and Repeel?" using the nicknames that had been given those two Marys. "Considering all that's going on in the compound with the Marys lately, do you think your roommates are homos, queer, or whatever?"

"Could be, maybe, possibly, likely, even probably. I particularly wonder about those Marys when they practice their ballet *relevés*. That's when they stand on their little tippy-toes. But truthfully, even if they are a bit short on testosterone, if they show up for work and do their jobs, I really don't give a flying fuck. They can bugger and blow each other to their little heart's content … as long as I don't have to watch."

DOING IT JUST LIKE THE GERMANS DO

Lee and Karl had been friends growing up together in a small town in northeastern New Mexico. They continued to be friends and fraternity brothers in college. If someone wanted to find the most attractive woman in the room, all they had to do was locate Karl. There she would be, right next to him.

Lee flunked out of college in his second year and lost his draft deferment. A board comprised of friends and neighbors deemed him fit to be conscripted. On the other hand, Karl had graduated—negating his military service delay—and then was drafted. As far as the local draft board was concerned, 'You can pay me now, or you can pay me later.'

Karl caught R&R flights from where he was stationed in the States to Frankfurt and made his way to Gutleut Kaserne, where he found and awakened Lee, who had worked the midnight shift.

As he awoke, Lee cried out, "Holy shit! Where did you come from? I didn't even know you were in the army. And how did you find me? We're supposed to be unfindable."

"Well, I first tried the army and got nowhere. Then I got in touch with your folks." Karl paused as his grin widened. "And here I am."

"There's an empty bunk," Lee replied as he sat up in his own bunk. "Get out of those miserable Class A duds and into civvies. We are gonna hit the town!"

"Great! And I want to do it just like the Germans do."

It was perfect timing, with Friday afternoon open and the entire weekend available to reminisce and chance upon new things to reminisce about later. They turned left out of the Kaserne and made the long walk to the Hauptbahnhof, where the strassenbahn departed and terminated.

About halfway down the first block, Lee dropped his keys deliberately, and as he stooped down for them, he glanced back. As he'd suspected, they were being tailed. Without commenting on their shadow, Lee said, "Frankfurt is one butt-ugly city. But the nightlife makes up for it."

"Remember, I want to do it like the Germans do," reminded Karl.

No, you don't want to, but, you're my guest. So, I'll do my best. I pray we're still friends when you're done doing it like the Germans do.

They took a strassenbahn through the center of Frankfurt to the Alte Oper so that Karl might see and get a sense of what Frankfurt looked like at the end of the war. Shortly before arriving at the site of the bombed-out opera house, they encountered a wurst stand. Lee inquired, "You likely haven't eaten for a while. Do you still want to do it like the Germans do?"

"Yes, and yes. Those kebab things look good."

"Don't even think about it. What you see on those spits is called shashlik, and heaven knows where the ingredients came from. Truth-in-labeling isn't big here in Germany ... so stay with the wursts. Wurst and beer are the Germans' two major food groups. Be forewarned, it's damn near impossible to find anything to eat in Germany that doesn't have some pig in it."

"OK. But remember, I want to do it just like the Germans do. You pick."

Lee deliberated about selecting because, in his opinion, Blutwurst was far and away the worst of the wurst, nevertheless said, "Germans, for some unknown reason, like Blutwurst, but your taste buds will never be the same. How about a side of sauerkraut also? Just like the Germans do."

"Sounds good ... go for it."

"You sure? You know about Montezuma's revenge. You may end up with the Kaiser's equivalent."

"Can't be any worse than some of the crap we ate in Juarez."

You have no idea how much worse it can be. However, if it's what you want to do.

Lee ordered, saying to the vendor, *"Für meine Freund, eine Blutwurst mit bröchen und sauerkraut* (For my friend, a blood sausage with a hard roll and sauerkraut.) *Und für mich, eine Bratwurst mit bröchen."* (And for myself, a bratwurst with a hard roll.) Then to Karl, "It comes with a big glob of mustard. That will help ... somewhat, to get it down."

After about the second bite of the Blutwurst, Karl's enthusiasm for *doing it just like the Germans do* appeared somewhat diminished as evidenced by the look on his face, as if undecided whether his stomach would withstand the onslaught—or not. But, with his macho image on the line, he managed to get it all down, saying, "Well ... that was different."

They made their way to the ruins of the old opera house, where Lee talked about its history. He explained how it had once been the largest and most elegant opera facility in the world. How it had been used by the German Army as a communications center during the war and about the booby-trapping at the end of the war. Then he talked about the futile and deadly attempts to remove the explosives, the Germans eventually giving up and fencing off the site.

Lee pointed as he remarked, "Look up there on the frieze. Do you see carved in the stone, *'Dem Wahren, Schönen, Guten?'* That translates as 'To the true, the beauty, and the good.' I find those words appropriate for today's young Germans as they look upon these ruins. It will remind them what their true, beautiful, and good elders brought upon this nation."

They again boarded a streetcar and made their way to the Eschenheimer Turm. Lee explained this was his favorite place to meet—or be stood up by—the fräuleins he made dates with. Then on to the nearest streetcar stop closest to the Altstadt. They were on foot for the rest of the journey.

At the Altstadt, Lee explained it had been a Roman outpost beginning around the onset of the Gregorian calendar. He led Karl around the reconstructed medieval Römer Platz square, pointing out the Rathaus, St. Paul's Church, the Bridge of Sighs, Old St. Nicholas Church, and the towering gothic Cathedral of St. Bartholomew. He thought about adding their histories and dates, but it seemed simpler to just say they had their origins in times long past.

"This area had the shit bombed out of it. Well, for that matter, all of Frankfurt got pounded. I read somewhere that thirty thousand tons of bombs ... tons, mind you ... got dumped on this city by our cousins and us. These buildings all burned, yet the walls and steeples we are now looking at stayed mostly intact. Those old stonemasons were clever. The half-timbered facades burned out and were replaced after the war. The Römer Rathaus has been the City Hall for oh ... six hundred years."

As they sat at the Goddess of Justice Fountain in the middle of the square, taking a load off their feet, Karl commented, "These people have at least two thousand years of history. Amazing!"

"Yeah ... at times, however ... they didn't handle it all that well. Particularly in the nineteen thirties and beyond."

"I guess it's been taken care of now? De-Nazification and all that?"

"Don't get me started on some of these Krauts and their forgetfulness as to who won the war, their Nazi Party membership ... some eight million of them ... or which front they fought on. Brings a new dimension to the term *collective amnesia.*"

"Sorry. Let's get back to me doing it just like the Germans do."

"Over there, underneath the Rathaus, is the Ratskeller, a vast labyrinth that includes a dance floor. There I met a young woman who had made her way out of Poland and across East Germany before the wall went up. I was falling in love with her ... and I believe ... she, with me. Nothing ever came of it. Anna was realistic. She knew about my security clearance and realized that being from Poland, she would never get cleared for us to be a couple." Lee paused for a moment, as if deep in thought, before saying, "Ah, well, that's the way the Mercedes bends."

"What?"

"GI speak here in Germany. Small-case b-e-n-d-s; not capital B-e-n-z. As if to say, something beautiful ends all crumpled up."

They left the Römer, and as they walked across the pedestrian bridge that spans the Main River, Lee said, "This bridge nearly survived the war. After multiple bombing raids in this area by ourselves and the Brits, it was still intact. Then, with just a few days left in the war, the German Army blew it to smithereens as they retreated. Now, thanks to the Germans' damned thoroughness, its restored and spiffy clean. I not all that fond of these Krauts, but have to give credit where credit is due." Once across the bridge they took a right and walked the hundred or so yards to Herr Burke's beer barge.

The barge was already crowded with GIs drinking beer and soaking up the rare sunshine.

Herr Burke with a genuine smile on his face, greeted them in English, "Good afternoon, guys. Nice to have you."

Lee made the introductions. "Herr Burke, my good friend Karl. Karl, the owner, Herr Burke."

"Find a place. I will have your beers right out," offered Herr Burke.

Once seated, Lee noted that their trailer was still with them. He'd found a place as far from them as possible at the aft of the boat, awaiting the appropriate time to make his move.

"Hey," said Karl. "This is great! A warm, sunny afternoon. Good beer. Right here on the river with its traffic bobbing us up and down, all those folks walking on the bridge over the river, and hundreds-year-old churches sticking up across the river.

"And this guy Herr Burke, not what I expected when I met my first German."

"Trust me, he's a rare exception of German men his age."

"So, what do you know about him?"

"Quite a bit, in fact. Late one afternoon, shortly after I arrived in Frankfurt, Herr Burke sat and began to suck down some beer along with a couple of other guys and me. It's a fascinating story. He was an escapee from a prisoner of war camp in Arizona. Want to hear it?"

"Does a bear shit in the woods?"

Lee recounted the story that Herr Burke had passed on.

Burke had been a conscripted submariner who was captured and placed in a prisoner of war camp in Arizona, from which he and a couple dozen other inmates escaped through a tunnel dug to outside the compound perimeter. He told how the officers intended to make their way to Mexico, while the enlisted guys planned to wait out the end of the war hiding in the nearby mountains and how their short-lived freedom ended when one of the escapees turned them in. He also mentioned how well Burke had been treated by a farmer and his family for whom he and other POWs worked.

"Burke wanted to remain in Phoenix and work for the farmer, and the farmer wanted the same. They tried, but the military bureaucracy insisted that all the POWs return to Germany."

"So, that's why this place is so popular with the GIs? For Herr Burke, it's merely payback time ... returning the hospitality."

"You got it."

Karl, shaking his head, said, "Helluva story."

The sun was setting. Lee suggested, "Why don't we go get a real German meal into you. There's an excellent restaurant back across the bridge where I've taken a couple of my Nazi Schatzies. It's a bit of a walk, but it's worth it."

Lee and Karl had their evening meal in an upscale restaurant near the Rathaus, located in a basement with low, vaulted stone ceilings. They planned on ordering a bottle of wine with the meal. Both had grown up in a small, rural cow town where the only folks who drank wine were the Eye-tal-yens. Lee's schatzies were amazed at his naïveté and lack of sophistication when it came to approving a simple bottle of wine and tutored him on wine tasting and acceptance. He gave Karl a heads-up about what was to happen.

"The wine steward will show up and display the bottle for you to approve the label. He will uncork the bottle and offer the cork for you to smell. Next, he will pour a little splash of wine into the glass.

You pick the glass up by the stem ... and only the stem ... then swirl it. You sniff for aroma. Swirl it again and hold the glass up to the light to check for its legs. Legs being that oily looking stuff that runs down the inside of the glass. The more legs, the better. Lastly, you take a sip, swish it around in your mouth and swallow, then nod to indicate that it's acceptable."

"You're shitting me! All of that to get a glass of wine?"

"Would I blow smoke up your ass? And remember, you're the one who wants to do it just like the Krauts do. Now comes the fun part if you care to try it. After you take a sip, let the wine steward see your face looking as if you swallowed a cockroach. That part of the drill is optional, although it's fun to watch the reaction since he'll pour the wine only after you nod. For myself, to speed up the process, as soon as the cork is pulled, I say, *Gehen Sie einfach vor und giessen Sie das Zeug,* meaning, just go ahead and pour the stuff. This breach of German wine tasting protocol is also optional ... it likewise aggravates the living shit out of them. There's a direct correlation between how many stars the restaurant has and how pissed off they get. I'll let you do the honors when the wine arrives. It's an interesting but unnecessary thing to do. But then, there's a bunch of stuff the Germans do that are interesting but not necessary.

"I'll do it. I'm, however, going to leave the options for another time."

Karl went through the wine routine as if it were an everyday occurrence for him. The meal was excellent, and the wine almost worth the trouble it took to get it.

"Now for the best part of the day," said Lee. "Back across the bridge to Dault Schneider's in Sachsenhausen. My favorite place in Frankfurt. You are going to love it. At least, I do!"

Dault's was in full swing when they arrived. As was common, there were a few middle-aged Germans. And as usual, accompanying their effeminate German boyfriends was an assortment of fräuleins looking to connect with one of the many GIs. All swaying back and forth, arms linked, to the oompah-pah music. The Horst Wessel variety of music would come later in the evening.

They found a couple of seats on a bench, and Lee said to Karl, "Link arms with whoever is next to you. Sway back and forth. Don't worry about the lyrics; it's likely they don't know them themselves."

"This is almost like a keg party in college except you get to sit on a bench instead of the ground. I like this."

"If you need to pee, go through the door labeled Herren and piss on the wall. Yes, piss on the wall! Just like the Germans do. You'll figure it out. Don't be concerned about the female attendant who watches you hang it out. She'll try to sell you a condom, but don't buy. First, in all probability, it will leak. Second, despite what you may have heard, your short-term chances of getting laid here in Germany are slim to none. Yeah, occasionally, you'll encounter a quick-to-bed Rosie Rottencrotch. But most German girls here in Frankfurt … I don't know about elsewhere in Germany … are like the girls in the States. They don't drop their panties until they are good and ready."

Before long, the trailer sat down across from them.

He's a persistent bastard; I'll give him that. Could be a MfS or even a KGB guy rather than the usual local rent-a-spy.

The trailer had the usual routine. He bought drinks, introduced himself as Herr Whoever, asked Lee's and Karl's names, and said he appreciated what the US military was doing for Germany.

The trailer then spoke the predictable, "You must be proud of the important things you do." Back to small talk to allow the GI to have time to think about bragging. At last, came the inevitable, "What do you do in the army?" Lee went into his *Ich-bin-ein-Spionageabwehr-agent* spiel. When he finished, the trailer left immediately.

"You speak German pretty damn well for a cowboy that spent most of his life looking at the ass end of your dad's cows. I thought they were Angus and Herefords, but must have been German-speaking Holsteins looking for some interspecies action … huh cowpuncher?" Karl asked.

"Up yours! For your information, I learned my German in pillow talk with accommodating fräuleins. No, truth be told, I have an agreement with our Kaserne librarian, and we *tutor* each other … linguistically only. And, I just know just enough of this throat disease masquerading as a language, to get through the day."

It was back to swaying with the music and drinking the cider.

A middle-aged German man who was sitting across and somewhat down the table had ordered a meal. Up to that point, he had been gregarious and swaying and singing with the music. When his meal arrived, Lee nudged Karl, saying, "Watch this." The German turned his undivided attention to the plate in front of him. Using knife, fork, and fingers, he devoured his meal without delay.

Karl gave Lee a quizzical look.

"During the last two years of the war and the two years that followed, the Krauts either starved to death or came damned close. Thus, they have this mentality that the food in front of them is perhaps the last they will ever have. In today's Germany, leisure dining isn't in their vocabulary, and it's only in the experience of a very few."

Later in the evening, the German girl came by to greet her favorite spy, doing her usual routine, boobs on his shoulder and hands through his hair, before returning to her boyfriend.

"Hey, that's one good-looking woman!" remarked Karl, a known connoisseur of the opposite sex. Then with a look of realization, he added, "I'm not keeping you from something, am I?"

"Nah. Just a casual kind of relationship."

Karl slurred, "If that'sh cashual, I think the non-cashual vershion would have you shtarring in a porn flick. How'sh about *Lee'sh Licentiousnessh Libido* for a title?"

"I'd tell you to go screw yourself, but you're too drunk to be offended. And besides, I need to get us back to the Kaserne."

They slept in the next morning. Around noon, Lee rousted Karl from his bunk, saying, "The sun is shining. We don't get many days like this. Let's make the most of it."

Karl sat up, gripped his head, and croaked, "Oh my God, this is my worst hangover ever. I'm nauseous, and there's an anvil in my head that some asshole is pounding with a five-pound hammer. Even my hair hurts!"

"Your headache is the apfelwein payback. It has something to do with the unfermented sugars. You drink enough of that shit, you go brain dead, which explains the uncalled-for behavior of a few of those Krauts … being true and typical Germans … we encountered last night. There's a shower down the hall and to the left. Let's go get some of the hair of the dog that bit us. A couple of beers are getting impatient waiting for us down at the beer barge."

By midafternoon, they were back on the always welcoming barge, lazing in the sun with a beer in hand. Herr Burke greeted them both by their first names when they came aboard. All was well in Deutschland.

A huge barge made its way up the river, leaving in its wake the smaller boats along the side of the river bobbing up and down. Karl raced to the rail in time to spew forth the toxic remnants in his stomach from the previous day's and night's questionable indulgences.

When he finished retching, Lee picked up Karl's bottle of beer and walked to the rail, saying, "Here, rinse your mouth out with this." Patting Karl on the shoulder, he added, "Oh, by the way … Congratulations! You've now done it just like the Germans do."

SHORT TIMERS

All conscripted GIs develop a short-timer's attitude as their tours of duty approach the end. It is a universal phenomenon: a recalcitrant mindset of having had enough of the army's regimented and often capricious ways. At this stage of their tours, they could give a Flying Wallenda, or some such euphemism, about what was imposed upon or demanded of them. Short of an Article 15 or a court-martial, they ignore, disregard, and even disobey. The long-standing acronym FYIGMO (Fuck You, I've Got My Orders) is frequently uttered. After everything they have been through and put up with, there is now a light at the end of the tunnel. Regrettably, this attitude often carries over into their behavior outside of the army and into the nearby civilian communities.

Those with fewer than one hundred days left in their tours refer to themselves as double-digit midgets.

The GIs have an odd way of articulating the number of days left until their discharge. It's simply X number of days and a wake-up, as if the wake-up didn't count as a full day. Nonetheless, the wake-up concept was necessary. One would hear utterances like, "Only twenty-one days and a wake-up," or "I am so short I can sit on a dime and my feet won't touch the floor." And, indubitably, there was always the profane, "I'm even shorter than the first sergeant's dick."

LOOKING FOR SWASTIKAS

Shortly after Lee had arrived in Germany, he became obsessed with finding a remnant of the emblem of the Third Reich somewhere in Germany—the Germans' beloved swastika. He explored dark corners of buildings, examined the coins he received in change, and always scrutinized the façades of buildings that somehow survived the war. The closest he came in his quest was in cemeteries where tombstones had their swastikas crudely chiseled out. *Teutonische Gründlichkeit* (Teutonic thoroughness) was indeed exhaustive, but Lee never gave up looking.

It was now mid-August. Lee was getting short and had the short-timer's mindset, reinforced by his early-out approval. He and the usual suspects decided to go to Rüdesheim for the annual wine festival, which drew immense crowds. To put it bluntly, the Wine Fest was little more than an officially sanctioned public event countenancing drunkenness by the masses. The 251st participants arrived early in the afternoon to ensure plenty of time to visit a few wineries and sample and purchase their individual bottles of the outstanding Rhine wine. By late afternoon, as the crowd was beginning to gather, Lee had consumed enough of the fermented nectar to qualify as being under the influence.

At this point in his inebriated fog, he decided that his legacy in Germany was to be remembered as the guy who ran across the many tables set up within the Rüdesheim town square during the Wine Fest. He jumped atop the first table, which immediately collapsed. Undeterred, he leaped atop the second, and it held—as did all the rest—as he made his tabletop way across to the other side of the square. The folks at occupied tables along his path appeared less than amused with his encroachment. As he jumped to the ground, he noted that some polizei were headed in his direction. Not to be concerned. They were short, chubby, and out of shape. Lee was tall, slender, and in shape—and his long legs were putting distance with each stride between himself and the local current-day Gestapo. As he breezed along a narrow cobblestone street, some local wannabe hero, sitting at a sidewalk cafe and seeing the situation, reached out as Lee ran by and grabbed him by the left wrist. Perhaps not the smartest thing for the local guy to do. With all his momentum, Lee swung around and hit him solidly on the jaw with the palm of his right hand. The aspiring hero-to-be, stunned, fell backward before releasing Lee. In the process, he pulled Lee down onto the cobblestones. When Lee attempted to regain his feet and start running, he sensed an excruciating pain in his left foot and collapsed back onto the cobblestones. It didn't take a podiatrist to tell him he had suffered a stress fracture or fractures of those little bones in his foot. Running was no longer an option.

The out-of-breath policemen arrived, took him into custody, and escorted him painfully to the German equivalent of a pokey. One of them, as expected, got directly into Lee's face while speaking only in German with an accompanying shower of spittle. Almost certainly he berated, threatened, and debased Lee's ancestry and his manhood while questioning the legitimacy of his birth—all at a decibel level reserved for rock concert attendees. Even with Frau Müller's tutoring, Lee understood little of the tirade, other than a few of the more blatant invectives. His lack of understanding may have been less a lack of German language fluency and more the fact that he was totally shit-faced. Eventually, he was agonizingly ushered into a windowless room with only one exit, which was locked.

The Status of Forces Agreement was likely Lee's salvation. That night, the local fuzz was overwhelmed—coping with an enormous drink-prone crowd—and didn't want to contend with the paperwork hassle involved in turning Lee over to the MPs.

Around midnight, the same bombastic police officer he encountered earlier came into the room and, in a reasonable voice, spoke in perfect English, "We are releasing you. Never, but never, come to Rüdesheim again!"

His friends were waiting for him. It was a military covenant that you never left a wounded comrade on the battlefield, whether actual or contrived. They transported Lee to the army's medical dispensary in Frankfurt.

Lee checked in and was told to wait until called. He gingerly limped his way to a chair, sat down and put his head back with his eyes toward the ceiling. Swastikas aplenty encircled the entire upper surface.

I'll be damned! I've been looking all over Germany for two years to find a swastika, and here are a bunch of them in an American-run building. I've been searching in all the wrong places.

Lee's name was finally called. When the medic took off his shoe, a small bone was about to puncture the skin. The practitioner gently pushed it down, wrapped a stretch bandage around his foot, saying, "You're going to need some surgery to set that. Come back tomorrow morning and schedule it. By Christmas time, with a little rehab, you'll be as good as new." He gave Lee a small bottle of pain pills. "Take them as you think you need them."

Back at the barracks, Lee sat on his bunk muttering to himself, "I have my early out, which means I'm out of here in September. If I stay around to fix this damn foot, I won't be out until December … forget that!"

He took an extra pain pill and maneuvered the bone back down somewhere close to where he thought it should be. Surprisingly, it was relatively painless. He wrapped the bandage again, put on his left boot, and tightly laced it. He hefted his duffel bag onto the bunk to be able to elevate the foot and climbed into the rack.

What's the old saying? 'God protects fools and drunks.' Tonight, I met both criteria, with room to spare.

With the help of the painkillers, he eventually went to sleep. Lee didn't show up the next morning at the dispensary for a surgery appointment. The army could not have cared less. Walking for the next several days wasn't much fun, and he often used the pain pills. Whenever he was about to give up and return to the dispensary, he thought about September versus December and painfully carried on.

THE LAST DATE

Lee had flirted with a fräulein at Dault's the previous evening. They met outside the restrooms and made a date for the following afternoon at the Eschenheimer Turm. Still, with nagging foot pain, he arrived early to verify that his apfelwein-induced appraisal of the girl the night before wasn't as bad as the hangover he had awakened with that morning. From experience, Lee had learned that a fräulein often wasn't nearly as attractive the following day as she appeared to be the night before when seen through the bottom of a glass. If she turned out to be anything other than a high number on the keeper scale, he would stand her up. Heaven knows how many times he was left high and dry at this location. Then the fräulein, possessing definite keeper potential and dressed to the hilt for the date, came into view.

She could be the one.

Anna's warning of what would happen at the train station at his end of his tour, came back to haunt Lee. Before she saw him, Lee stepped aboard the next outgoing streetcar without knowing or caring where it was bound.

That was a shitty thing to do, but I can rationalize it as being the least painful for both of us in the long run.

Lee had the paperwork informing him that his request for an early out to return to college was approved. It indicated he was to travel on the troop ship the *USS Gordon* from Bremerhaven to Fort Hamilton in New York City, where he would be discharged from active duty. But he didn't have the orders to allow him to travel.

Not having orders to travel is like sitting on the pot with a severe case of diarrhea and not having any toilet paper. In both instances, one can't get up and go without the appropriate piece of paper. Otherwise, things get messy.

Time was getting short. The last day of late registration at the university was about two weeks away, and he had not received his travel orders. Lee had almost given up on the early-out. He didn't object when Mac sent him on TDY to Bad Aibling. But as soon as he arrived, a message came that said, "Get your ass back here now. You have to be in Bremerhaven day after tomorrow."

Lee caught the night train back to Frankfurt, slept a couple of hours and got up early the next morning.

Clearing post would typically take seven to ten days, having people check me out at places I've never been. I'm going to do it in one day if it kills me. For sure, I'm going to get my security debrief, take my money out of the bank, and clear with the armory, then go from there.

Off to the Farben Building he went, where Chief McDuff debriefed him—with the usual warning of ten years in jail at Fort Leavenworth and a ten-thousand-dollar penalty should he reveal any classified information—and then initialed the form. Lee now needed only nineteen more signatures to finalize his Clearing Post Form. The chief took Lee's security clearance badge and escorted him out of the SCIF. Just before stepping on the paternoster, Lee turned and asked, "By the way, Chief, how is your supply of burlap bags holding up?"

No response. The warrant officer just glared at his antagonist.

If looks could kill, I'd already be a maggot-infested corpse. Trust me, Chief ... the feeling is mutual.

On to Chase Manhattan Bank and back to the Kaserne, where he fired up his old beat-up Pontiac station wagon on about four of its cylinders. He drove a couple of blocks down Gutleut Strasse toward the Main River and parked on a side street next to a drain alongside the curb. Taking a screwdriver, he removed the license plates, cleaned out the glove box, and locked the doors. He took a couple of steps and dropped everything into the drain—keys, license plates, screwdriver, and all.

Then back to the Kaserne and into the basement where the gun guy signed off.

Down at the far end of the hallway was the library. Lee checked the form. It was on the list.

I ought to take the time and have the courtesy to say goodbye to Frau Müller.

Sure enough, there she was, dusting an already immaculate bookshelf. She initialed the form. Lee, to show his appreciation for all her linguistic assistance, spoke in almost perfect German, *"Es war eine Freude, Sie Wissen!"* (It was a joy to know you!) This brought a mist to her eyes.

As he stepped out of the library, he gazed down the long row of prison cells that had held the WWII POWs and paused for a moment in silent respect.

There but for the grace of God and the passage of time go I.

It was already mid-afternoon. The next stop was one floor up at the company clerk's office. On the clerk's desk was a cracked beer stein filled with various pens and pencils. Lee sat down and pointed at the beer stein saying, "Let me have those." The clerk complied.

Lee initialed the remaining seventeen slots on his Clearing Post Form, using a different pen or pencil from the mug for each fabricated set of characters. Then, tossed it to the clerk saying, "There, I just cleared post."

The clerk picked up the form, stuck it in a folder, and said, "Gotcha! Say, didn't you have a piece-of-shit POV?" as he placed the folder into a file cabinet.

"It's all taken care of, and, thanks to you, who says it takes days to clear post? If you can make it, some of my asshole buddies are having a going-away party for me at the EM club around seven o'clock tonight."

"Gee thanks, but I've got a Nazi Schatzi. We have plans for this evening. If you know what I mean?"

I do indeed. Take her out. Feed her at a nice gasthaus. Get a couple of drinks into her. Then, let her take you home and boink your brains out.

"Yep, I know what you mean. Been down that road a few times myself. "Lee slapped the desk a couple of times and uttered a cautionary, "Take care."

Lee went upstairs and, as he packed his duffel bag, noted with a certain degree of satisfaction that the cord to the FDL's radio was now about one foot in length.

Next-up, to the EM club to say goodbye to some great guys. Then I'm the hell and gone outta here.

A dozen or so of Lee's friends gathered around a couple of tables at the EM club, drinking their nickel Lowenbrau beer and eating pizza. They reminisced about their episodes and misadventures with Lee, while not bringing up anything that happened at work other than Chief McDuff's burlap-bag-experiment debacle.

Enter Derek, with his newly arrived girlfriend on his arm. Next to him was the other Lee with a drop-dead-gorgeous creature at his side—An absolute ten on the keeper scale!

Well, so much for my pen-pal, blind-date theory.

The other Lee caught Lee's eye, glanced at the stunning woman on his arm, then back at Lee. He mouthed a silent yet exaggerated, "Thank You!"

Lee glared back, shook his head, and mouthed a likewise silent but more exaggerated, "Up yours!" Both chuckled and exchanged a short, sharp salute.

Lee kept checking the time. Someone inquired, "What's with you?"

"This is one train I ain't gonna miss."

At about nine o'clock Lee stood up and shook hands around the table, saying goodbye. He picked up his duffel bag and headed for the exit. A few of his better friends joined him and took turns carrying Lee's duffel bag on the long walk to the Hauptbahnhof. Lee shook hands once again. There were promises to keep in touch, knowing it would likely not happen.

Lee found and boarded the night train to Bremerhaven. Thoughts of Anna flooded his memory as he stared out onto the platform. Her words, "We will fall in love. The day will come when you are on the train to Bremerhaven, and I am left standing at the station. We will be waving goodbye forever," rang in his ears.

Bless you, Anna! You beautiful, pragmatic woman.

Lee slept most of the way to Bremerhaven.

AT SEA

Around dawn, he awoke on the outskirts of Bremerhaven. The trainload of GIs was transferred to the dock where the *USS Gordon* awaited their boarding, along with some four thousand other troops bound for the land of the free and the home of the brave. Before boarding, all had to be ordered alphabetically, something to do with having a manifest should the good old *Gordon* not make its way across the Atlantic.

How come all the ASA-ers are flown to Germany, but sent home by troop ship? As far as the army's concerned, we are just perishables sitting on the shelf. Our use-by-date has expired, and we are put aboard this sea-going trash can, waiting to be dumped.

By the time they got to those with surnames beginning with W, it was late in the day, and Lee was shown his domicile for the next ten days. The troops were to bed down in bunks stacked high in the hold. The earlier arriving troops occupied all except the top one or two tiers. There was not enough room in what the navy called berths to accommodate their duffel bags, and they lay cluttered about on the floor. After Lee clambered to one of the top bunks, he soon learned there were two options for a sleeping position. Either you chose to be on your back or your stomach, and you entered the bunk with that in mind. There was not enough space to sleep on your side or, for that matter, to rotate from the back to stomach or vice versa. Having been relegated to the top bunk turned out to be a blessing. Sir Isaac was again proven correct. Vomit is one of those things that flows downhill.

The *Gordon* made its way down the English Channel with a rather pleasant rocking motion. When it turned west, the ship's captain put the pedal to the metal. It was September after all, and he had to cross the North Atlantic. The *Gordon* wasn't due to dock in New York Harbor for ten days, but the captain was going to get the unpredictable—and at times downright dangerous—part of the voyage over as quickly as possible. The passengers' comfort was at the bottom of his list. What was once as gentle as a rocking chair now became an out-of-control roller coaster ride.

Lee eventually managed to fall asleep despite the sound and smell of the retching occurring below him.

THE MOTION SICKNESS THEORY CONFIRMED

He awoke the next morning, squeezed out of his top bunk, and climbed down past a bunch of GIs in various stages of nausea. The verb *to puke* and all its tenses came to mind.

He has puked, he is puking, and he will puke. You, poor pitiful pukes.

Lee headed to the head, cautiously making his way to the showers on the walkway above the inches-deep vomit splashing against the hull as the ship tumbled about in the sea. He bathed, lingering in the warmth of the hot saltwater shower, then stepped into the brutally cold freshwater shower to rinse off. Despite his brief stay in the cold water, when Lee emerged—shivering and his teeth chattering—his manhood was about the same size and shape of a peanut shell. After shaving and dressing, he left and found the galley.

When entering, he saw it was meant to serve food, but there was no one eating. "I must be early," Lee said.

A server on the chow line replied, "Nope, you're not. We don't get many customers this part of the trip."

The bill of fare was light and fluffy scrambled eggs. Not green in color with the stench of sulfur as was standard issue in army mess halls. Ham, bacon, and sausage were choices, or all the above if you desired. Real biscuits with sausage gravy, exponentially better than the army mess halls' watery chipped-beef-gravy version served on a slice of toast. The army's offering was fittingly known as Shit On a Shingle (SOS)—an appropriate distress signal whether at sea or in an army dining facility.

As Lee was sitting down, another GI entered, went through the line and joined him at the table. The ship was rocking side to side, and the meal trays on the rails tended to drift away from in front of them. "I guess you hold the tray with one hand and eat with the other," said the GI. "Dang, this Navy chow is good. Best I've had since I entered the service. My favorite breakfast is biscuits and gravy. This is damn-near perfect."

Lee agreed, "A biscuit-and-gravy breakfast is also one of my favorites."

Changing the subject, he offered, "I'll bet you often rode horses when you were growing up."

The GI swallowed a large mouthful of food before replying, "How'd you know that? Matter a fact, my dad was the foreman of a large ranch just west of Amarillo. I spent a lot of time in the saddle."

"Amarillo, huh? We're practically neighbors. I grew up on my dad's ranch in northeastern New Mexico. My name's Lee."

"Mine's Ken."

"Ken, I have this idea. Call it a theory if you like. It's that people who often rode horses when they were young don't suffer from motion sickness. Dad owned a cutting horse that I swear was the only creature on God's green earth that could go in two directions at the same time, which this ship, as you've no doubt noticed, tries to do."

Ken, having cleaned his tray, wondered, "Can we get seconds?"

"Do you see anyone in the line?"

They had seconds. Twice.

Shortly, a few more GIs came in and were eating.

Thoroughly sated, Lee declared, "I'll be Gawd-damned if I'm going to go back to that barf-fest I just came from. I'm going to grab my field jacket and go topside to get some air."

"Me too. I'll see you in a few."

They found a structure on the deck and hunkered down on the leeward side. After a while, some of the GIs Lee had seen in the ship's galley came up and found shelter out of the wind at various places around the deck.

Lee said, "I'm going to research my 'Ride horses as a kid and don't suffer from motion sickness' theory. Want to come?"

Ken sat up in time to catch a blast of the North Atlantic near hurricane-force wind in the face along with the ever-present saltwater spray. He dropped back down saying, "Not only no, but hell no! Good luck, and try not to get swept overboard."

Lee made his difficult way around the deck asking the GIs—who a short time ago had eaten but not suffered from nausea—if they often rode horses when they were young. The responses were mostly "Yup," or "Yeah," and one responded with, "I've been thrown off more horses than most folks been on."

Lee dropped out of the wind, hunkering down next to Ken, shouted gleefully, "Theory confirmed!"

THE REST OF THE VOYAGE

After a couple of days, most of the GIs found their sea legs. Continual upchucking slowed to sporadic. As GIs lined the rails of the ship watching the dolphins escort them across the Atlantic, they learned to be nowhere near someone vomiting over the side of the vessel. The updraft off the ocean picked up the barf and haphazardly distributed it to all standing nearby. Over time, the rails became crowded. If someone wanted a place to watch the accompanying dolphins, all he had to do was make a gagging sound and dash forward. By the time, he reached the rail, there wouldn't be anyone within ten yards on either side of him.

Correspondingly, the chow lines grew in length until someone wanting to eat three squares a day had to stand in line all day. Stand in line, eat breakfast, go to the end of the line and repeat the process for the other two meals of the day.

After five days crossing the turbulent Atlantic, Newfoundland came into sight. When the ship's captain turned southward, he went from full steam ahead to just enough propeller thrust to allow for steerage. After all, he wasn't due in New York harbor for another five days. The journey became excruciatingly boring and frustrating as they drifted down the New England coastline. Even the escorting dolphins abandoned them.

Frustration turned to insubordination. Disobedient GIs began ripping off their uniform name tags to hide their identities. Word came down from on high that anyone without a name tag would be denied entrance into the galleys to eat. The ASAers, having never worn name tags, found themselves once again—to the very end of their tour—cursed by the intelligence community's mindset about name tags. Eventually, they found someone familiar with their situation and were issued meal passes.

At long last, in the distance, the skyscrapers of New York appeared.

EPILOGUE

Having watched the sun come up, Lee—still in the same spot on deck—would soon see it set. Lady Liberty was resplendent in the sun's last gleaming. Finally, the line began to move. Lee shouldered his duffel bag and, as he started down the gangplank, took one last look back. The Lady, as she had done for countless others before and would do for untold numbers yet to come, appeared to nod her head and whisper, "Well done, my good and faithful soldier."

Made in the USA
San Bernardino, CA
28 November 2017